I0822792

Nocte

NOCTURNAL SOULS
BOOK ONE

LANA SKY

Nocte

Note By Lana Sky

Cover Design by Caoimhe Coleman
Interior Formatting by Lana Sky
Editing and Proofreading by Katie Crum
Alpha Reading by Jessica Rita Rampersad

Acknowledgments

Thanks so much to everyone who supported this draft along the way, including the many beta readers who provided encouragement! A special thanks to Kat, Caoimhe, and Jessica Rita Rampersad for working tirelessly to help make this book the best it could be.

Please keep in mind that this story includes dark, graphic, and explicit content matter that may not be suitable for readers under the age of 18—or for readers who are uncomfortable with the following subject matter: explicit sex, and graphic depictions of violence.

PART ONE

The Citadel

CHAPTER 1
Niamh

I *must* be shunned for my own benefit.

I've been told as much my entire life. That I am ugly. Ungainly. Unworthy. An abomination of my race. A fae's only purpose is to embody perfection, neatness, and order above all else. We are boundless. Eternal.

Any deviation from the path is a harbinger of death and destruction.

They tell me, and tell me, and tell me so...

Grateful for their shelter and protection, I have found it within myself to internalize those teachings.

I've made peace with my fate.

What I cannot stomach, however, are the lies. To be fair, I've only found one in my time exploring the alcoves. Just one. A tiny lie that disrupts order and contradicts the rules they enforce. A lie that entices me to entertain a dangerous line of thinking—what else might be possible?

There is a book that claims the *vamryre* never stray beyond their compound. How could they? Linked in their twisted mental landscape, they cannot bear to be separated from one another for even a second.

Even a second.

Yet *he* is always alone. With pale skin and cold eyes, he looks like them, moves like them. But his thoughts... They show across his face as if written there in brilliant black ink. Murderous intentions.

Violent fantasies.

He is *all* anger—not like the rest. They stick to their covens and enclaves, traveling in pairs of two or more, never alone. Never silent. It's how they function, you see. The vamryre. *They are like bees in a hive*, or that is how the old scholars referred to them as.

Together they hum with a buzz of emotions, the thoughts of many contained in one. According to another elder, if you cut one of the creatures they would all feel the pain. Never do they frown or pout or show any outward distress.

He is the exception.

Here, where no one else can see, he glowers at the world. The first time I saw his face still sticks in my mind. Beautiful beyond compare, yet frozen like the marble statues on the outskirts of the tower compound, battered and unfazed by time.

Initially, I thought he was simply curious. A creature compelled by his masters to explore beyond his boundaries. Upon finding this place, he probably wondered why a lone fae was allowed to stay here. Live here. Shelter in hiding and in secret.

Such a fool he was to wonder, or so I thought.

It wasn't until the third day that I realized the truth, and I felt a creeping, tingling sensation all over my body. The unease festered and festered until I came back here yet again and found him lingering on the outskirts of the courtyard.

The vamryre isn't here out of curiosity.

He is hunting. While the Citadel's law prohibits them from taking prey within its walls, they do so anyway. Vamryers, are incapable of adhering to boundaries fully, after all. It is in their nature to test all rules, other than those their masters give them.

He sees in me something to feast upon.

Yet it is hard for me not to feel pity for this beautiful, poor vamryre. If he seeks to prey on me, he must be weaker than the rest. Desperate.

Surely, he is an abomination too.

In any case, I am as curious about him as he is about me. How do the vamryre deal with one who makes a mockery of their laws? I am not sure. They are beholden to their own twisted set of values, far different from those that guide the fae.

The fae punish those who stray from the fold. Individuality is shunned. One might think vamryres do the same...

But he is here. My mind spins as I watch him stand in the same spot he always has—near the rear wall where the crumbling stone has left a divot in the once-impenetrable structure. He looks strong enough to have caused the damage, though I know a storm did years ago.

Still...

There's a softness to his beauty that I don't expect to find as I creep closer to watch him. Viewed from beyond my nose, he looks so small. A spot of glaring white on a gray landscape. Not like sunlight. Something harsher and destructive, like fire. Lightning. He burns my eyes, searing the longer I stare. A painful and beautiful spot.

Then he looks up.

My heart stops. I jerk back and nearly lose my footing on the slanted roof tiles. What does he see from down there?

A girl.

A woman.

A pale creature with long hair the color of midnight and sunken, mournful eyes that I sometimes glimpse on the polished floor when I've finished my chores. I am not bright like the other fae with their pink skin and flowing hair, the color of starlight and amber. They have wings as well, while my back is just a lumpy maze of bones and scars.

My physical appearance is how they knew I was different from the day I was born.

But my mother...

He moves again, snapping me back to awareness, the vamryre. He has such a penetrating gaze, like the ritual knife used to draw blood by the elders during their ceremonies. During their punishments. Sharp and precise, yet with a serrated edge meant to slice, cut, and butcher.

He butchers me. Slices through my core and eviscerates the fearful, furtive part of my soul accustomed to hiding. In the presence of other fae I must not be seen, but he isn't fae.

And he sees me. Those eyes suck me in whole, and I can't look away like I should. He is a curiosity, one far more interesting than any I could find in the archives.

Whatever interest I held to him, however, was fleeting. He turns and walks away, scaling the wall with an effortless ease. His red robe billows out behind him—the color all vamryre wear. I'm left staring after him, unsure if he was real or just a figment of my imagination. Years of isolation have rendered me so desperate for company I've imagined it.

Strange. I've never thought of my life in those terms before—isolation. Loneliness.

It is not my place to feel despair at my circumstances. They are what they are, and it is only due to the benevolence of the council that I have survived this long, sheltered in the walls of the Citadel. The vamryre wasn't the only one to slip into these ruins unnoticed. Another visitor sneaks in to see me, but he is different.

We are blood.

Yet I'm not allowed to think of him. Instead, I tiptoe back to the edge of the rooftop and follow it to where an incline of tiles forms a steep, makeshift path upward. From there, I must grab onto the edge of the nearest window overlooking the courtyard and pull myself inside. Once my feet hit the marble flooring I have to move quickly, dashing down the hall and up the lone stairwell leading to the bell tower.

This place is so familiar to me I could navigate the creaking wood panels in my sleep. Eyes closed, breath baited. I know how to avoid the loose floorboard that comes right after the doorway and how to tiptoe to avoid making too much noise and risk disturbing the workers below. I can even tell just from which direction the wind blows if a storm is on the way or what time of day it is.

And now, I can tell—as that gust of wind brings with it the sharp scent of incense—that I am not alone. Someone is here.

Someone important.

I drop to my knees instantly without bothering to face the newcomer directly. I know that scent and the air of authority it carries.

"L-Lord Master," I choke out the title. "I'm sorry, I wasn't expecting—"

"Stand." Their voice radiates the command and wisdom garnered from decades of life. For the figure standing before me is the oldest soul of all the fae, transcending any other title or even gender. They simply are the Lord Master, their previous self irrelevant.

Tall, they threaten to pierce right through the low ceiling of the bell tower—and even the rafters seem to strain just to avoid the head of long, gray hair framing a set of silver eyes. Piercing eyes. They appear to see everything and nothing at once, gazing through me while rendering me frozen.

This figure has been the sole continuous presence throughout my entire life. Twenty-four years—a pittance in comparison to theirs. Yet they somehow have aged in that time more than I have, becoming colder and sterner with every passing year. Fae lack the persistent youth of the vamryre. How old is the white-haired vamryer who watches me? He looks to be twenty but is probably twenty decades or more.

"Your greeting, young one." Lord Master's voice is ice, washing over me in a callous sweep. As I process their words, my heart sinks and I shuffle forward, my head bowed solemnly.

"Greetings, Lord Master. I thank you for the blessing of your presence." Those are the words all fae must greet our wise elders with.

Yet several more slip out of me unbidden. "I wasn't expecting your arrival today."

"Young child," the Lord Master replies. "Need I remind you? You are to expect nothing. Request nothing..."

Their subtle inflection is a demand for me to continue.

"Require nothing. Desire nothing," I finish, still eyeing the floor. "You are correct as always, Lord Master. I forget myself."

But I never forget anything—especially not when it comes to the carefully choreographed moments of my life. Only three days in my life matter each year, precisely three. One is the naming day, the anniversary of our birth. The second is the solstice to commemorate the births and deaths of all fae. The last and most essential falls upon the final day of the year—the commencement of the high council—the only one of those days even remotely close to today.

Those are the only times of the year when the Lord Master visits me. Never in between.

"You were gone, girl," Lord Master says, their voice eerily flat. "Where?"

"I...Nowhere." My heart won't stop racing as if betraying me with every beat. *Liar. Liar. Liar.*

"It is noon," the Lord Master says. "Your chores, child. What do they consist of?"

I swallow hard, relieved by a relatively simple question. "I clean the archives and dust the catacombs. I sweep and return the books to their proper shelves. I repair and catalog the older volumes."

And I read those volumes, huddled over candlelight—a skill that isn't allowed. When I was younger, the Lord Master taught me only the runes necessary to recognize a title and return it to its proper shelf. The bare minimum. Yet I went further. Not out of disobedience, I told myself then. I learned to fulfill my sole purpose all the better.

But a well-meaning sin is still a sin.

"The Citadel Mother was kind enough to show me to the catacombs and the archives," the Lord Master remarks, drawing my attention back to them. "You were not there."

I stiffen. "I… I was—"

"Though you were born ungifted and forsaken, you do possess one small quality, child. What is it?"

I clear my throat and croak, "Honesty, Lord Master."

"Honesty," the Lord Master echoes, turning the word into a dirty sin. A lowly crown. A curse. "With that in mind, I want you to answer me now. Where were you, child?"

There is no point in lying. "I was on the roof, watching the courtyard."

Out in the sun.

The silence is deafening. I can't stop shifting my weight from foot to foot. The poor Lord Master is so stunned by my debauchery. It takes them several tries to choke out a response.

"Where you can be *seen*?"

I shake my head. "No, Lord Master. I remain out of sight always…" My voice breaks. I lied. The vamryer saw me, but no one is allowed on these grounds. No one. Therefore, it cannot be a lie to say…

"Is there an event taking place?" I ask. Suddenly, that lone contradiction makes far more sense. "One involving the vamryer? I am sorry if I—"

"Vamryer?" The Lord Master's cold tone chills me to the core. "Recite your purpose to me, child. In full."

"I am an unwanted creature, claimed by no clan," I say softly. "I owe my life to you, Lord Master, and the sanctity of the Citadel. Honesty is my only quality, and obedience is my only task. I must never be seen and never be heard by those untouched by my wickedness."

"Does your task include venturing beyond those walls?" they ask, their voice an angry hiss. "Or questioning?"

"No."

Since I was a child, I have never left the grounds—at least not in the strictest sense. The roof is part of the tower complex, as are the winding caves beyond the catacombs. Never am I seen, therefore...

It isn't a lie to say as much.

"I am sorry, Lord Master," I say, desperate to fill the silence. "I shouldn't have—"

"You must atone."

My heart drops to the pit of my belly. Atone. I must. For I have sinned, so I must atone in the hope of forgiveness.

"Did you hear me, child?" the Lord Master snaps. I haven't moved.

"Yes." I spin around and finger the front of my plain gray robes. They are so ugly in comparison to the Lord Master's—a brilliant white that radiates purity and perfection.

My cheeks flame as I unhook the metal clasps holding the front of my robes together and let them fall just enough to expose my lower back.

"Recite your purpose," the Lord Master commands, their steps slow and assured as they move closer.

"I..." My voice breaks. Shakes. But it mustn't. I must never reveal any hint of pain or fear. To do so is to sin. To wallow in wickedness. So, I swallow hard and say, "I am an unwanted creature, claimed by no clan—"

Slicing pain cuts into the flesh along my spine. A sharp single line. The blade is polished—I know that much without turning around or looking back. Polished to shine and bestowed with ritual meaning. Every time I disobey, it cuts into my flesh.

Intentionally. Unintentionally.

In either case, atonement must be paid. Blood must be spilled. Scars must serve as lasting reminders.

"Enough," the Lord Master replies, silencing me mid-recitation. They step back. "Make yourself decent."

"Yes, Lord Master." I raise my robe and redo the clasps. Then I turn to face them, my head lowered, my eyes downward. Shadows play across the wooden floor as they stow their ritual blade back in their robes, still coated in blood. Always coated in blood.

My back sears. Eyes burn. But I mustn't ever show any pain.

"The commencement of the high council is nearly upon us," the Lord Master says, their voice stern.

I flinch at the abrupt change in subject. Has my transgression been forgiven? No, I sense. There is another motive for why the Lord Master made their way all the way here, beyond the high ramparts of the upper Citadel. A motive other than to catch my sin and issue punishment. But what?

"Yes, Lord Master," I intone in response.

"You understand what the ceremony entails, do you not?"

I nod and find myself wringing my fingers together, though I don't know why. "Yes, Lord Master. It is the one day of the year when the members of the high council gather before the entire populace and recite the rules that guide and fulfill us."

"Those of us who call themselves citizens," the Master corrects. A reminder meant to clarify one point—I am not included within that descriptor. I am a shadow hovering on the outskirts. So why remind me of such?

Unless...

A sharp, electric sensation darts down my spine, and I struggle to classify it. Excitement?

"That day is the most hallowed among our kind, and this upcoming one marks the centennial. A hundred more years of unity under one covenant. A glorious day. One I thought I would never live to see."

I nod again. As aged as the fae and vamryre are, it was only relatively recently that both races, along with the lunaria, finally made peace. Their covenant is fragile yet binding. A hundred years mark the first century of any real, lasting peace since the dawn of time. A testament to the wisdom of the elders that compose the council.

Or so the archives claim. Personally, I've read more than one account of the violence and bloodshed that raged before the peacetime.

"Do you understand me, child?"

I blink. "I—"

"I know you haven't witnessed such a ceremony, but I believe you still understand the significance?" The Lord Master is wary. How stupid am I? Do I even know the customs of the world in which I am shunned?

Of course, I do. Every detail and every custom I know well.

"Yes, Lord Master. Every year, a youth from one of the assembled races is offered to stand before the council in a reenactment of the original signing of the treaty," I say.

Silence in response. My belly twists as the seconds scrape by, with only the crowing of birds high in the rafters to fill it. I'm uneasy. Sweat drips down my brow, and I watch a drop splash onto the wooden floor. A dark thought takes hold—that is my life in the grand scheme. A splash that will mar the world for but a second before fading into nothing.

A tiny, pathetic drop.

"You understand that for the centennial, certain exceptions can be made. Must be made. It is a special day, unlike any other. A day when even our flaws can be acknowledged."

I frown, unsure.

The Lord Master continues, "A day when even those who may not be accepted upon regular circumstances may be asked to participate."

My heart skips. Stutters. Stops. They couldn't mean... I couldn't...

I look up and meet their cold, lifeless stare with a hungry, questioning one. "Lord Master?"

"You must keep up with your duties," they say, that glimmer of hope forgotten. "On the eve of the ceremony, I may come for you again."

With that, they leave, their robes swishing out behind them.

But I can't forget it. The chance to leave the Citadel for the first time—and to see a ceremony up close. It's a cruel temptation, one I know I could never have. Yet....

I want it more than anything I ever have. *Almost* anything.

Still, I want it so badly it hurts.

I want it badly enough to forget that I deserve nothing.

CHAPTER 2
Caspian

For us vamryre, freedom comes at a price—our souls. After death, no great equalizer will right all wrongs, reward the good and punish the bad.

There is only *more.* More existence. More agony. More suffering.

More.

It's an endless dance, and no one is left standing at its end. As a new pair takes their place in the twisted fucking waltz, only bloodied marks remain on the floor. The thread is what we vamryre call it, this horrible game of life. A woven tapestry composed of too many souls to name. A purpose that binds us in perpetuity.

Our master dresses it up with intrigue and claims that our being chosen by him is a gift.

A calling to Godhood.

He spends eternities trying to find new ways to glowingly describe what, in essence, is a curse. A festering charade of living that we carry on for his benefit. Oh, how we play pretend for *him*.

The reality is that we are all dead without the benefit of coffins for comfort. Though we pretend to be creatures that care little for our immortality, we will stop at nothing to extend it. This is what we are by nature as undead, lingering beings shunned by nature.

We want, and we take, and that is *our* truth.

We are no better than the mortals who supplicant us with their warm bodies and decadent blood. We hate them. We envy them. We cut their lives short to meet our own ends.

Over and over and over again.

This creature, however, meets none of the criteria our masters crave and desire. She lurks on top of that goddamned bell tower, always scraping. Waiting. Watching. Like a rat or a mouse. Some scurrying creature born in filth and darkness, she lingers in the shadow, never showing her face to the light. Worthless. Disgusting. Vermin.

So why was she, this foul creature, presented to me?

Why does Cassius want me to kill her so brutally?

Don't care.

I relish the chance.

It must be a test.

Or a reminder—I am always a dog on his leash.

His slave. How ironic that the promise of this realm is freedom, where all races live in supposed harmony. Bullshit. I hate these damn walls of stone. This sprawling city of glass and gold. A pretty, gilded cage of invisible bars. Our *beloved* Citadel.

It's a prison—but to think as much is to sin.

No matter, according to Cassius, I am all sin.

Caspian, he warns, his thoughts seeping into my own. I wince, feeling his pull from halfway across the city. As if space matters. Through centuries, he has had a hold over me. Over us all. Though the others crave his presence, squeaking like monotonous mice—*Our beloved Cassius. Our Master. Ours...*

I resist, biting deeper into my thoughts. Those fragile, pathetic recollections I can call mine.

Her. She is mine. Cassius may have commanded it, but a toy given by another is still, in essence, owned by the one who has it.

Therefore, she is mine, that ugly, little, deformed fae.

I have her in my grasp, and I don't care if it's part of someone else's game. I'll crush her. Break her. Scatter the pieces at Cassius' feet. I'll do his bidding with a smile, but in the end...

He can't make me do it cleanly and quickly. He can't stipulate that there be no lingering. No drawn-out moments until the end.

He can't make me waste what little time I have, freed from under his thumb.

Caspian!

The force of the command brings me to my knees in the middle of a fucking street. A glistening avenue lined with buildings of glass and gray stone. Our perfect, perpetual city. Strange looks are cast my way, and I can see the pathetic fleeting thoughts that cross their isolated brains. *Strange vamryre. Must stay away.*

Good.

They can run and hide all they want. When Cassius has his way, they will all be pawns to dance and sway at his whim. No longer will I be the only one to—

You dare to disobey me, boy?

Boy. Still crouched, I grit my teeth. Trying and failing to stand, I growl in frustration. How he loves to throw that hated word in my face. He relishes in the anger that heats my skin. He believes it puts me in my place. Swallowed by a mind as vast as his, I am a mere boy in comparison. A worm. Insignificant wiggling pest.

But he's the one who plucked me from the mortal masses. At *his* behest, the others turned me. At his begging.

He chose me.

Caspian, come.

My reply is terse, spoken out loud and within. "I work." Belatedly, I add, "As you wish, Master. I do this work for you."

Come, he snarls, unswayed.

No. No! "I work," I say, knees shaking, muscles straining. "For you. I do this for you!"

He relents—because he has no fucking choice *but* to. I can sense him lingering like a cat waiting to pounce. A lion, perhaps. He wants so badly to roar and take charge.

But he can't. His own words tie him.

He can't be implicated in this great scheme, oh no. The rest of the high council wouldn't like that. This sin is all mine. He would have me wait until the ceremony to strike. Maybe I would.

Until she looked at me, the little broken bird. So fragile. I see those black eyes even now, and I hoard the image away from Cassius and the others. It's mine. They remind me of something. A color I used to love. I think. Ebony. Black, black, black.

Doesn't matter, Cassius says, batting the thought away, out of reach. Bastard.

When I see her again...I'll poke those eyes until I remember more. Oh, how I want to play with my little bird, locked in her stone cage. What point is a surprise attack, anyway? No. True betrayal is crueler than that. It's stealing away inside the victim's skull and making a home there.

It's turning their own body into a despised enemy.

It's becoming their puppet master before they even realize they're being strangled by the strings.

I want that little fae to hurt. Can't explain why, but I want those black eyes wet with tears. It will be fun.

Easy, Caspian, I sense Cassius warn. Always warning. Always twisting. He told me once that my darkness was what drew him to me.

A gem among stones. A black heart, a perfect match for his own. Oh, how he resents that weakness. He reached out and took a pretty trinket for his collection.

He took me.

However, his virus did not infect me as perfectly as the others.

I do not love Cassius, my benevolent master.

I hate—

You don't, he replies, his tone so damn assured. *My loyal Caspian.*

Oh, how he loves to turn my disgust into a game at my own expense. I hate him. Love, love, love.

My master, my creator. Oh, how I love and adore him.

"No." Teeth gritted, I keep moving, pushing past a group of startled fae, single-mindedly focused on one goal. Cassius won't take this from me. I won't let him. "I do this work for you," I say. I lie. "For you, I do this."

Sweating, I reach my prize and brandish it in a fist—a delicate blossom taken from a cart sporting hundreds of the damned things. Smelly things.

The merchant—a dark-skinned lunaria—eyes me and sniffs. Only they, the wolf kind, can leave this damn realm and ferret back mortal trinkets to hawk for coin. Or so they think.

"I want it," I say.

He grunts and names his price for it—two silver—a fortune these days. All for what?

A stupid flower. A rose to be exact, white, and pristine among the dark stone surrounding it.

Cassius wants me to wait and strike like he would. Like a snake with fangs bared and poison at the ready.

But where is the fun in that?

I will do this my way. My own devious, deceitful way.

I will kill her on my own.

At the ceremony.

Maybe before.

Her life is mine alone to take.

CHAPTER 3
Niamh

Only those entrusted with safeguarding the repository are permitted to enter the catacombs below the Citadel proper, where the old knowledge is stored.

To enter without permission is forbidden.

As a keeper, my only role is to protect this place from outside eyes, but as I hear the sound of approaching footsteps, I swallow. My lips twitch. Maybe I smile.

"I can hear you," I call out tentatively. Quietly.

"I can see you." The voice is disembodied, and I can't tell which direction it originated from. Still, I spin around. My lips twitch again. It's a smile—not really. To do so would be an insult.

For one such as myself should never dare to greet an unblemished fae as an equal.

"Day," I say instead, wrestling my lips into a neutral line. "You came."

He steps forward from behind a row of wooden shelves. Bathed in lamplight, his eyes twinkle though his lips also remain in a flat line. Once I strived to find any resemblance between us. Any at all. Maybe the shape of our eyes was the same, though his are green, mine black. Our hair, at one point, might have been the same dark hue until his took on the redder tones of a fae at the height of youth and beauty.

Once... Perhaps in the womb, we were the same.

Watching him now, Day and I couldn't be further apart in both stature and status. He is so beautiful, destined to head house Aurelius, with his rightful counterpart beside him.

That is the one miracle of my birth, one could say. Poor Day wasn't born alone without a half to share his future with. Upon that fateful hour, the house of Aurelius was rewarded with two healthy fae children suitable to uphold the family name.

And one shameful spare.

Pairs are inherent to the fae. Like the night and its lover, the day, we must accept life's duality. Every true fae is born with a twin, a rightful counterpart. Three children in one birthing is unheard of. Forbidden. Taboo.

Three parts of one whole cannot exist.

"You're frowning," Day points out, his voice musical in the stuffy air. "Do I not look dashing in my ceremonial robes?" He extends his hand and I lower my gaze for the first time. He is right. Instead of the usual green garments that are a hallmark of house Aurelius, he wears silk in a brighter emerald hue, trimmed in gold.

Ceremonial robes. He showed me them once before, years ago, though they were far less ornate back then. Simple robes to mark his transition from a young Dawn to an adult Day. I wish I could have seen him then, standing tall before the elder council. Oh, how brave he must have looked, with our sister Day beside him—*his* sister. Day Aurelius and Day Aurelia. Were I included, I'm not even sure what moniker would be left for me to take.

Therefore, I technically have no name, though I devised one for me in secret. It feels like a small, invisible ball of warmth tucked next to my heart, known only to me. Maybe one day I will tell it to Day.

Maybe one day.

"You look so grown up," I say instead. "Accomplished."

"You've been learning new words without me," he scolds, but his tone is playful.

"Yes." Again, I almost smile. "I found an old thesaurus the other day. I will read it to you."

The back of my neck prickles as if warning of the Lord Master's disapproval—but what the high elder doesn't know does not hurt. I use my skills only to further my work in the archives.

But *if* I were discovered, my sin alone wouldn't be exposed. It was Day who taught me this rare, special magic: how to convert these strange runes written on old parchment into sounds. Then words. Then stories.

"Perhaps later." He nods, stroking his chin, now absent of any hair. One day—in decades perhaps—he will grow a beard before transitioning into the role of Night of House Aurelius. For now, his youth is his crowning glory unblemished. The planes of his handsome features are devoid of any wrinkle or flaw, and his red hair gleams like a living flame.

"Though I am *accomplished*," he replies, his eyes sparkling with pride. "After the ceremony, I will have a place on the high council. A true place."

"With Day Aurelia," I add.

His lips quirk downward. "Day Aurelia," he repeats, but his tone is flat. "She won't enjoy the role like you would."

Something uncomfortable twists in my stomach. I turn away and dust the books nearest me with my bare fingers. These old books remind me much of myself, abandoned in the dark, cared for only out of necessity. However, it doesn't make them any less valuable than the sparkly volumes on display on the higher levels. They hold their own secrets and hidden bits of knowledge. To those who care enough to seek them out, they matter. Maybe once every few centuries, but it's vital all the same.

"She won't," Day continues, his eyes narrowed. "She will be too busy sneering at the others to tend to our duties. Such arrogance is beneath House Aurelius. She has no humility. No pride in her modest role as a woman. Some days it's as if she thinks herself an *Aurelius*—not an Aurelia." He scowls, and my heart pangs with guilt.

"Then it is your role to guide her," I say gently, but I understand his frustration. The role of a fae is their only purpose, and that of an Aurelia is to support her fellow Day. To be beautiful and fleeting. To be honorable and obedient.

"She is not easily guided," he grunts, shrugging off the suggestion. "She doesn't listen to a word I say. She's defiant. Flighty. Easily distracted by trivial things. *You* would enjoy the main Citadel beyond these walls."

I can't stop myself from sighing in longing. I've only glimpsed bits and pieces of the famed Citadel city, heart of our society, in old volumes and through the windows. And...

From the roof.

The Citadel proper is the building at the city's center where all ceremonies take place—a huge, sprawling complex mockingly close. The main chamber is meant to be crafted out of pure black stone. Breathtaking is the only word to describe it.

"See?" Day prods. "You would enjoy it, and you would know your place; *by* my side and not in front."

He nods in approval at the imagery, but it seems like an unimaginable fantasy to me. Even now, to walk behind Day would be an honor well beyond my reach.

"How can I interact with those I am not allowed to speak to?" I ask of the row of books before me.

Day scoffs. "Hypothetically, of course. In this imaginary world you would be allowed to. By my side, no one would dare deny you anything—" He curls a fist, and his lips quirk upwards. Almost a smile. "I would be respected. They would have no choice."

A world where I would have been born a normal fae. It stings to think about. Perhaps it's just the remnants of my punishment that plague me so? My back is sore, chafing with every brush of my robe's coarse material. Restless, I slink deeper into the shadows where I know Day won't follow. The dark unnerves him. Threatens. Fae belong in the daylight, relishing in the open sky and taking wing in the sun's warm rays. Only unwanted creatures seek the dark for shelter. Vermin and vamryre and, of course, me.

"You won't be able to visit me, then. Once you ascend," I say. "You would be too busy with your duties on the high council." Why do I sound so sad?

"I will come anyway," Day demands, taking a step toward me, in half shadow. "I always will. No matter what. As the heir of House Aurelius no one would dare stop me."

No matter what. I cherish those words even though they are the antithesis to what I know in my heart. Even though they are a lie —a nice one—I cherish them still.

Poor Day will never admit out loud what we both know in our hearts.

Eventually, he will become an elder, perhaps even a Lord Master. If not, his magic will form the very veil that shields our realm from the mortal world, proving vital even in death. For eons, his soul will live on in the Citadel's foundation.

By then? I will be gone.

I will be dust.

Although it's a chilling thought, it shouldn't bother me. Honesty is my sole purpose. To despair is to regret, and to regret is to feel shame. I am not allowed to indulge in either emotion.

So, I grit my teeth and tell myself that I am fine. Content. At peace.

Then an errant thought slips into my mind, unbidden. Before I can stop myself, it's flying off my tongue, posed as a question, "Day, have you ever seen a vamryer?"

He laughs and I go rigid. My cheeks flame at the amusement sparkling in his eyes. "I forget how naive you are," he admits, his tone playful. "Vamryer are not allowed beyond the Citadel proper and certainly not in here. I see them at the ceremonies, or on the street. To speak to one is to speak to them all, for they are all husks controlled by their elder three. Mindless vermin, far beneath your curiosity."

I nod along. Mindless vermin. Not creatures with their own will. Certainly not a beautiful male who creeps into this very complex to watch me sin.

"Of course," I say, still nodding. His wisdom should ease my confusion and put it to rest. It's time to stop asking questions. Stop wondering.

In spite of that logic, the feeling persists long after Day leaves.

When my chores are finished, I should return to the bell tower. I start to, only to wind up on the roof as the sun begins to set below the horizon. So marks the time when the fae retire and the lunairia take their reign. The time of the vamryre, of course, is dusk and dawn, and though it is wrong, I claim my time in the few seconds of sunset. Just a handful of seconds, all mine.

At least before him.

The vamryre's smell reaches me even before I see him. Sickly sweet and pungent, so different from his usual icy scent. When he appears at the mouth of the courtyard, I see why.

In one hand he holds a white rose—a rare occurrence in this part of the realm. Any awe I might feel is smothered by wariness. Why is he here?

As if knowing the workers will flee rather than confront him, he stalks forward, boldly and unashamed. He is vamryre, and at their core, they are dangerous. Killing to them is what flying is to the fae. A way of life. A favorite game.

Why doesn't that unsettle me? I wait for the uneasy feeling, but it doesn't come.

"Hello, little fae."

I blink. Stare. It's another long second before I realize that he spoke to me. His eyes don't waver, his head upturned, gaze predatory and mocking.

I should disappear. Obey my only role. Never speak. Never be seen.

My lips part.

"Don't be scared now," the vamryre taunts. His voice is ragged, as though he is always on the verge of a laugh. Or a growl. "Come closer, little bird."

"You don't belong here, vamryre." That strong voice. I don't recognize it. It's a shadow of the stern Lord Master's, but the part of me cowed by authority shivers. Then I realize: it was mine.

The night creature smiles, and my breathing stops.

"So, it speaks."

It. That word itches more than Day's delusional fantasies. *It.*

I step back.

He lunges forward, standing almost directly below me. His rose looks so fragile in his grasp. So delicate, quivering in a stone-like grip. Pity for it is why I reach out. Without meaning to, I reach out, letting my fingers tease the empty air.

The vamryre grimaces. I think he meant to smile. "Come."

"Why?" I say. A question. A statement. Why bring that rose to me, if he has?

"Fly down to me, little bird, and find out. Secrets should be whispered."

A secret. A whisper. It's dangerous, a deceitful lie. I know that vamryres used to feed on our kind once—fae kind. Could this one be desperate enough to seek out a half-fae unprotected by the council?

If so, it would be a smart course of action. Were I in his shoes, I would do the same. And if so… I would want that prey to run. To scream. To make it fun.

How boring would it be if they put up no fight at all?

Slowly, I inch forward, unsure of how to proceed. I've never climbed down from this height. Never roamed the actual courtyard floor. I never have, but I don't feel afraid. Perhaps…thrilled. Disobedience has never been this exciting.

"Jump," my visitor says to goad on the rebellion. "I'll catch you."

He won't. I can see it in his eyes: the glee and the hate. He wants me to fall and bleed. He wants to test me. Can I fly like other fae, or is my deformity more crippling than it looks?

He's right.

I hate that he is right.

There isn't time to think. So, I step forward and raise my arms.

And I fall.

Thudding pain. The ground slams into me, driving the breath from my lungs. It hurts. Hard stone digs into my ankles, cutting and ripping. The front of my robes is covered in dust. My knees smart, bloodied and torn. Then, just as the sharp pain bites deep, I'm lifted into the air. Spun around. Set down gently on a crumpled piece of wall with the vamryre standing before me. Between my legs. Too close for comfort.

"You're bleeding," he says, his eyes glowing, teeth peeking from his upper lip. Sharp teeth. Fangs. He's ecstatic. Surprised. I've made it too easy for him, but I've also made it more fun. He lives for fun, this strange vamryre.

I thought his kind wanted only what the others wanted. Craved only what they all crave. Power. Wealth. Luxury.

None of which can be found here, in an old building that serves as a monument to their loss of freedom. The council elders want us to believe that all races live in harmony. The old texts say otherwise. The gossip circling even this old, neglected part of the Citadel claims otherwise.

The vamryre fought unity the hardest of all. In the end, it was only self-preservation that made them join forces with the fae and ultimately create our other realm. By that time, only three of the pure vamryre were left. Centuries later, only they and their spawn remain still.

Which one created him? A vicious one.

"You let me fall," I tell him, craning my neck to see his face.

Neither of us is surprised.

"You knew I would," he tells me, but he frowns at that. I wonder what he's thinking—which, should, in essence, be what every vamryre is thinking. They are one and the same after all.

So, what do *they* want from me?

Blood. In his gaze, I can see only hunger. This creature isn't like Day or Lord Master.

They pity me. Despise me.

He wants to devour. Me. The stone I'm perched on. The sky.

He doesn't care. He'll take anything he can sink his teeth into, leading to a stranger realization. Titles and status matter little to him.

"I can hear your heart beating, little bird," he murmurs, bringing his face near mine. A perfect face composed of impeccable bone structure. Lips unnaturally pink. Eyes unnaturally bright. Teeth unnaturally sharp. "I didn't know you perfect fae could bleed."

I am. Smears of red seep from a patch of missing skin on my right knee. As I watch, more blood comes forth. Drip drop.

I'm horrified. The wounds inflicted by my "punishments" are invisible to me, on my back, hidden by my robes. I've never even seen them for myself. Just felt the neat row of scars.

My blood is a novel sight. I gape. Stare.

The vamryre is electrified. He breathes in, pale nostrils flaring. Then his tongue shoots out along his lower lip.

I feel like I'm falling all over again.

"We bleed," I say. Then, I correct myself. "I bleed."

"You make it sound so novel." He rakes his fingers through my hair. The touch is harsh, snagging at my scalp. At the same time, it renders me paralyzed, awed by the sensation. He is ice cold, devoid of warmth.

He is the first stranger I can recall to ever touch me. Ever.

"What is your name?" His gaze rakes over me, bright and alarming. "Are you a Day or a Dawn?"

I frown. *Dawn. Day.* It is how we are named in accordance with our clan title. Since I have no clan, I have no name, not one sanctioned by our covenants, at least. So, I made one up.

I say it, and he scoffs. Sneers. In that cold, hissed voice, he repeats it, and I have goosebumps. "*Neeve.*"

He makes it sound harsh and vile.

"Niamh," I repeat. So soft and gentle. I love it still, even in the face of his amusement. It's all I have, and I love it still. "I found it in an old text. It's an old mortal script—" I break off, betraying a forbidden secret. Mortal lore shouldn't appeal to fae. Especially not a name, ancient and beautiful.

But to me, it was a marvel. If one could not be blessed with a clan moniker, then what could be better than choosing one?

He sneers. "You fae. Is that your family name?"

"I found it in an archive," I repeat. "What is your name?"

I don't care. It's not a mystery. All vamryre are named for their masters, one of a collective. The same could be said about the fae, but our family names come with a wealth of heritage and ancestry. Vamryres are just dolls, meant to please their owners.

"Caspian," he says in disgust.

I don't know why. It is a simple name that sounds nice to the ears. C must be the initial of his master, from which all the names of progeny are derived. I am not familiar with their hierarchy, though, just the name of the main leader who signed their end of the treaty: Nataniel.

"Your name isn't in the archives," I say.

His eyes gleam even more. "Your archives. You fae and your historical references. I thought your kind named each other like categories. Boy. Girl. Day. Night."

He laughs at our sacred traditions, though again, they are not mine.

"What do you want with me, vamryre?" I ask.

His smile falls. "What could I possibly want with a lone little fae?"

His voice deepened. I think he aimed to scare me, but I have nothing to fear. As long as I have the shelter of the Citadel and the grace of the Lord Master, what more could I want?

There is one thing, a part of me murmurs. One secret thing too sacred to voice out loud. A private thought. A wish.

"I brought you something." He raises the rose I'd forgotten he had. So beautiful and fragile it quivers in his grasp.

I take it, surprised by its softness. Its sweetness. I sniff the air and gasp in shock.

Caspian laughs, and the sound echoes in a dangerous rasp.

"I knew you'd like it," he declares.

I eye the object in question. Do I like it? I shouldn't, of course. It is a forbidden taboo—an imported luxury from the human realm that vamryres indulge in, but fae should shun.

I read about them all in the archives, roses.

However, none of the texts mention how sweet they smell. Pungent but soft in the same breath. I inhale again. Sigh. In this realm, such a bloom is a rare, coveted luxury.

It had to cost a fortune.

"Look at me, little bird." His fingers run through my hair once more. "Do something for me in return," he commands, his lips near the base of my throat.

"Is that how this goes?" I ask, mainly to myself. The archives are scarce when it comes to vamryre social customs. I don't know much about how they conduct themselves. Perhaps this type of exchange is unique to them? Given their transactional nature, I wouldn't be surprised.

But how should I respond? The fae don't…

Wait. I am an abomination.

Though, the vamryre doesn't seem to care to hear my response. His eyes wander, creeping over my gray robes and downward. When he spies the naked flesh of my thigh, where the skirt rose up, he grasps it with the flat of his palm.

I tense, my next breath trapped in my throat. He is ice, his skin flawlessly smooth but a dangerous strength resonates through his touch. He could break this limb if he wanted to. Shatter the very bone. A dark intent lurks in those scarlet eyes when I look up. Perhaps he intends to do that to me.

"I've always been curious what fae blood tastes like," he says. "Let me bite—"

"No!" I bat his hand away and jump down from my perch. Chuckling softly, he watches me go.

"It is forbidden," I say. Then I fumble my tongue and add. "Besides, I am not recognized as fae. Not officially—"

"You smell like the fae." He smiles in that beautiful, icy way. "See me tomorrow. Right here."

"No," I say, inching back toward the shadow of the building proper.

"Come," he commands, his eyes flashing. Then he cocks his head and beams. "I'll bring you something else, not-fae. Spend the night wracking your little brain as to what it might be. Consider what I am owed in return."

I owe him nothing. Nothing but a fortune in exchange for the rose. A foul rose I should return.

But I don't. As I clutch it, something the vamryre said echoes in my brain. *It's night.* The sun has already set, the best part of my day missed.

"Tomorrow," the vamryre says, drawing my attention back to him. "You bring me something in exchange for that—" He nods to the rose I still hold.

I want to let it go. I can't.

Personal items are fleeting. Besides my name, this is the only one I have. I cradle it to my chest as if to protect it from the vamryre's gaze. Another term from the archives comes to mind as I watch him: unhinged.

He is unhinged incarnate.

"Until tomorrow, little ebony bird." He turns and lopes up the ruined section of the wall with a grace that catches me off guard. From the roof, his movements looked jerky and unnatural. Animalistic.

Up close...

He is fluid and sure, much in the way a true fae would be before they take flight.

Not that I would know. I've never seen it.

CHAPTER 4
Caspian

I hate him. Cassius, the all-knowing. Cassius, the brave. He makes up those fucking titles to adorn himself with, always including his name. That name.

It's why he named me Caspian—as unique from his own as he could come, or so he said.

So he says.

Yet the others—countless many that compose his collective of souls—all have names deriving from his. Cassius. Beneath him swell an army of brothers: *Cassander, Cassper, Cassador.* Among them lies a harem of sisters: *Cassie, Cassandra, Cassidine.*

Then there is me, Caspian. His broken one. In fact, he named me differently from them. To prove it. To remind me. To torment.

I hate him. I hate him.

You love—the thought comes from outside my skull, bearing down like the stern hand of a parent. Scolding. Guiding. Warning. *We all love Cassius. We all love Caspian.*

As if the vamryre know any damn thing about such an emotion.

We feel nothing. It's why we like to masquerade as we do, luring fae, human, and lunaria alike. Oh, how we fucking love to play pretend. Those fools eat it up. They play into our hands, ripe for the taking. Ripe for the killing. Ripe for becoming yet one more of the undead, a new pawn in the Three's collection.

But her...

She irritates. Pale-faced and wide-eyed, she should have trembled head to toe with fear at the sight of me. Tears should have sprung to those strange, black eyes. Damn. It should have been easy.

But she resists, stubborn and unwilling. And yet she felt...

So soft. Unafraid. Another word trips into my brain, as unwelcomed as ebony. *Ivory.* The color of skin like the petals of that infernal rose. Delicate ivory.

Like a rose, she was fragile and weak, with limbs like petals that could be easily plucked. It was only natural for her to tremble. Even if they craved my touch, so many others before her shivered in apprehension. Instinctively, they knew to fear me. To hate me. To want to run from me.

She didn't. Her gaze held mine, those eyes unyielding. They relented to my touch as if she wasn't afraid, and I...

I wanted to taste her. *Me.* Not Cassius or the others. Her taste would belong to me.

Come, Caspian.

At night his command is too strong to resist. Cassius is awake at full strength, his veracity running through me. I am enslaved to the pull of the collective, those blind, dumb bastards. Their thoughts suck me in, pouring over the fae with disgust before scurrying away.

She doesn't interest them. They can't understand Cassius' greater plan.

Because he is, of course, why I have any interest in her at all. His will commands it.

There is something wrong with her, the broken fae with black eyes. They all can see it. Smell it. The nearer I am to her, the more revulsion they feel. As if cringing from an insect, they pull away from my thoughts. It's brief, but I get a glimpse of silence. Absence of thought.

I should loathe that emptiness.

You do, Cassius' voice in my head urges, potent with slavish devotion. *Resist it. Resist her. Kill her at the ceremony and be done with it.*

I will.

After a little longer play. He owes it to me after what he did to Cassiopeia. Loyalty is a foreign concept to our kind. There is only our master. Only the enclave and the collective. Only the vamryre.

No. I don't give a damn what Cassius thinks—what they all insist I think. Cassiopeia wasn't a mindless slave in a hive mind—what the other races call our collective. She resisted. We would tangle and clash our thoughts together. Sometimes, the clamor blocked him out.

Sometimes his voice overpowered us both.

I want her back.

No, you don't, Cassius' voice demands. *Cassiopeia was a traitor. She betrayed us all.*

How? We can't fucking know. He won't let us. No matter how hard I try to unravel the twisted thoughts, he keeps me at bay. It's only when I think of the fae creature that he lets me close. Slithering over my memories of her, he darts away once more. Apart from his plan, he has no interest in her, that broken thing.

He doesn't see in her what I do. Oh, she does her best to hide it. Maybe it would be more fun if she did? That hunger in her eye. That blind acceptance of pain. I know it well: *desperation*. She'll make this game too damn easy.

Good.

Centuries at Cassius' beck and call, and I need a good distraction. I've earned it. Earned her. He said I was a disgusting mortal. Evil, callous, and cruel. That was what drew him to me. Sometimes, he'll let me get snippets. Fragments of thought.

A boy. A man. I can't see his face, but I can hear his laughter. Cold as ice, my own voice distorted back. How I envy that bastard. How I wish I could remember.

You don't, Cassius claims.

But I do. If I taste her blood, I may remember. Fae blood is potent, rumored to—

Forbidden, Cassius snaps, monitoring my thoughts as always. With a sharp tug on my psyche, he aims to draw me back into line. His good, obedient, little Caspian. The creature he so badly wants me to be. A cherished pet I never was. There was a time when I treasured words like ivory and ebony. When I knew the terms beyond their superficial definition.

But how?

Enough! Come home, Cassius tells me. Beckons. Demands.

With night having fallen, there is no choice. My limbs move and carry me through the heart of the Citadel, away from the bell tower. Our home rests on a hill above the city, sprawling like a grasping spider, our web endless. We dwell within the most enviable luxury. Our master loves us so well.

When I enter the main hall of the manor, three siblings stand to greet me. "Welcome home, Caspian," they chant.

I can't even remember their names. There's so many of us now. Hundreds of insipid toys, each one as empty and uninspired as the last. Their minds were so easy to mold beneath the weight of his. Almost too easy. He's grown bored of the malleable ones, hungry for another rebellious entity to consume.

Like you, he hums. *My Caspian.*

Hate. Hate. Hate.

"You've done wrong," a sister says, stepping forward. Her eyes are beady red, her smile as rich and expressive as one painted on a doll. She's a puppet at the moment, controlled only by him. "He wants to see you, our beloved Master. Come."

I want to resist but denying him is futile. He is in my head—burrowed deep within my skull, laughing at my attempts to shut him out. One day, I'll silence that laugh. I'll render him eternally quiet.

"Enough!" Though her lips are moving, it's Cassius' voice she speaks with. "Come now. You've had your fun."

The others avert their gazes. It's not that they aren't enjoying my impending scolding. Their glee licks through our connected minds like the buzzing of bees throughout a hive. They'll watch and savor my punishment.

Cassius prefers to pretend these moments are private. I don't know why. He prefers to have me walk up the long winding hall to his chambers alone, where he sits on a velvet chaise, alone. When it comes to me, the bastard always desires to be alone.

Not the others. Not his perfect, unflawed toys.

"You've been restless, Caspian," Cassius declares as I approach him, sinking down to one knee. The action isn't mine. This close to him, there is no choice but his. No will but his. Only here in my mind can I rebel.

I hate this bastard.

No, he insists. *You love only me, your savior. Your master. Your—*

"I was doing your bidding," I grit out. Doing his bidding. Spending his fortune. Learning forbidden words he wanted me to forget: ebony and ivory.

Insolence! An audible hiss resonates through the mansion and through the mental collective. Another sin. One can't interrupt Cassius. It isn't done.

Yet, he smiles and, instantly, all are quieted.

"You are correct," he says, his voice like frozen honey.

Unlike his two counterparts that make up the vamryre council, beauty is the main trait that Cassius desires to hone, despite untold centuries of life. His—our eldest brother Nataniel prizes wisdom and collects his little tokens with their intelligence in mind. *His*—our sister Pol cultivates strength in her section of the vast collective mind. She seeks out mortals and immortals alike with a bloodlust on par with her own.

Cassius is different. He likes to claim that his oddity makes him unique among his equals, but it must be a lie because he *makes* us believe it. Beauty and character are what appeal to him. Sex and adoration are the only talents he deems worthy.

"You are restless tonight, Caspian," he repeats, but this time, the full weight of the collective echoes him.

Restless, dear Caspian, dear. Our dear, dear brother.

"I'm doing your bidding," I snap. "I always do your bidding. But I remembered something—"

Something lurking in those ebony eyes that haunts me still.

"Words," I spit out. "Words you wanted me to forget, but this is the part you won't let them hear, right?"

I can feel his smile widen like a string being pulled taunt. A warning. Yet, for a second, the rest of the mind grows silent. Only he can do so at whim—turn off the din of the others, create a secluded hole where he and his chosen prey can linger.

Is that what he did to Cassiopeia? It's been days, and I can't hear or feel her. I only know the bastard hasn't killed her.

To do so would be to admit failure, and dear brother Cassius is never wrong.

"Look at me, child," he commands.

My head jerks up, and I take in the creature lounging before me. He somehow manages to be both revulsive and appealing. Disgusting and breathtaking. A face and body that can attract both men and women, but I despise those gleaming red eyes. Hate. Hate.

"You've enjoyed playing with your toy," he says.

My upper lip curls at the word. The way he says it drips with disdain, but maybe it's the only one that fits. Enjoy.

"Yes," I admit. "Let me do more."

Poor little fae. She seems so damn innocent, locked away in her crumbling tower. The fae must tell her that she is a scourge, unknown to the others.

Lies. The secret has been out for all twenty-four years of her life. We all know. Her existence festers. Besides, the fae couldn't keep secrets if they tried. Those high and mighty bastions of haughty birds. The day she was born they had to reconcile with their flawed perfection. They haven't been the same since. She with eyes of ebony and ivory skin threatens their entire fragile balance...

I'm not sure if my memory goes back that far or if I'm just leeching off Cassius.

"My thoughts are your thoughts," he quietly scolds. "We are one, dear brother. It pains me that you resent us so."

Me and us. How he uses those terms so interchangeably. He wants the rest of his followers to abandon all sense of self. Become one with him.

Yet he can shed us just as easily as a silk robe. We matter little to him. His scars penetrate our bodies and minds, but in the end, the most lasting mark we can make on him is dissent. Being the off-note in his perfect symphony of sycophants. Hating him relentlessly.

"Wrong," he tells me while lifting the edge of his embroidered tunic. A perfect body chiseled from living stone but with one small flaw. "You are the only one of my many children to ever harm me." He's smiling. He relishes the pathetic attempt. He savors it over and over.

Why?

He thrives on control, and one day, decades ago. Days? Years? One day in the near past, I came after the bastard with a knife taken from some fancy display deep in the mansion. I tried to plunge it into his stomach.

No, that's wrong. The image in my head blurs and resets, clarified. Me *and* Cassiopeia.

"You miss her," Cassius says. "Our disobedient one."

He smiles wide.

"Yes," I say on cue. "She's served her punishment. Bring her back."

"I alone say when she has served long enough," he reminds. His glee licks through the back of my mind, exciting the others even if they're kept in the dark. I can visualize myself as he sees me. Bowed low, pretty little head upturned. Anger blazing in red eyes. Cassiopeia isn't the one he's punishing.

It's me. Always been me.

"Such an egoist you are," he murmurs, practically laughing. "Even now, after so long as a superior being, you still believe that the world revolves solely around you, little Caspian. Always raging like a mindless human. Hoarding meaningless words. Ideals. I've long tried to coax that out of you. How perfect you could be if you wanted to achieve it."

I hiss through clenched teeth. "Don't want..."

"Don't want what?" He raises an eyebrow innocently. "Finish your statement, brother. As you said, we are alone at this moment." He raises his hand, gesturing for me to continue.

I can't. He is subtle in his mastery, but I know the sudden dryness in my throat isn't real. Neither is my inability to find words.

The bastard loves to exert his control in small ways. He loves to watch me struggle on his proverbial leash.

One day, I'll strangle him with it.

"Your little fae bird—"

As soon as she is mentioned, my ears perk up. He suddenly has my full attention, and his pleasure settles over me like a sickly sweet perfume. He likes my attention, oh yes. He craves it.

"You do realize that your role only matters during the ceremony? Perhaps it was a mistake to tell you so soon?"

He's lying. Dear brother Cassius never makes mistakes. He told me for a reason. He lets me play with her for a reason. Because of his disgust for the fae. He wants her to suffer. Wants to shame and embarrass them.

He wants me to hurt her in order to hurt *them*.

"Those creatures have paraded their treaty over our heads for long enough," he says. But that's all he'll ever say. The real reasons behind his anger are locked up tight, well beyond my reach. Even his—our—brethren don't prod it. They let him fester in silence. They think he's too inept to act.

Cassius knows they underestimate him.

He is counting on it.

"Beautiful things are always overlooked," he says softly. "We understand this, my dear Caspian. More than you realize. Those who see beauty in the world are discounted. Ignored. Dreamers, they call us. Starving artists—"

"You want me to ruin the ceremony," I blurt out. Pretty words sound intriguing when uttered by the fae bird. Ugly when spoken by him. Wrong. I'll draw his attention away to anything else. "Why wait that long?"

The reasons why don't matter to me. I want to rip. Bleed. Kill. Without Cassiopeia, what else is there to do?

If I linger in this den of sheep, one day I will become like them. Their thoughts are a mindless hum: *we are one, one...* My brain will turn to mush like theirs.

And he will rue the day. He is my tormentor but I am his only source of amusement. I know it.

"So deviant you are, little Caspian. But yes, you are my agent of chaos. My knight," he purrs. "The fae have lorded over us all for long enough."

He will never make a move against them. He can't.

I can. I will.

But...

"I want to play with her," I say. Dumb, silly words, but they're the only ones that feel like me. Not pretty and fanciful like him. I'd speak in grunts if I could. I wonder if that little fae would shudder then.

"You can't harm her before then," he warns. "That is an order, Caspian."

Too late. I picture her blood. Hell, I can still smell it. Sweet and fragrant despite her abominable form. Far better than the itchy rose she sniffed with a longing she thought I didn't notice. My mouth waters. Tongue dampens. Damn, I want to taste her.

“Be careful,” Cassius warns, his tone stern for once. My little rebellions don’t faze him but this does: risking his precious plan. I’m only a small cog in it, that I know. Cassius would never ever trust the entirety of his plans to me.

In fact, I’m probably a backup. A last resort. My dear master, he has something else in mind.

“Such little faith you have in your own skills, my brother,” Cassius scolds, still serious. His voice sounds different. Less flowery. More grated, betraying his real age. This man’s life has spawned countless civilizations. He doesn’t waste his time on trivial nonsense.

Unless it happens within the walls of his domain.

“But that one stipulation cannot be undone. You’ve marked her pretty skin once. That should be enough.”

It isn’t. I want to bite her. Make her bleed more. Scream. I want to see fear in the little fae’s eyes. More forgotten words might spill into my mind when I do. Such as new, pretty words for the color red.

“You will,” he promises.

I flinch at that. Cassius never promises me anything, but he means this.

“You will have your bloodshed soon enough,” he adds. “That I can promise you, my dear boy.”

Yes. I nod. Oh, yes, I want it. But...

I remember something else. Fragments of a memory he doesn’t want me to fully grasp. Someone. Female, her voice a mocking imitation of his...

"Cassiopeia," I grate out her name and it's like yanking away a blindfold. I see her. Remember. My sister in bondage. She was punished, and he promised... "I do your bidding. You free her."

Was it our agreement in the first place? I can't remember. He dangles the true memory just beyond my reach, chuckling the harder I try to grasp at it.

"Our dear sister, Cassiopeia, who attempted to betray us all," he says, his voice low with disapproval. "Do my bidding in this matter, save your bloodshed until the ceremony and I will consider..."

No. Liar!

"You promised."

"I will reconsider her punishment," he says, smiling. Gloating. He holds all the cards, and we both know it. The whole damn collective knows it, simmering with the echo of his smug glee. He threatens to let them back in. To shatter this moment.

As pathetic as it is, I lower my head in deference. I don't want this quiet to end just yet. It's almost like my thoughts are mine alone. I only have to contend with his. Even so, I can grasp at thoughts just beyond my reach. Almost touch them. *Ebony. Ivory. Art. Museum. Canvas...*

"Are we agreed?" Cassius wonders, greedy to be my sole focus, always.

"As you wish, brother Cassius. I won't hurt her."

Yet. I won't leave marks. I'll make her bleed in ways that won't draw her pretty blood. Don't know how, but I will. I'll find a new word at the sight of her pain.

Sadist, Cassius interjects, supplying me with one I already know well.

"It is in your nature," he says out loud, sounding sad. Sounding pleased. "Always has been, before I rescued you from mortal obscurity. A fact that you have never forgiven me for it seems."

Forgiven. But what is there to forgive? He made me a perfect, immortal creature.

No. He corrupted me. Ruined. He—

"I saved you. One day, my dear boy, you will see that. I am your lover. Your only. Your savior. But for now, you may have your fun."

His permission is a gift. I'll take it anyway. *Yes.* I picture her, the fae. Those black eyes, pale skin. Ebony and ivory. I'll rip her to pieces before this is all done. I'll smear her blood all over the Citadel stone. I'll relish it all.

And, for once, he won't stop me.

"Just remember," he says. "Keep her in one piece until the ceremony. But have your fun."

He doesn't approve. The fae unnerves him. Disgusts him. She isn't a pretty, sweet thing ripe for the plucking like my "siblings" are. She is ugly and different and distasteful.

But what really bothers him is that I want her.

Never, not once, have I ever wanted him.

CHAPTER 5
Niamh

My days are simple and orderly. I wake up before dawn and gather the firewood for the two large fires in the heart of the underground archives. I must do this in darkness before the others wake up. Even when my lungs are filled with soot from stoking the fires alone, the old stone rooms are warm and comfortable.

Then I go to the main archives, wipe the floors, and clear the loose scrolls and bound books. The workers leave them for me to find, left open on desks and in stray corners. My duty is to collect them all like wayward children and tuck them back in amongst their brethren. Every volume has a place, no matter how dusty or tattered or neglected. Every one. When nestled in their home, they seem to sigh and settle into the cobweb-coated shelf with content. Yes, there they belong.

They don't despise their nature or rail against their fate. It doesn't matter that they may not be read as often as others. They matter, for they are in the Citadel halls, which means something.

Even for living beings, it means something.

I toil away like this until the sun begins to rise over the horizon. Then I tiptoe back to the empty east wing, climb into the bell tower, and then into the room above.

I am meant to stay there, out of sight, until sunset. Sometimes, I do stay.

Sometimes the itch for fresh air is too great, and I creep up onto the roof instead. Or sometimes I want solitude and head into the deepest depths of the catacombs where few venture.

Only Day will visit me now and again, and on those three important days of the year, I will be seen by Lord Master. Otherwise, the workers leave food for me at the mouth of the bell tower, but I never see or know any by name. One of them must have helped care for me when I was younger. Stern hands and a blurred face are all I can remember. Should remember. We live in two different worlds, much like how the mortals dwell alongside us in their own realm, oblivious to our very existence.

My heart pounds. It's forbidden to think of it—at least for me. The other races are feasibly allowed to transverse between the two worlds but there is a process.

What that entails, exactly? I'm not allowed to know. Fae, lunaria, and vamryre alike can leave and see those things mortals hold dear.

Once, a long time ago, I found a volume covered in dust at the very back of the shelf. I lied before—not everything has a place. It's a lie I tell myself; maybe one day I will believe it.

I have to believe it.

But this volume did not belong. I knew it with one look. The cover, though battered leather, was once a glossy sheen embossed with the title: sketchbook. On the first page, depicted in color and inked lines, was a building the owner thought important enough to transcribe in breathtaking detail. Not just any building, either. It wasn't composed of the stark gray stone that forms the walls of the Citadel. It was vibrant. White marble columns and gleaming steps.

Beyond that page was a wealth of other sins to discover: one of them being defacement, written in someone's hand on the inside cover. *Collin Webber.* A stranger who so permanently marked what he once saw as his. Owned. Possessed. My guess is that he created the images that fill the rest of the narrow book. Pages upon pages depicting the most wondrous things. Drawings. Paintings—some scribbled as belonging to The Museum of Art, the very building on the first page.

I'd never seen anything so bold. Beautiful. My favorite page is so worn it's nearly broken free of the binding. Still, I flip to it almost every day and gape. The use of color was wild and seemingly random, and yet the image was perfectly clear: a park with various people spread throughout, each one as lively as the next.

Artwork, I learned this collection was called. A sketchbook.

Never would I admit as much out loud—it would be a sin to—but that book contained images of the most beautiful things I've ever viewed. Collin Webber was the owner of his own realm contained in pages. More beautiful than the Lord Master, even. All of it created by mortal hands with nothing more than pigment and brushes.

I'd give anything...

Wait. I clear my head and shake it firmly. I own nothing. But if I did. Well, I would give anything to see such artwork in person. To look upon the strokes up close. Are they as realistic in person as they are in the drawings?

I will never know. Only fae are allowed to leave the realm, them and the other races. Even that vamryre could leave if he wanted to. Maybe he has.

I couldn't ask...

But to do so would be to humor his request. Tonight. I don't want to.

Yet, I do. The question won't leave me alone. It buzzes around and around in my head, and then I remember that, yes, he has. Not only has this vamryre been in the mortal realm, but he lived there once. Was mortal once.

He would know better than any.

Asking him would be wrong. Forbidden. Though, picturing those wild red eyes, I doubt he would mind. He radiates a wild energy that seems antithetical to how vamryre should be, according to the texts I've read. He has none of their poise. Their aloof mystique. If anything, he seems unhinged, like a bloodthirsty lunarian. Yet, his beauty alone designates him as one of the blood-sworn few. I wonder who his maker is. Not Nataniel, known for his quiet patience and icy wisdom. Clearly, he is the spawn of another.

I shouldn't let thoughts of him persist—but they do.

All day, he lingers in my skull, taking up space for useful knowledge. Obedience and honesty are my two redeeming traits. I have chores to tend to. Silence to maintain. I must remain hidden.

But as night falls, I am there, perched on the edge of the sloping roof, watching and waiting.

He won't come. The vamryre played a cruel trick. Cruel because even he knows what the rest of the fae do. I'm tainted. Unworthy. Unwanted.

"Little fae."

I startle, swaying on the edge of a tile. As if born from the darkness itself, the vamryre appears at the base of the tower. His eyes glitter in the dark, his hands empty.

"Jump down to me," he commands. "I'll catch you."

"Liar." I don't know where the refusal comes from. My legs still smart. I had to use parts of my robe as makeshift bandages. Even so, it isn't my place to refuse anyone, even a vamryre.

Aware of that, he smiles, his teeth bared. "Come. I won't bite."

He will. I can see the desire displayed clearly in his gaze. His teeth practically quiver with the urge to clamp down over flesh.

Yet, he seems restrained as well. As if he's balanced on tiptoe, ready to spring into action for another reason.

My throat tenses around a swallow. Oh, how he unnerves me. I start to back away, toward the safety of the bell tower. Then I remember.

My question. My heart races and my tongue dances, poised to ask it. Eyeing the vamryre, I say instead, "Don't let me fall."

His eyes narrow a fraction. "I won't."

He will. Even as I shuffle close to the roof's edge, I can see that he never moves. Doesn't even twitch. Still, I throw myself forward anyway. A little pain will be well worth it if he answers my question.

So, I brace...but the cold, hard impact never comes. I'm cold, then hot all over. His hands are on me, his arms so rigid the embrace hurts. His skin is ice, his gaze electric, igniting the skin of my neck. I hear him breathe as he sets me down. A harsh inhale. A hiss. An audible swallow.

My entire body quivers, though I'm not sure why. It could be shock. No one has ever touched me. Now this. He held me in his arms, just for a second before scuttling back as if I burned him. Did I burn him?

My eyes sweep over his hands, but they're unblemished. Perfect, even. His flawless skin seems to mock me with a quality I will never achieve. I wouldn't blame him if he cringed at the sight of me.

I look up into his eyes.

He is oh so very hungry.

"Caspian," I say, tasting his name. It's dangerous, like having live embers on my tongue.

He winces at the sound. Grimaces. Sneers. "Little *Neeve*," he replies, stressing the wrong syllable.

I say nothing. It's strange to hear someone call me that out loud. Even Day doesn't know it. I don't think I could tell him. He calls me sister and that is a gift enough. It would be wrong to expect more. Ask for more.

But near this vamryre, I find the strength to say, "I want to know something."

His nostrils wrinkle as his eyes narrow again. Then widen. "You want." I think it sounds mocking at first. Then my mind replays his tone and I decide he sounded cold instead. *Want.* He said it the way Day did when he spoke of our sister Day Aurelia. Anger. Bitter. Jealous?

Of me. I'd laugh if his gaze wasn't so stern. He pins me in place with that look. Holds it for so long I can't breathe. He'll drain me dry if I let him. I need to blink. Run. Anything.

I can't move.

"Speak, little fae." He advances a step, looming above me. His height is something I notice only now. With one blow he could strike me down. With one stride, he'd swallow at least four of mine. "What do you want?"

My throat trembles. I can almost hear the Lord Master scolding me from their place high up in the Citadel proper. Then I shake my head and remember: Lord Master isn't here.

"I want to know if you've been beyond."

"Beyond?" He cocks his head, his nose wrinkled. He is so strange. On him, curiosity is nearly indistinguishable from rage. He lives in anger and yet it suits him. Those cold, fiery features seem alight in the darkness. Day with his polished words and careful nature would warily ask me to continue.

Caspian, chin in the air, commands it. "Beyond where, little fae?"

I gesture blindly. "Beyond the realm. In the mortal world." My mind races before I can help myself. Beyond the realm. These walls. This gray, dark solace. Beyond rules, and regulations, and stiff order.

"And if I have, why does it matter?" His smile is sweet, his gaze deadly. "You can never leave."

I can't and I know this. I know this.

It stings to hear him say it. It irritates.

"You can leave," I toss back. "So, have you?"

However, I can see that he has not. His anger fades in favor of a brief, momentary glimpse of confusion. Has he left? He doesn't know.

I suppose his master doesn't let him question as much.

What a shame. I start to turn away. Lightning-quick, he lashes out and snatches my wrist, yanking me closer.

"Don't turn your back on me," he warns.

I wrench my arm away. "I would have humored you if you could give me what I wanted," I say. Then I wince. It's so mean. So greedy to be so transactional. My cheeks hollow, and my face goes pale. Then I remember, he isn't fae.

"Ah, so you are one to value repayment," he says, like a snake hissing a warning.

Too late do I realize my mistake. I've provoked him worse than the sight of blood on a skinned knee. He stalks forward, pushing me back.

"Do you?"

Back.

"If so, you owe me. Do you remember?"

For his rose, still tucked in a hidden corner of my room. I remember. He gave it offhandedly, with only mocking in mind. I know it.

Even so, I can't deny...

It's my only possession, rotting away. Petal by petal, it is all I have. Even if he demands it back...

I want to keep it.

"Do you?" His hand cradles my jaw, aiming for my throat. I feel the kiss of a nail, unnaturally sharp. He teases a vein with the tip of it, barely grazing at first... Then biting a little deeper.

I wince, breathing heavily, chest heaving. He is too close. My senses are overrun with this strange creature. It should be a bad feeling—worse than being on the wrong end of Lord Master's wrath.

He's too foreign to process properly. I go numb in the wake of his touch. I'm enthralled by the power of his stare. It lingers and stabs and swallows parts of me that draw his interest: my throat, my chest, the heart beating beneath. He looks at me the way the Lord Master does when eyeing the walls of the Citadel during their visits.

As if he owns every last inch.

He reaches for my hair again and I resist the urge to swat his hand away. Why? I don't know. It's a foreign sensation that jolts through me as he winds a dark strand around and around a twisting finger. My stomach churns. My skin heats.

He watches my reaction and he smiles. My fear excites him. Though, am I afraid? Fear is meant to be an unknown emotion to me. I live in the safety of the Citadel, what could I possibly be afraid of?

The answer: everything. I'm afraid of this quiet place, all I've ever known. I'm afraid of what lies beyond it. I fear the look in this vamryer's eyes and most of all...

I'm terrified that I won't be able to take hold of something I desperately want. I'm greedy. I want something badly enough to sin for it.

Head tilted, I say to the vamryre, "You can go outside the realm. Can't you?"

He laughs and lowers his face to mine. Up close his beauty is searing. It's packed into every pore, a delicate and violent mixture of strength and loveliness. He never has to think of the effect he might have on someone should they see him. He wields his beauty as dangerously as any weapon. Yet he seems careless with it, also. He doesn't seek to sway or impress me. He doesn't care to.

"You owe me something, little fae," he murmurs in a low voice, ignoring my question. He heard me, though: that brief streak of irritation crossed his face. For whatever reason, the topic of leaving...aggravates him. Frustrates. "What should I take in return?"

My pulse jumps. I'm rendered frozen as he inhales my scent. His very lungs seem to pull on the air, sucking bits of myself down into him. Rather than furrow his brows in disgust he... He hums.

"Give me something worthwhile enough and perhaps I'll enlighten you on the other realm, little bird. Give you another treat."

Like the rose.

He's lying. Yet I can sense that deep down he doesn't mean to. Perhaps his master's hold on him is far greater than he realizes. Still...

It's something. Anything. I'll grab hold of it, even so.

"What do you want?" I ask him. The words have scarcely left my mouth before I feel his own lips nudging the arteries straining in my throat, forcing me on tiptoe to grant him better access. I know what he wants.

"No," I say as firmly as I can manage. "It's forbidden."

But so is this.

"So is this," he grates out through clenched teeth as if I've become one of his collective and he can read my thoughts as easily.

"No. No blood."

He hisses in annoyance. He doesn't like that word: no. He must hear it a lot in the complex where they live—which is odd to consider. Vamryres are supposed to be one and the same. Yet his very nature is to resist.

"Then what?" he demands, his lips still pressed incessantly to my skin. As I remain silent, he deduces his own answer: what he can't bite, he will touch. His hands turn into grasping claws, gripping at the fabric of my robes. He doesn't discern between soft flesh and bone. He treats it all with the same rough, almost desperate groping. He captures a breast against his palm and squeezes it so hard I gasp. Then he's onto prodding my ribs. Hips. My thighs.

A strange thought comes to mind: he's never touched another. Not like this. Just to feel, with no care given to the body on the receiving end.

When he brushes a part of me that holds no interest—like my hands—he moves on with little attention given. But when he comes across a part he likes. He grips it, digging his nails in, making me wince. I'll feel his hands on my upper thigh for days.

"S-Stop," I choke out when he starts to wind up my skirts.

He does, panting, his head lowered, eyes downcast. "What?"

I don't know. I don't know why this feels so dangerous or why my heart is thundering like mad. I don't know why the thought of him stripping this layer of fabric unnerves me so much. It feels wrong. At the same time. It doesn't.

I want what he knows, and he wants... Something to do with contact. Feasting on me in a way that doesn't entail drinking blood. Should be an easy trade.

But he is so hard to decipher. I don't think he even knows exactly what he wants.

"Tell me about the other realm," I try.

He scoffs and pulls away, bored already. Then he stops. Whirls around. Lunges into me, pinning me back against the hard stone.

"I want to know what a fae tastes like," he counters, a challenge. His eyes glow, his upper lip quirked at an angle. "Let me taste—"

"Can't bite," I insist, though what good would mere words do against fangs? I can see them, threatening to pierce the flesh of his beautiful mouth. He wields them carelessly. In fact, I wonder if he has ever bitten himself by accident.

"No blood," he echoes, his gaze unreadable. When he pushes a knee between my legs, I freeze solid. He uses the foothold for leverage to bring his forehead to mine. When his lips descend, I'm sure he'll ignore my request. Bite.

He doesn't. At least not yet. He presses and presses, forcing my lips apart. His tongue shoves forward, brushing past mine. I stiffen at the contact.

He hisses, his mouth moving while still pressed to mine. "Do you fae not know how to kiss?"

Kiss. I should know the word. I think I do, but the meaning doesn't come. My head is swimming, my body alight with the feeling of him. I don't like this: kiss. It feels more dangerous than biting.

"Now tell me," I choke out, pulling back as far as I can. "You got what you wanted."

His eyes flash. He wants to deny it. But vamryres are transactional, or so I've read. It's in his nature to accept this payment, whatever it was.

"I *could* go to the other realm," he says, and I feel my eyes widen. I half expected him to deny me my prize but here it is, an exchange for an exchange. "The process is easy. If I wanted to."

Easy process. Easy. My brain won't let go of those words. It feeds on them, and that greedy ache within me grows fervent. I need more. I need to know.

"How?"

"Now, now, *you* are owed something," he says, sounding on the verge of a growl. "This is my gift to you: the ceremony..."

I suck in a breath. "What about it."

"They aim to show you then," he says with mocking derision. "Parade you before them all. Acknowledge. Does that make you happy?"

Does it? I don't know. I don't...

Stepping back from me, he laughs. "Until next time, little fae." He adjusts his robes with a flick of his wrist. I know little about vamryres, but he should be disappointed by his inability to feed from me.

Instead, he smiles in a menacing way, sated by something else I'm too ignorant to understand. Perhaps he enjoys unnerving me and vamryres can also feed off of pain and discomfort. It would make sense.

Long after he turns and stalks into the darkness, I'm still thinking about it.

And for once, I almost forget my greedy hope in favor of another mystery. What exactly did he take?

And why do I feel so empty without it?

CHAPTER 6
Caspian

She's waiting for me tonight, my little fae. I can smell her full of hope and innocent glee. She thinks she got something from me the other night.

She didn't. Her quest is meaningless, her curiosity pointless. The other realms hold no interest. No interest.

It's Cassius who tells me that—who insists it. Over and over, he inserts himself, growing louder the closer I come to her. *Ignore. Stay away. Remember, Caspian.* Usually, his anger toward me is minor amusement at my resistance. He enjoys it.

But when I kissed that little fae...

He grew enraged then. He hated me.

Good, because I will *always* hate him.

You don't, he tells me as I spy the fae lurking on her rooftop. *You love me. You are loyal. My Caspian—Mine!*

Not by choice.

But she is mine, all mine, and oh, how he hates it. He can't touch her, but I can. He can only force me to kiss him and the others—others who need to be lured to him and placated with false fantasies of what immortal life will be like. Lies upon lies. Shielding himself from their regret is why he never collects new toys himself.

Except once. *You*, he murmurs at the back of my skull, the lurking snake. *Only you, my Caspian. You were special enough to draw my eye as no one else has before or since...*

Bullshit. He took me, and ruined me, and broke me. The same way I'm going to break her.

"Niamh," I call to her, watching her throat jerk around a swallow. She doesn't like the way I say her fake little name, I've caught onto it. I love to say it wrong. I repeat it louder and watch her squirm.

Then she counters me with a soft, "Caspian," and my joy is snuffed out. She says my name like it's a dirty thing. A creature that will bite her if mishandled.

Just like I will. Yet something comes back to me when I hear that hollow voice. Almost. Another name... Another feeling other than hate.

What is it?

"Come," I snap, impatient.

She hesitates and bites her lip. Despite her plain features, I catch myself staring. Damn, her mouth is beautiful. It's not like Cassius' and his harem of pretty dolls: perfectly pink, plump, reddened from the previous drink. Hers are pale, and chapped by the wind and the lower is fuller than the other. It's ugly and lopsided.

I need to feel it again.

"Jump," I goad her.

With one last glance downward, she throws herself into the air and I watch her fall. So slender and delicate, she is. I consider letting her hit the ground and ruin more of that pretty skin.

You can't, Cassius warns.

But I've already lunged to catch her—he never told me to.

I sit her down and push her back against the wall, face upturned, eyes wide and innocent. Perhaps a different kind of innocence than the kind Cassius claims. Makes us mutilate. The mortals he craves are so very hopeful. They believe our bite will cure their ills and make them happy.

It does, he claims.

It doesn't. It makes us bitter, distorted angels just like him. He prefers us that way. Little shattered mirrors he doesn't have to see his own reflection in. Hateful, vicious things.

However, I can see myself reflected in her eyes. A pale creature with an unholy red gaze. Cassius' sadist. He wants to swallow her whole, she can see that. Even so, she doesn't shy away. She'll let him engorge himself on her—for a price.

"Ask your question," I snarl, cutting to the chase. She couldn't hide her intentions if she tried. Such a greedy one when it comes to knowledge. I wonder how she'd react in Cassius' library. The one he keeps locked up tight and warns us away from.

He doesn't remark on that. So, I'm left to imagine it. The little fae might wet herself with glee. Would I give it to her? Maybe.

For a price.

"Tell me how to get to the other realm," she demands. This is the one aspect of her I dislike. She isn't haughty like other fae, with their holier-than-thou demeanor and noses upturned to the sky. Her arrogance isn't an act. She demands and expects her quarry in return. There is no game with her. No chase.

Whatever I ask, she'll give. Except blood.

She even says it as if reading the intention that crosses my mind. "No blood—"

I silence her with a kiss that makes her wince. I slice her mouth on my teeth. *Yum.* I taste her blood after all. A hint. A glimpse. It's so...

Fucking good.

My blood surges with need and desire. I'd rip her open if I could. Tear her to pieces. Drink and drink and drink.

You can't, Cassius warns.

I don't need him to hold me back. If I break her now there won't be anything left to play with. No pretty little limbs to touch and feel with squeezing handfuls. No tiny throat to gasp and no living body to flinch as I ram my tongue inside that wet, warm mouth. She is a broken puppet at my disposal.

Unlike Cassius, I can't break her mind on a whim. I can't smother her urge to resist. I've got to make her want it—want me. I've got to coax this lamb into letting me slaughter her piece by piece.

So, I step back and let her breathe. She pants, struggling for air, her hands clutching her chest. I've ripped her robes open. Pale flesh lurks beneath the heavy fabric, out of my reach. She struggles to pin the material together. I grab the edges from her. Pull them apart. Stare.

It's hard to tell whether she's ugly or beautiful. Her body is gaunt, sickly thin. Nothing like the plump little beauties Cassius likes to hunt. He picks them out like a butcher would the primest rib. Those lazy, spoiled mortals, drunk on life and power and prestige. He especially likes the kind whose wealth has seasoned them like fine wine. He can taste the aristocracy as he drinks them up. Perhaps he believes it makes him wealthy as well. Poor Cassius.

He would never want her. Never ever want to shove himself into that delicate, tiny body and see if he'd fit. Make himself fit. He'd never crave what he could easily have.

But I do. My cock stirs to life with a searing, alien emotion. Lust. I want her.

You can't, he warns. This time, his concern isn't about the blood. This time, he isn't asking. I feel his will slam into me, a weighted battering ram. *No sex. No touching. No more kissing.*

But why? He makes me do it to the others. Makes me lure and seduce his chosen few. He lets me fuck them, and suck them, and package them prettily for him. For *him*, he lets me have them.

Not her. She isn't for him or anyone else. Locked in her tower, she'll never be touched again. Never be seen. And when I kill her —*when* not if—that poor little body won't be in pieces large enough to be felt.

She's mine at this moment. I can fuck her body and Cassius will never know the feeling. I can make her unlock this caged memory and usher new words into my fractured mind. A million seem to explode from nowhere, here and now. *Gracile. Docile. Impeccable creature of ivory and ebony.* Mine to take and ruin. All mine—

I said no, Caspian!

I wince and pull back. My skull is on fire, his anger a rancid poison. Stupid motherfucker. He can do that when it suits him—hurt me when it suits him. I'm a dog on his leash.

"Are you alright?"

Her voice. The concern in it makes me recoil. It isn't forced or faked. How dare she? I whip around and find her pressed to the wall, hands trembling, robe open, body on display. I look at her and forget the rest. Even Cassius. For a moment, he is a quiet, angry voice in the back of my skull and I wouldn't have it any other way.

Defying him hurts—excruciatingly. But when I kiss her again, the agony evaporates. The glee feels better. Rebellion feels incredible. I take my tongue and shove it deep. Hard. I'd shove my way through her throat if I could.

In her, I discover even more words. Sensations. Thoughts. *The warmth of sun on my skin. Charcoal-coated fingers. Acrid smoke...*

She sputters and presses on my chest. When I let her free, she gasps for air, her cheeks flushed pink.

I can hear Cassius again, gnawing away. *Stop. I said stop!*

"Name your price, little fae," I croak to her. She knows what I want. She can already see. For the first time, those black eyes are wide and afraid. Good. Good. Good. Good.

"Tell me how to get into the other realm," she says but her voice doesn't break. It's steady and stern in a way Cassius' could never be. How the hell can she do that? She shouldn't be able to...

Still, I'm captivated, sucked in. His voice is even quieter now, a whisper. *Caspian!* If I please this little fae, maybe he'll go silent permanently. Forever. Blissfully fucking quiet.

"Don't know," I admit, but that isn't the answer she wants. She'll pull away and Cassius will return. So I look at her, and I lie. "But I can find out. You'd like that, wouldn't you?"

Her hope. Fuck, it's brief. It glimmers in her eyes like a shooting star, gone in the next breath. She smothers it deep down where I can't see. But it's too late. I know what she wants and she craves it so badly.

Boy, will this be fun.

"Be a good little fae and maybe I'll tell you how," I suggest, twisting the knife. Hope is like that, painful and deep, too deep to pull out.

Maybe I'll discover the real answer. It can't be hard, but it must be a secret. Cassius knows but he hoards the answer. I can feel him tugging it out of reach, tucking it beyond my view.

Stop and I'll tell you, Caspian. Stop this. Stop! Or I'll change my mind...

I wrench away from her. The bastard. He'll take my fun away.

Her startled gasp is intoxicating, however, tempting me to ask...

"Why do you care?" When I turn back, she's watching me, still half-naked, wringing her delicate fingers together. She's doing it on purpose—with every twitch of her hands, the opening of her robe widens, until the sleeve of it threatens to slip off a slim shoulder entirely. Damn her. "Cover yourself!"

She blinks and then does, wrapping the torn halves of her robe tight, pretending they're whole again. Cassius is even louder. *Caspian! Come—*

"I want... I want to see a museum," she blurts out. "It's where mortals store their paintings. Their art." She assumes I don't know the term.

But I do. Somewhere deep in my thoughts—mine, not Cassius'—that word triggers a bell. Words. *Color. Pigment. Linseed oil.* I curl my fingers, remembering something. A sensation. Wet. Soft... I just don't know what any of it fucking means. So I smile and lie. "I've seen one. I can take you there."

It's a building. A place in the mortal realm, I know that much. A place where they horde things—old things. A stupid place I'd never visit.

Unless she asked me to with those wide eyes. Begged me to, bloody and bleeding. Maybe I'd give in. It could be the last sight she ever saw.

The thought has barely crossed my mind when that hope begins to swell in her again. She can't even contain it. So full of fucking hope and wonder and the disgusting things that Cassius craves in his prey. It almost makes her pretty, almost. That look in her eye is almost enough.

"You have? What was it like? Did you see the—" She says something. A forbidden word that Cassius blocks out. He's clawing his control back bit by bit.

Caspian, he growls. *I'll make you pay. Make you suffer. Ungrateful wretch—* I'd shrug him off like any time before, but... This time feels different. Angrier. Oh, I've made him very angry.

Good.

"I could take you there one day," I lie, and she eats it up with a startled gasp. Her longing is disgusting. It creeps over me, drawing me closer to her, shutting Cassius out again. The bastard will make me pay for this—*oh yes, how you will pay.* But lying to her is a game too delicious to resist. It tastes almost better than her blood, so damn sweet. I need it. Just one more drop. "What would you give me in return?"

She swallows hard, her throat trembling. Then she says, "I know what you want. I don't care. I'd give you anything."

A laugh rips out of me, but inside I'm irritated beyond all belief. Anything. As if that word means a damn thing. But to her, it does. Anything means *anything*. I'll have her little soul in the palm of my hand. Mine to break. Shatter. Twist and morph. She's mine. All mine.

You are mine, Caspian, Cassius growls. *Come home to me. Now! That is an order—*

"Prove it," I spit out to her.

She flinches, wrinkling her button nose. I'm sure she'll refuse. Renege on her previous offer. Good little fae don't promise their bodies to vamryre after all.

She juts her chin instead and runs a pink tongue along that awkward upper lip. Then she tilts her head as if to offer her throat to me—she doesn't. No, that would be a step too far. Instead, she issues the next most dangerous taunt: a twitching, trembling hand inches toward the front of her robes. She fingers a carefully hemmed collar.

My vision flashes red. Cassius's rage, not my own. *Come,* he growls. *Now!*

All I can see is a slender patch of pale skin shielding a racing pulse. The thrum of it floods my eardrums, a siren song. She'll give me anything? Only a fool would spurn such a bargain. Cassius can't punish me for that—it's what he taught me to do, isn't it? Prey.

"Tomorrow," I bite out to the fae. Cassius is raging, and his summons devolve into shooting stabs of pain ripping through my skull. I ignore him, focused only on her.

She should shiver with gratitude, thankful for my merciful acceptance.

Instead, she shakes her head. "No-No. I..." She sucks in a breath and bites her lip.

Ah, I see. I'm not the only snake to visit this fragile, little bird. The thought is unwelcome. It itches. Who else has touched her but me? Who? Who? I sniff her, pulling her scent into my lungs. Interpreting every little nuance. Next time, I'll test her. See who else's scent has tainted her.

"Tomorrow," I tell her. Then I turn and give in. My body moves of its own accord, back to the mansion. He will punish me for this, old Cassius. Maybe even take my toy away.

As if he could. It's too late.

I'll scratch my name into her flesh if I have to. I'll take her life for him—that is a given. But in the meantime...

In the meantime, I won't let anyone stop my fun.

Only I can end this game.

CHAPTER 7
Niamh

There is a book I have in mind, one I have yet to read. A dangerous one—a forbidden one, only the Lord Master wasn't the one to deem it off limits to me. I doubt they would care. But I have. I've sought to protect my mind from anything that might sully it. What need would I have for such knowledge, after all?

I am alone. I'll die alone.

The vamryre, however, has peculiar tastes. He wants one thing from me, even if I'm not sure exactly what it entails. I know of it, the act between two creatures meant to create new life. Mortals use it for fun.

So do the fae. They pretend like they don't, but I can hear them, the other workers sometimes. They gossip and speak freely out of earshot of their betters. They speak of trysts and fun and other taboo subjects.

Dirty subjects.

My fingers shake as I pry the particular volume loose from a collection near the middle of the archives. It isn't dusty like the others deeper in, and a simple, brown cover and dark script seem relatively anti-climactic for what it contains. It's only after I finish my chores that I find a corner and read by lamplight in the few minutes I have before the other workers awaken.

With every word, my cheeks flame. My eyes widen. I feel like a child learning about the wonders and magic of the fae—then learning in the same moment that I will never be able to experience such wonders for myself. Only, *this* act I can experience. Maybe with the red-eyed vamryre.

A worthy trade. I tell myself that over and over. In exchange for information on the mortal realm, any price would be worth it. And it is. I don't need much convincing.

I continue to read, fingers shaking, unease growing. I push it aside and study this volume the same way I would any other text. I strip any emotion from the act and interpret it simply. Limbs and bones. An organ that goes there, a reaction here.

Nothing serious. Nothing vital. It's less taboo than giving up blood.

"Sister?"

I never even heard him approach and my body relatedly has to remember how to work. I startle back, dropping the book entirely. The clatter is violent, echoing throughout the room. At a glance I can tell that no one else is here—yet. No one but Day.

He watches me warily, his head cocked, a question in his gaze.

I stammer. "Day. I didn't hear you."

"Are you busy?" He gives me that almost smile and stoops for the partially open book. I nearly trip in my rush for it, but he's too quick. His friendly demeanor lasts right until the second he scans the title. Then his lips shift downward and scarlet creeps across his high cheekbones.

"I was returning it," I say. My voice sounds odd. Then I realize that it's because I lied. Even accidentally. Even a little bit. I have never lied. The panic doesn't sink in as I reach for the book. My hands are upturned waiting and empty.

Because I can't take it. Politeness dictates that I wait for him to return it.

He doesn't. Instead, he steps back and flips through the volume, an eyebrow raised skeptically. When he scans the last page, he laughs outright and slams it shut with none of the care that should be taken. *Thunk!*

"I'm surprised they keep such tawdry trash in here," he says, his voice too loud. I scan the room like a hungry mouse. There's no one here, but my heart is racing. No one here, but a part of me still despairs. I lied. I'm filthy, less than tawdry trash.

"I should return it," I say weakly. Finally, he slowly lowers the book into my grasp. I turn and nearly run past dozens of towering shelves deep into the back corner. There, I shove the book back and then jump away as if burned.

What on earth was I thinking, reading such things? Despite my disgust, my brain is already processing the newfound information and storing it away for later. What I once never considered now seems imminent. Inevitable. Sooner or later, the vamryre will do those things to me. Wicked, sinful things.

"You are distracted today," Day remarks. It's a second before I process his low tone. Then I see the confusion in his eyes. "Are you not happy to see me?"

"Yes," I blurt out with a nod. "Of course. Always!"

It used to be the moment of every week I lived for. Wait... Used to? No, it is. No one else could take his place, because he is fae and we are blood. He sees me even though it is forbidden to. The risk he takes is so great I could never repay the kindness. Never.

"I'm sorry, I am just... Thinking about the ceremony," I say.

He scoffs and some of the light returns to his expression. He's himself again. "How silly to worry about something so boring. Though, this year is supposedly a 'special' anniversary." He sneers. How silly.

To me, it is everything. I would give anything to leave these walls, if not the realm. Anything to see the Citadel proper with my own eyes. Would I ask such a thing of him, my dearest Day? No. The risk would be too great, and his presence is enough of a gift. Besides, there is nothing I have that he could want.

He isn't a rabid dog hungry for a bone.

"Should I leave if you are determined to ignore me? Me, the only one that bothers to speak to you like an equal? Who teaches you purely out of kindness?" His voice rises. "It's only because of me that you can even enjoy this damn place as you do!"

I stiffen and nearly sink to my knees in contrition. "I'm sorry," I breathe out. I'm so sorry. I'm being so rude—so horribly rude. It's as if the vamryre has infected me, stripping away my manners as easily as he did my robes.

My skin grows cold at the memory. At the same time, a deep-seated shame heats up within me, but it doesn't feel like shame should. It's not painful to endure. It causes my heart to race and my belly to flip.

"I'm sorry," I repeat to poor, confused Day.

"I accept your apology. Now get up." He nods and adjusts his bright green robes—his normal style this time. "What shall you read for me today?"

My lips twitch though it would be obscene to smile. "Whatever you like."

His choice is the same as always: a volume from the olden days. One rife with bloodshed and violence and depictions of the horrific wars that eventually led to the Treaty of races. He gobbles up every word and licks his lips every time I mention the word death.

"What a shame we don't live that way anymore," he says when I finish a particularly brutal passage. "Out in the open, rather than here—hiding in a false realm like herded animals. Forced to walk alongside scum like lunaria and vermin like the vamryre. Safe in here, you don't see. You don't have to deal with their infernal stink." His nostrils wrinkle, his disgust palpable. "The other day, you asked of vamryre. I will tell you of them: a slavish horde controlled by three. Cassius, Pol and Nataniel—the only one with real authority. Soon, they will not traipse around, flaunting our rules as they do."

I swallow hard. Cassius must be the master from whom Caspian descends. One of the three, yet Day makes it seem as though... They will not maintain their status for long. Am I curious? I shouldn't be. Yet, I don't implore him to stop. Instead, I ask, "Oh?"

He sneers. "Our high council will put those bloodthirsty rats in their place. At the ceremony, the entire realm will see the way. The *rightful* authority is not with some pointless treaty, but with the fae alone."

My heart twinges. The boast would sound odd coming from anyone else. Coming from Day, descended from one of the very figures who composed the first council, the words are merely reflective. Right?

Yes, I tell myself. It was the fae, after all, who devised this realm—a haven from the chaos of the mortal world where they were persecuted to near extinction.

"Sister?" Day claps his hands loudly enough to draw notice. "You may continue reading."

"Of course." I read to him until our hour is up and he has to leave. He does so quietly, his head bowed, flaming red hair blazing a path through the shadow. I'm not exactly sure how he sneaks in. Perhaps there is a tunnel or a passage somewhere. Maybe one day I could be brave enough to ask him—

Stop! I shake my head firmly and return to the bell tower, my hidden haven. I should read or attend to fixing the old books the workers leave for me. There is so much work to be done.

Yet I pace instead. I pace in circles and tear at my hair. I adjust my robes—my remaining set. The other one is ripped beyond repair, folded, and hidden in the same corner where I keep the sketchbook of art. And now my rose. His rose.

I own nothing. I am nothing. It is the way of the world.

One vamryre can't change that—even if he holds the potential to upend my entire world. Expand it beyond the boundaries I have been taught to always obey. Damn these greedy feelings.

I close my eyes and try to drive him out of my mind through sheer will. It's futile. By nightfall, I'm creeping onto the edge of the roof, watching and waiting. My body is alight with all the shameful things I've learned. It's like I've been given a million pieces of silver—the exact price of the only thing I've ever wanted. I'll spend it all without a second thought. I'll throw it all away just for a glimpse. A chance. A tiny piece of hope.

He has my hope in his fist, the vamryre does.

Over the course of the night, he shatters it into a million tiny pieces.

Because he doesn't come.

As far as he was concerned, it was all a game.

CHAPTER 8
Caspian

I disobeyed. Therefore, I should be punished.

Oh, how the bastard makes me pay.

A simple game of torture is his favorite.

I sit in a room with nothing in it. No furniture. No window. No him. No light, either.

Should be paradise in theory. I'd kill for a world without him.

But then he plays, oh, how he plays. He twists my thoughts to suit his needs and makes me see what he wants me to be. In my own damn skull, he makes me play pretend. As a benevolent master with me as his slave.

I can't resist—not when the fantasy is his creation. The only thing I can do is watch as this simpering, twisted wretch wears my face and submits to him. Moans for him. Begs for him.

I'd rip off my skin if I could. Gouge out my eyes. I'd tear my throat to pieces if only to give him the satisfaction of watching me choke on a pool of blood at his feet.

But he won't let me. In this dance, he holds all the cards, a cruel puppet master. I can only sit and watch. And watch. And seethe.

His fantasy begins the same way they always do. I thank him for rescuing me from the bonds of mortal life. Oh, how I simper and carry on. What a fucking fool this fake Caspian makes of himself.

Usually, he shows me what he wants from me in these deranged mental theaters. Disgusting shit. Twisted shit. I have to beat it out of my mind later—literally. I ram my face against a wall until my skull splits, and the pain rips me in half. As I heal, the others will whine and whimper. They've grown weak in their immortality, sheltered like the well-fed lambs they are. It's Cassius who enjoys my agony. He enjoys it too damn much.

The only way to forget is through the pain. To numb the part of my brain only he can touch and exploit for his own uses. He never lets the others see these sick fantasies of me. Only he and I can play this game.

And now her. He takes my fantasy of Niamh and corrupts it. It's *him* that I watch sling her against that wall and rip at her delicate robes. He is the only one in those dark, haunting eyes. He is the one who breaks her. Who makes her scream. *He* paints that ugly face with tears.

No. No. No.

It should be me. Me!

During his torture, I normally feel hatred, not this. This is rage. Anger. *No.* She's mine. *Mine!*

Suddenly, his fantasy breaks. The fake Caspian lunges, eyes blazing, a knife conjured from nowhere. Maybe I created it. Maybe it's a memory...

"Enough."

He's here now, in this room, and I'm back in my own skin. Fists clenched, teeth bared.

Cassius isn't smiling either. "You go too far, boy," he snarls, and his face reveals itself for what it is: a mask of skin stretched taut over a skeleton that should have long since faded to dust. "Your disobedience is a novelty to me."

At least he admits it. To hear him admit it...doesn't fill me with the glee it should. It sounds like a warning.

"But outright defiance? I will not allow it." His voice raises and echoes throughout the house. Our siblings cringe and shudder. He isn't like this: angry and unseemly. All because of some stupid little fae.

A fae who is *mine.*

"She isn't yours," he corrects, flicking through my thoughts as if they were a swarm of flies. He sees me watching her, well before I ever approached. Then he sees me touch her. Kiss. Crave.

He knows what I really want: to remember. To take her. To feel that body envelope mine in a way I've never craved anyone. Never him.

No! He hisses. Anger makes him ugly and strips away the beautiful veneer. Any other time, I would revel in this. I did it, finally. I pissed him off well and truly.

But I'm not gloating. His rage carries a risk this time. He can batter me. Hurt me. Torture. But I don't want him to—

"It was a mistake to trust you with such a vital task," he says, and my vision turns red. "I'll ask one of your brothers instead. Then sweep your memories clean."

"No!" My teeth are gritted, muscles chorded, body on all fours like a snarling beast. I paw at the blood-red carpeting. Can't do much more than that. Still, I snarl, "She's mine. You gave her to me!"

"Wrong." He raises his hand. "I did no such thing. Tell me why I should let you keep your little toy? Your recent naughtiness does not warrant a prize."

Bastard. Motherfucker. Piece of shit.

I think every fucking insult I can muster.

He laughs and laughs. *This* is the Caspian that appeals to him. A monster fixated only on him. But her...

The fae complicates things. Ruins things. He can't let me have her.

Then I won't remember. Won't remember that I will *never* want him.

"I may change my mind," he says, his voice a slithering snake winding around me. "For a price."

I hate him. He's thrown my own words back in my face. On the receiving end, they aren't so much fun. They are a demand. A test.

How badly do I want her?

You don't, he tells me, his smile wide, voice inescapable. *You don't want her. You will surrender. Give in. Be my good, loyal Caspian. Your past is gone. Dead. Accept it.*

I do. I will. The past is dead.

"One of your brothers will take over from here," he repeats, but I know a knife is hidden within that offer. None of our brothers have their own will, not anymore. They'll do his bidding, and it will be *him*. Him touching her. Killing her. Tasting that sweet fae blood.

No. I'll kill him first. I'll kill them all first.

"Now, now, Caspian." He clicks his tongue, and in an instant, I'm flat on the ground, writhing in agony. It's as if he dropped a ton of bricks onto my skull and stripped away my ability to heal. Then he goes further, oh dear, Master Cassius. He turns my brain into a sieve and lets the others in. I'm inundated with them all. Stupid, mundane, insipid creatures that only think of him. Long for him.

Cassius, our lord Cassius...

Through gritted teeth, I counter him the only way I can. "N-No. No! I...want...her."

"Insolent wretch!" The pressure relents, and he begins to pace, his robes swishing out behind him. Then he stops. His smile returns. Damn. I know that look. He's devised a new plan. A more twisted game to play, he and I.

"You can have her," he declares. "For a price. Whatever you derive from that fae, you must also give to me."

Fuck. No. No. No. I'd rather die. But I can't let him know. Can't show that he has me dangling on a string. "I gave her a rose and a lie," I hiss. "Is that what you want, Lord Cassius?"

"No," he says with no inflection. "You gave her a kiss. A slow, savoring kiss." His disgust laces the air. I can only imagine how angry he was after that. To lose control over me. To watch. "That and anything more, you must give to me. Or, you can carry out your original plan. Attack her at the ceremony. Nothing more. Nothing less."

Sick fucker. He thinks he's won. Thinks I'll back down without a fight. I should. Nothing is worth touching him. Enduring him. Nothing. Nothing!

"Until you square our debt, you are forbidden from seeing her," he says. "Not until the day of the ceremony."

There is not much time left until then, of course. He's already taken one night from me. I've spent hours locked in here, at his mercy. What has she gotten up to in that time, the little fae? I picture her face. I see those eyes.

Worth touching Cassius for? No. Never. *Never!*

"Then we are agreed," he says. "The ceremony is in a fortnight. I can ease your mind before then. Wipe your thoughts clean."

Take her away, those minutes I stole. Minutes when I wasn't crushed under his thumb. Seconds when I did what I wanted. Without him. Seconds when I almost remembered...something.

Are those memories worth a kiss? A dance with the devil? No. No...

"Wait." The word rips from me just as his consciousness descends on mine. I get a glimpse of his true self then, old Cassius. So very badly does he crave to wipe my fae away. Replace her image in my head with his. Maybe then I'll crave him?

Never. Never.

Regardless, I step forward, hands clenched, head bowed. My hackles raise with every step. I hate this. I hate the way this monster's eyes widen in shock and desire as I draw near. When he reaches for me, trailing a finger along my jaw, his hand shakes and I have to choke down my revulsion. He wants this more than he wants her gone. A chance to touch me if I can touch her? A fair trade.

A sick trade.

A bitter bargain I will make, for I need to see her again, sweet little Niamh.

As Cassius traces my mouth with the pad of his thumb, her fate is sealed. For this, I will make her pay. As he crushes his lips to mine, I count the ways I'll make the fae return the favor.

She will suffer as I suffer.

It's just that she's so damn naive...

She might enjoy her punishment.

CHAPTER 9
Niamh

Here in the archives, apart from any race, I have learned to create my own creed by which to live by. A purpose. That of a fae is to fly on the rays of the sun, majestic and wise. The lunaria live by the light of the moon, powerful and bold. Aloof and mysterious, the vamryre dwell in shadow, comforted by their distorted truth.

And I…

I thrive in disappointment. Resilience. Honesty. I have learned not to expect anything from anyone. It was a lesson I thought I'd ingrained within myself.

Apparently not. The vamryre and his offer was a test, one I failed miserably. I dared to hope.

Never again will I fall for such a distraction. I will tend to my studies and my chores with vigor. I will clean and order the archives. I will ignore that hidden sketchbook. I won't think of him.

I won't.

It's been two nights, going on a third. How pleased he must be with himself. He dashed my hopes, but to what end? My mind can't conjure up a reason, and that is what unsettles me. I don't know why he came to me in the first place. Why he taunted and touched. Kissed. Toyed.

There should be a reason. One that explains his behavior—all vamryre have a motive, driven by the will of their master. He has to have one.

In the end, what matters is not his motives. I could have used him in my own greedy way. I could have glimpsed, maybe...

No. I shake my head and refocus. Rather than wait on the roof, I linger in my room until the complex falls silent. I've never noticed how enclosed this space is—a narrow box that spans the length of the bell tower. I never realized how cold it is—the wind whistles through the thin windows and their fragile shutters. My only source of light is a candle, not the fae magic that illuminates the rest of the Citadel proper. The flame on the wick dances as I cradle it to my chest and tiptoe down into the archives. Upon finding it empty, I creep back, back to the furthest, most darkened corner.

No one comes this far in. These shelves hold the books of least interest to fae kind. Some of these books have not been touched for hundreds of years.

I crouch down behind the most neglected shelf and...

I don't cry. It isn't allowed. I just breathe. In and out. Out and in. Then I bite my lip and dig the nails of one hand into the flesh of another. The pain is sharp and sweet, but it doesn't penetrate. I have to dig deeper. Scrape. My nails, however, are a pale imitation of the Lord Master's blade.

Still, as I scratch, my mind grows numb. Until, clarity. I can think. The thoughts aren't quiet like they should be. They're bitter and lingering, fixating on the vamryre no matter how hard I try not to. It's wrong to hate. Taboo. Forbidden.

But if I could...

I'd despise him.

"Little fae. Is this where you hide at night?"

I blink. Stiffen. Freeze. He can't be here—I conjured this hallucination from thoughts alone. It's why negative emotions are forbidden. They seep into our psyche and stain. Corrupt.

The vamryre standing here isn't real. He does, however, have a scent. This hallucination can also move, advancing toward me, pale enough to reflect what little lamplight there is. Despite his kind's aversion to daylight, down here he is the sun. He is blinding.

However, something isn't right. His steps are different, lacking the predatory ease. They're stilted. Stiff. As if he's fighting through lead with every inch he advances. Like it hurts him just to come near me.

Those eyes blaze, burning bright. They peer into me and turn any hesitation I had to dust. My body has already become accustomed to our transactions. The questions I thought I'd put behind me surge back to the forefront of my mind. I can't resist. My lips part, and they tumble out one after the other. "I waited. Where were you? What do you know? Tell me about—"

"Patience." He snaps the word, utilizing it like a whip. "So eager, little fae. Little Niamh."

My heart stops. It's the first time he said my name without the mocking. The cold nonchalance. There is power in every syllable. Hot, molten hatred.

The hairs on the back of my neck stand on end. He pins me with that stare alone. I'm suffocating with every second, feeling his hands wrap tight around my throat. Only a heartbeat later do I realize that he's never moved.

He's still standing there just beyond the nearest bookshelf. The shadow cast from it drapes him like a cloak. It is only those crimson eyes that remain visible.

"Tell me what you want. I..." I lick my lips and change tact. "I know what you want."

I've studied it. I'm ready. My body tingles with anticipation. I'll sacrifice it and any other part of me he wants. I need to know. I have to.

"And what do you want?" he counters, his head cocked at a menacing angle. "Say it out loud, little fae."

I do. "Tell me about the other realm. The mortal one."

He cocks his head and leans against the nearest wall. His skin clashes harshly with the dark stone. He's a creature of light and darkness. A representation of all the races in one. Fangs bared like the lunaria, blood red eyes of the vamryre, the confidence of the fae.

But what does that make me?

A creature in the shadow of all three. A hybrid of immortality and something else. An enigma that lingers in obscurity, ignored by all but the corrupt few. An illness. A disease.

"Why should I do that, little fae?" That voice is colder and sterner than any I've heard before. "What will you give me?"

My lips tremble. I run my tongue across them, but it doesn't seem to do much. Still, I swallow hard and say, "I know what you want."

At least before I did. Tonight, he is different. The mention of corruption doesn't excite him. He grimaces as if the thought is too repulsive to contemplate. In the blink of an eye, he lurches closer as if drawn to me. Pulled. His hand flies out, fingers outstretched. They brush my hair and then grasp a handful in a fist, yanking me toward him. His lips brush mine and hover. Not quite contact. Something in between. I can hear his ragged inhales, drawing my scent into his lungs.

And I...

Go limp. My back arches. A strange ache pulses through my belly, moving downward. It's like the hunger pains I feel when I've gone too long without eating. Harsher, if that is even possible. Pressing my knees together is the only way to find relief. Sanity.

Suddenly, I am unable to meet the vamryre's gaze. I have to stare down at his throat and watch it jerk as he swallows. I shiver with every controlled movement. Jump. His mouth nudges my jaw without warning, urging me to face him. Present my mouth again for him to brutalize.

I shouldn't.

I can't stop myself. It's as if my neck begins to twist of its own accord. In a blink of an eye, I find my chin tilted, my lips parted, mere inches away from his.

Then, all at once, he steps back. "No," he tells me. "I don't think you're worth it."

Like that, he turns away and stalks toward the mouth of the archive. How he got in, I suppose I'll never know. I should be relieved that he is gone. I should hope my brain conjured him as a brutal reminder.

I'm not supposed to hope for anything. Ever.

Disappointment is all I'll ever know.

CHAPTER 10
Niamh

I wake up with a renewed sense of mind and a stronger resolve. I know my place and I will seek comfort in the dusty corner of this massive shelf that is our realm. I will take the Lord Master's wishes to heart. I will obey and cloak myself in honesty.

When the ceremony comes, I will perform however I am asked to.

I will clean and hide. Hide and clean.

When I creep into the archives before dawn, I do so with my hair pulled back, and my head bowed in deference to no one. Obscurity is all I require. Even Day...

If he comes, I will turn him away. No one should penetrate this dusty, cobweb-covered solitude. It is all I deserve.

In resignation, I begin cleaning. I wipe the floors until they shine and return the books to their shelves. Then I dust and sweep and...

I nearly choke on a hard swallow. The back of my neck prickles—it has from the very second I entered this vast chamber. From the moment I sensed him, even if I didn't want to. I've tried to ignore him. Pretend. Will him away.

He isn't here. He is a figment of my imagination.

He is right behind me. The primal rasp of his inhalation teases the air. Inescapable. Was he here all night? Watching and waiting for me. Or perhaps he meant to prey on one of the other workers? No. Drinking from them would risk prison or worse.

But me...

No one would care if he hurt me.

I wait for him to make himself known. My heart races—he has to hear it. He must feel how my skin heats and catch the hitch in my breathing. Damn him, he knows.

He says nothing.

So I keep walking, moving deeper into the catacombs. The darkness shrouds me, a familiar friend, but it's heavier than ever. The solitude descends, and too late do I realize my mistake.

No one comes here. No one...

Except for Day for a few brief hours a week.

And *him*. Caspian is behind me. Against me. Pressing his body into mine.

I can't contain the sound that rips from my throat. A gasp. A whimper. A cry.

It's a noise that strikes a match and sets him alight. His hand captures my mouth, sealing the lips shut. Then his body acts as a battering ram, shoving me into a shelf, as if he means to crush me into it. His free hand creeps over my body, grasping through my robes to grope the flesh beneath. My throat. My collarbone. My breasts. He grips one tight, so hard I lurch on tiptoe. It hurts, but in that pain lurks something else that shouldn't be there. It makes my head feel lighter. Dizzy. It makes my lips part against his palm, and another broken noise slips out.

He groans then. For a second, I think I've hurt him. Bitten.

But I haven't. Although his mouth finds the crook of my throat and suckles at my flesh, he hasn't either. A sharpness rakes over my pulse point: teeth. Still, he doesn't bite.

In spite of this, I'm bleeding, drained of something more vital than blood. The feeling makes my body go limp. It makes it easier for him to grind his hips into mine. Wrench me to face him. It is this overwhelming, draining emotion that makes my lips part in anticipation, even before his tongue plunges between them. He drives into me so hard it hurts. Stars dance before my eyes, and the blood rushes through my eardrums.

I can't breathe. My hands fly to his chest, aiming to push him away. My grasping fingers snag the edges of his robes instead. Grips them for dear life. Holds on as he drains me dry.

And it is a tormenting, torturous, incredible way to die.

When I am kissed by him, I lose myself in the violent nature of it. The hunger betrayed by his grasping hands that roam my body. Tug. Grab. Knead. That ache within me returns, gathering in my abdomen. Then lower. Pressing my legs together isn't enough to stifle it. I can't...

Abruptly, he pulls back, but there isn't a smile on those beautiful lips now. In contrast, he seems even more lovely, with a look of horror corrupting his features. The first time he kissed me was a taunt. The second, a game.

But this...

With a third kiss, he's committed some horrific sin that rattles him to his very core. It guts him. Disgust fills his eyes as he looks at the fingers still grasping me. His upper lip pulls back from his teeth, exposing his fangs. He'll bite me now, I know he will.

He kisses me instead. Harder than the last. Grasping my skull, his fingers tear through my hair. His chest presses against mine as if he is trying to crush my beating heart with force alone. Each brush of his lips feels sharper, tinged with fangs he doesn't bother to restrain. My blood is a symphony humming through my veins, reaching a crescendo as his nails scrape at my scalp, locking me in place.

He breathes his darkness into me. Like a wildfire, the corruption spreads from my belly to my entire body. It steals my breath away, and I feel that foreign pressure building within me, pulsing. Unbearable. Only by rocking my hips and grinding my knees together can I smother it.

The vamryer notices, tearing his mouth from mine. His eyes blaze as he looks down, lips glistening—but he doesn't move. Using his leg to push mine apart, he grinds his knee against the source of the ache instead.

And it is...

Violent. Searing. Fire.

A broken sound rips from my throat. My head rears back. I can't find the strength to stop him or even remember if I should. I only need relief. Anything...

Then, too quickly to bear, he jerks back, out of reach. "Fuck him," he hisses. "Fuck. Fuck. Fuck!"

There is a look of torment in those eyes. Yet before I can pull away, his hand slides down to my hip, stroking through the fabric. I shouldn't find comfort in the action, but I do. He wants me, the only bargaining chip I have to trade. Whatever his hesitation, I'll make him push past it.

I have to.

"What's wrong?" My voice is a breathless gasp.

"I can't," he hisses. "Already owe him. Fuck him."

"Who?"

My voice makes him stiffen, and those eyes fixate on me once more. It's like he's seeing me for the first time.

Disgust isn't there, though. That dangerous hunger returns for a second, and I know exactly what he wants. He's never stopped wanting it. However, something has held him back.

Maybe it's the same rules that should restrain me.

No matter; I know what I want. What I crave. What I need.

"Tell me about the other realms," I murmur, my voice soft in the echoing space.

"I can't." He breathes out as if pained. Then he lowers his skull to mine, our foreheads meeting, lips a hair's breadth away. "What do you want to know?"

My mind runs wild. There are so many things. So many more questions. One day in, I've already broken my new rule. The hope is back, and it's too potent to resist. In his arms, I'm suffocating with greedy, filthy need. I'm drowning.

And he is my lifeline.

"I want to know *everything*," I breathe out. "What is it like? How can I go? I want to go. Take me—"

No. I bite that back so hard my tongue stings. Too hard. I've made myself bleed.

"And what will you give me in return?" he asks, his voice practically a whine. "Your body?"

He uses both hands to capture my waist while raking his gaze over the body in question. Small in comparison to his. Thin. Pale. Sickly.

Even so, his eyes gleam and glow. For this, he's just as greedy.

"Is that what you'd give me? You'd let me fuck you if I wanted. Shove my cock between those pretty little thighs."

My cheeks flame at the vulgarity. Never outside of that infamous novel have I heard such language spoken. But I don't deny it.

And he groans, his throat rasping. "You would," he snarls. "You would. But I don't want it, fae. You aren't worth it." He steps into me, shoving his knee between my legs like before, but this time, his hand follows, inching up, up, up. "But I *do* want you," he grates, prodding at that part of me, unshielded by fabric. "I'll take—"

Suddenly, he stiffens, head cocked, eyes narrowed. He frowns and steps back, pressing a finger to his mouth. A heartbeat later, he fades into the shadows.

And then I hear it. Footsteps, bold yet soft. Day.

I can't move fast enough. My limbs don't seem to work, and I'm left tugging my robes into place as he steps from behind the nearest shelf. His gaze is warm, his half-smile firmly in place. Somehow, he doesn't sense the vamryre lurking just out of sight. Somehow.

Though he is all I can feel. All I can focus on. His presence cloaks me in an icy chill that even poor Day, despite his namesake, can't displace. As the seconds tick by, the furrow in his brow deepens. He is unsure.

"You should be happy to see me." The statement isn't a question and yet it shatters my mind state all the same. Am I happy to see him? Yes. No. I fear for him.

Caspian's vile emotions are so easy to read. Even with my eyes closed, breath held, I'm sure I could sense what he's thinking. His anger has a smell, like sulfur and fire. Like smoke.

How can Day not sense him?

But he doesn't. His smile is gone now, his gaze wary. He runs a pale hand along the front of his green robes—an uncharacteristic display. What in the hell is wrong with me?

"I... I am always happy to see you," I choke out in a whisper. My voice can't seem to penetrate the quiet. My heartbeat surges, seeming so much louder. It tolls like an alarm bell, sounding suspiciously similar to a name. *Caspian! Caspian!*

"You're shaking. Are you cold?" Day's frustration has turned to concern. He grabs my forearm and steers me toward the hearth at the front of the chamber—or, he tries to. Something happens the second his fingers make contact with the fabric of my sleeve. It's like I'm electrified—struck by lightning like the bell tower is during a particularly fierce storm. Jolted. I trip over my feet and crash into a shelf, knocking books off their perches and sending a teeth-grinding pain through my shoulder.

He shouts in alarm, Day does—but I barely hear him. I can't hear him. All I can see is a creature molded from the shadows, threatening to descend. I shake my head. I'd plead with him aloud if my voice worked. *Don't. Please.*

And somehow... The shadow stills and fades back into the darkness.

"You're ill." Day's tone carries a knowing dip in inflection. As if my pale presence confirms a deep-seated fear. As if he finally realized that I'm broken and might corrupt him with my taint. He steps back, and it hurts. I don't know why it does.

The vamryre leaves me in disgust, and I hate him.

Day cringes from me and alarm, and it hurts me.

"I'm sorry. I'm fine," I rasp. My right hand won't stop stroking my left shoulder. It aches and aches. My eyes water if I touch it. It burns if I don't.

Still, I push the pain deep, deep down and smile.

Day is at ease again. He steps out into the main chamber and beckons for me to follow. We're at our familiar corner within seconds, and all should be well again. Should be. His visits bring me such pleasure—at any other time. When he isn't in danger. When I'm not gritting my teeth in agony. When a bloodthirsty creature isn't watching us from the shadows, leeching anger and bitterness into the air.

Unconcerned, Day heads to the nearest bookshelf—the one that contains his favorite volumes. He picks up a well-worn leather book, a different one than the other day.

"Read to me?" He asks, or rather, demands.

But it is a request I always fulfill so happily without question. When a monster isn't near, hungry for me, seething that his meal was cut short.

"Of course." I take his preferred book like I always do and flip it open to the first page. Then I read. I try to. My voice is a croak, but I try so very hard to.

Luckily, Day doesn't notice or care. He gets his story told in a halting, hesitant near-whisper. Even so, he nods, content.

When I finish, I return the volume to its proper shelf. Then I face Day. Smile.

He doesn't leave. Instead, he leans against a bookshelf and watches me. He lingers. It's the first time he's done this. My fingers tremble as I trace the spine of another book. Wait for him to speak.

"I've noticed that you've been distracted lately," he finally says, his disappointment clear. Suddenly, my heart hurts more than my shoulder. I've upset him. All my fault.

"I'm sorry—"

"I think I know why." He tilts his head to eye me solemnly, his hands clasped at his front. The stance is so similar to Lord Master's that I blink. At the pinnacle of youth, it's like Day has morphed into an elder overnight. Then his half-smile returns, and the illusion is shattered. He is still my almost, not really sibling. We are blood again.

"I'm sure you heard the rumors." His tone is a prompt, but I don't know the correct answer. What to say? What to say?

I stammer. "Rumors?"

He nods, a red eyebrow raised in suspicion. Or is he merely skeptical? "About the ceremony."

Ceremony. Ah, that ceremony. The one the Lord Master hinted about. The one Caspian claimed I would attend. The centennial anniversary of the only order our society has ever known.

"The ceremony." I nod.

Day's brows furrow. Wrong. I've given him an incorrect answer. "Perhaps I misunderstood." He starts to leave without uttering his customary goodbye. It's not that he's angry, but that he's stuck in his head, much like I am. But why? Over what?

Suddenly, he stops. Spins, the edges of his robes swishing out in an emerald wave behind him.

"The book you were reading," he says. "The other day. I'm sure you know."

My cheeks flame. I can't breathe, and the shame has nothing to do with the taboo topic tucked away on that very back shelf. It's because of who is here to hear it. My filthy indiscretion. That, more than anything, has caught the vamryre's interest. I can feel him listening, hunting for any topic to use against me.

"I... I was returning it," I rasp.

Day frowns. Then he sighs. "I am ascending early on the centennial."

He says it so casually, which it is anything but. An asteroid has just struck, destroying my entire world in the violent aftermath—and it happens completely in utter silence.

Day will ascend. He will marry his chosen bride, his counterpart. He will live in wedded bliss in the high Citadel.

He will never ever see me again.

"You didn't know." His tone is cautious but relieved. I didn't lie to him—I never would. Whatever fear he's held silently has been put at ease. His smile returns, but this time... It's nearly full and almost fills his eyes with mirth. "Are you happy for me?"

"Yes," I croak. For him, ascension is everything. He will become a full Day with all the rights on the council. His purpose will be fulfilled.

I will be left behind. How selfish of me to care about that instance of his happiness. How greedy to want him to stay here forever.

"That isn't all," he says. "We are House Aurelius, the most pure. Due to our status, I can make decisions that others cannot."

My mind is buzzing so loudly that I barely hear him. My body hurts. Brain hurts. My skull is two sizes too small, and my heart will soon grow tired of beating if the vamryre doesn't leave soon. Boom. Boom. It hammers into me, overpowering whatever Day tells me next.

I only hear snippets.

"Choose my bride..."

But she's already been chosen. His counterpart—our sister Day—as is custom. She's been chosen for him since birth, destined since we all drew our first breath. She is everything I'm not, but jealousy isn't what I feel.

In a sense, it is relief.

He'll go live the rest of his life in bliss, and he'll never see the mess of me that Caspian makes.

Because I saw his intentions clearly. I can almost hear him shouting them, even in the silent dark.

I'll break you, little fae.

I'll gobble you up whole.

"Goodbye, sister," Day says. I realize he's never left. Not yet.

As he does, my feet move of their own accord as if I mean to follow him out. Run. Chase. I've barely entered the ring of light that shrouds the main chamber when a hand comes from the shadows and yanks me back, back, back.

He drags me to the end of the archives and shoves me into a dark alcove where the candlelight can't reach. He's so heavy. I can't move him, even when I press both hands to his chest and push. He is stone, crushing me, slowly, slowly...

He's not. He has me pinned, both hands on my shoulders—my poor, injured shoulder—but his fingers shake. He wants to grip me tighter. Push me away. Then he compromises, bringing his face in close while letting his hands fall.

"Read to me," he intones in a cruel mocking imitation of Day's fae-like cadence. Coming from him, the accent sounds slippery. Sickly sweet. A mask. "Is that all he wants from you, the pretty fae? A story?"

He's implying something. But what? I don't know. It stings anyway. I try to press my body flat to the wall and squeeze past him.

He blocks me in so easily, and his mouth draws nearer to mine.

"Perhaps that is what I should make you do in exchange for my kindness? Read to me?"

"N-No," I choke out. I never could. These books are sacred precious things that look so fragile in his hands as he snatches one from the nearest shelf. He rips it open to a random page. As his eyes scan the text something strange happens. Confusion. Irritation. Aggravation.

He throws the volume across the room and it hits the wall with a bang.

"No!" The poor, dear thing. Its cover is dented, forever mauled. All because I failed to protect it. I stoop and cradle it to my chest. Then I whirl around to face him and snarl, "You stupid brute!"

The words hang in the air, harsh and angry. Oh. I never say such things. Never ever. Day would be ashamed and shocked. He might swear never to visit me again.

Caspian laughs. Head cocked he advances, predatory again. Hungry for me once more. Paces away, he extends his hand.

I'd rather die than give him this book. I clutch it. Hold it so tightly my fingers turn white.

He smiles in that sinister way. Then he demands, "Read it to me."

"No!"

He reaches for another. Another to mutilate and maul.

I scramble to flip to a page. My fingers smooth over the parchment, as if to soothe it. Poor, poor thing. I'm here now. I'll never let him hurt it again.

But he's creeping behind me, his breathing audible and heavy. "Read," he commands into the nape of my neck.

I look down and do so woodenly in a mindless monotone. There is none of the flare nor excitement like when I read for Day. Because Caspian, he doesn't care—

"What is that?" he demands. "What does it mean?"

I stop. Breathe. Re-read the passage for myself and struggle to decipher it. Of all the things he chose, this is a text on fae history. An older text, less valued than the pristine copies on display in the Citadel proper. Just a draft.

And yet for once, the vamryre is interested. His curiosity wasn't faked. He wants to know about the Fae ruler I just mentioned. Some king in the olden times, long since forgotten.

I should shut this book. Shut him out. Refuse.

But he is insistent. "Read," he commands.

So I do, haltingly. Brokenly. Hoarsely.

And he listens to every word, rapt, as if gobbling them up the way his kind do blood. Word by word. Drop by drop.

He listens—but not in amused silence like Day does. He takes these words from me and churns them up in his collective hive mind. What he makes of them? I can't know. I will never know.

But it's strange. Like speaking into an endless void.

CHAPTER 11
Caspian

She makes her magic so easily. She interprets her symbols and precious books at a glance, then spits out the words. Creates worlds. Makes me fucking see the things she intones. Even when she isn't trying.

Even when she doesn't want to.

Making her read for me is like forcing a bird to sing. It's pretty, all the same. An incessant song.

Damn her.

The smell of her is as intoxicating as it is vile, reminiscent of dust and forgotten things. Like fresh air and sunlight. Rain, and heat, and sweetness.

With every breath I breathe in, Cassius rages and raves. Her mere presence infuriates him. My nearness to her. How I struggle on the tightrope he's made me walk.

Every action I inflict on the fae, he'll make me inflict on *him*. One kiss already. What is one more? I start to reach for her. Then stop.

She's still reading. Still emitting that little voice into the air. Compared to her, Cassius is a whisper now. I can barely hear him. As she drones on and on about some obscure, forgotten thing, the bastard can't touch me. Can't exert his presence.

He wants to.

Under this fae's dark spell, I am once again beyond his reach. That is what makes her so dangerous to him. Not the jealousy. It's her power to hold sway over me where he can't. Because I'm hungry. I'm restless. I want her so badly it fucking hurts. My throat aches for her blood. The thought of being buried inside of her makes my cock throb.

Can't bite. Can't fuck. Doesn't matter. As long as I don't have to hear him again, I'll torture myself to the point of madness...

Until she falls silent.

"Read," I snap.

"It's finished." A tremor runs through her voice. "I've read it all."

All. I've been leaning over her shoulder for hours, devouring this sweet songbird's tune like a vulture. Her tune has run out. Now should be when I bite. Kill. Strike.

But I won't. As soon as I kill her, Cassius will have me back under his thumb, with no plaything to distract from him.

Using my body, I push her onward, onward, toward that towering collection of books. I make her grab one—all I have to do is pretend to reach for it first. Then I tell her, "Read it."

"I can't." Her voice is barely audible, almost choked out. Sweat enhances her scent: I can see drops of it, dripping down her neck. "It's late. The day is wasted. I... I need to sleep."

Sleep. Day. Wasted.

I don't care. Let the fae sleep after I've ripped her to pieces. I want her awake and alert now. She needs to read.

"Do it."

"I can't." She pushes back, newly emboldened like a mother hen protecting her flock. A flock of paper and leather that smell like dust. "It's time for you to go." Her voice flits between a whisper and a shout. It's like she took lessons from Cassius once and then forgot them: how to be an arrogant prick and order your lessers around.

Unlike his voice, hers doesn't irritate me. I want to hear it more. In more ways. How can she stretch it? What other magic can she create? How will it sound to hear her scream?

"When," I snap.

Her fingers run through her mane of black hair as she stiffens. It's so damn long, reaching past her narrow waist. Then she cocks her head and inhales. "Tomorrow. No... Tomorrow. Please go."

Go. I let her think I do. I watch her scramble to the bell tower, her gray robes hanging off her gaunt frame. She's easy to follow. Easy to watch.

Taking off her shift, she washes her limbs. Eats a hunk of stale bread. Goes to sleep.

In one small way, I will give the fae their win. They have one advantage over the vamryre. Sleep. They can turn their minds off and escape into a world where none can follow.

We are not so lucky. Cassius is our morning, noon, and night. There is no rest from him. No respite.

Yet, even in her dreamworld, the fae doesn't find peace. She tosses and turns. Whenever the wind cuts through the crumbling plaster and old wood, she shivers.

Then she wakes up before dawn and shuffles to do it all over again. This is her existence, scurrying in the shadows, hoping to avoid notice. I think she truly believes it matters whether she is seen or not by the hordes of other fae that call this complex home.

She's wrong.

They all know of her. They talk of her in harsh whispers. How they despise her.

Except for *that* one.

He's different from the rest. Most fae are pretty, flighty, flaky things. They huddle beneath the sunlight and shun those they deem unworthy—which is everyone that isn't fae.

Not him. Sneering, he looks down on his own kind. He charms the lesser fae females that flock to him. He fucks them in secret, caring little for them after. Yet, seeks *her* out like a wolf hunting prey. Fitting because that's my role. Only he has no idea how to play it. No idea what he wants. He sees her, and watches her, and the little fae is none the wiser.

She thinks she's humoring him.

He's studying her.

He thinks he can take her for himself.

I'll kill him first.

Even now, I can sense him, creeping his way toward her little hovel, hoping to slip inside. He isn't allowed to, but he does so anyway. Boldly he shuns their little rules. He is confident that she belongs to him alone.

She's mine, though. Only she isn't. The cost is too great. Too steep. Cassius has tightened his leash and made my boundary clear. I can watch the little fae but I can't touch. To do so is to incur a debt I must repay to him. Disgusting, sick fucker.

I owe him one kiss already. That's why he sits back, content to let me play another day.

Eventually, I must pay my dues.

But no more. She isn't worth any more.

Even so, I haunt her worthless steps, deep into their dusty, suffocating archives. The fae spread the rumor that their vaults of knowledge are safe and secure.

A lie. It's too easy to slip in and walk around unnoticed. Those haughty fae have their noses too far into the air to notice. They think that the threat of discovery alone keeps them safe and hidden.

Even Cassius is surprised by how easily I can creep in amongst their stone. He's never tried, but he's wanted to—that much he lets me discern.

However, he is lazy and unmotivated. I am not. I have a prize to hunt. A toy to play with. A body dressed in ugly rags that beckons to me even in this dark, dank crypt.

Cassius' price tag isn't the worst part, nor is the looming death hanging around her neck. It's the fact that she knows I'm here. She's known all along.

Rather than quiver in fear, she waits for me to make myself

known. Eventually, the little fae becomes impatient. Hunched on the floor, rag in hand, she asks, "What do you want?"

"You know what I want," I reply. But that isn't quite the truth. She knows what I want but can't have. I'm here for another reason. A foolish reason.

"Pick up one of those books and read to me, little fae."

She shakes her head. Picks up her rag. Tries to clean. She fails. Her hand shakes too badly to manipulate the rag correctly, but fear isn't the reason.

"No. They... They are not a game." Disgust paints her words with a fae-like haughty sheen, but she couldn't sound like them if she tried. Even here in her chosen domain, she isn't arrogant enough. "These books are important. Not toys."

She truly believes that. It amuses me just how deeply she believes that. As if none of the shit in this stuffy room is as fragile as paper. One small flame and it's all alight. All gone. Poof. Dust.

Telling her so would make her snap. I like her better this way, fragile and delicate. I'll use her books against her the way Cassius has used her body against me. She wants my mercy? I'll make her dance for it.

"Read to me little fae, or..."

The threat dangles in the air, unspoken but just as sweet. Just as potent. She jumps as if I've pulled a knife out and slashed at one of those leatherbound covers.

"I can't," she insists. "I have to clean. I can't stay here all day."

Partly the truth. Mainly a lie. The others avoid this place like the plague. Oh, how the fae pretend to exalt knowledge and wisdom and their history-laden bullshit. In reality, they prefer to play, and gossip and fuck. They hate this place. They hate her.

Yet they allowed her to believe that it all matters. That this place, which she treats so sacredly, is important. I want to crush her delusion. Tell her just how little they care.

I don't. Cassius wants me to. He's purring encouragement at the back of my mind, lurking there like a coiled snake, waiting to strike. *Come, Caspian. My loyal one. My little sadist.* He wants me to dash her little fae hopes and dreams—which means I can't. I won't.

Even if it hurts her, I will never please him.

"I want you to read," I tell her. Her lips part but before she can speak, I add, "You want me to tell you about the other realm. The mortal realm. Don't you?"

She stifles a gasp as she falls silent. Ah, I've got her. She can't wiggle away from her heart's desire. She'll jump through any hoop just to achieve a glimpse of it.

Though, she's not as dumb as I thought. "You've told me nothing," she points out, chin in the air. "Even after..."

I lick my lips, recalling the toll she's already paid. One kiss. Two. Three.

"Yet, you've told me nothing. I'm starting to think that you know nothing."

Ah, maybe she's right. Perhaps she's wrong. Our collective mind hums at the mention of forbidden knowledge. I'd run myself ragged trying to break down Cassius' mental barriers—not that I have to. I'll make him a trade. A small piece of knowledge for...

Another kiss, he replies in an instant. Greedy bastard. There is no time to regret or despair. No time to hate him either, because in my mind unfurls a kernel of information, brilliant and bright.

"There is a way out of the Citadel," I tell her, and watch those black eyes widen. "A secret way where one can pass without needing clearance from the elder council. Another tunnel, underground. A forgotten portal."

Is there? Cassius, the bastard, doesn't clarify. He could be feeding a lie through me to this little fae. But, hell, I'd lie to her forever if it made her eyes widen like this and her throat clench.

"Really?"

Oh, her hope is such a delicate, fragile thing. I'll dangle it and toy with it. I'll tease it to the breaking point before snapping it.

"What will you give me for more?"

Her eyes narrow and she casts a downward glance at her body. That shapeless, haunting body. The one I lust after like a dog in heat. I want to tear the robes from her skin. My fingers twitch but I force them down to my sides. I can't.

But she can.

No, Cassius warns. *Toe your boundaries.* Stupid bastard. He thought he'd won, but he hasn't. His game can be beaten.

"Take off your robe," I tell her before she can question.

She stiffens. One pale hand flies to her throat, but not to the clasp holding her poor excuse for a robe together. She runs her finger along the pulse point as if to draw my attention to it. Taunting me with one of the many parts of her I can't have.

Stupid, fucking Cassius. How I hate him. Hate. Hate...

My thoughts go quiet as she stands. I forget to think rebellious thoughts to needle the bastard with. I forget Cassius completely.

She has my attention in the palm of her hand, that slim pale hand that she uses to finally tug the opening of her robe apart.

A memory creeps in—one I don't want. Hundreds. Maybe thousands. All the people I've lured for Cassius. Seduced for him. Plied for him. Fucked for him. They would eye me shyly, men and women alike. They'd strip as if their body was the only one that existed. As if I hadn't seen them all before. Male. Female. Thick. Thin. Dark. Pale.

One and the same.

My skull is full of ripe, beautiful, imperfect, ugly bodies I could compare her to. Then she opens her robe and lets it fall to the ground.

I come up short.

No one is like her and perhaps that's a good thing. No one Cassius craves anyway. Her flaws are numerous, her appeal to him in the negative degree. We vamryre in our collective all have the same cravings, the same tastes.

It's what he wants us to believe.

As I look at her, all I know is... I want. Me, Caspian. I want her. I need her. I'll have her.

Wait. Wait. WAIT!

A million warnings sound off in my skull, all unheeded. For now. I can't kiss. Can't fuck. But...

Cassius can't demand a damn thing from me if I look at her. "Turn around," I command.

Confusion flits across those eyes, but she complies. Has no choice but to. With slow, shuffling steps, she spins in a circle, putting her back to me.

I look, expecting more pale skin and visible bones. I find as much —and more. Someone has hurt her far worse than a skinned, battered knee. My hand shoots out, fingers grasping...over nothing. I force it down by my side. No touching.

Instead, I inspect her the way I would anything else. Some poor, desecrated thing.

Once—no, recently—someone took to the little fae over and over again. With a knife they made neat, clean cuts. From her neck down, they form a macabre row. A mocking imitation of wings.

I've seen scars before, on bodies vamryre and mortal alike. They are silvery with age. Sparkling reminders of violence.

Not hers. They glow, a strip of fresh crimson as if her blood still glistens there. Fresh. Bleeding.

"Enough," I say.

Dutifully, she spins around to face me. "I don't know."

Her reply rings out in response to a question I never asked. Maybe I did. *How? Who did this? For what?*

She shakes her head. I must have asked her again.

Not that I care.

She shivers as I approach and backs herself into a corner. Poor little fae. I can hear her pulse tapping into the air. I can taste it in my throat. *Thump. Thump.*

Yet she hides it well. She holds her head high and stares into my eyes, as though she isn't afraid. As though she isn't tensing in anticipation of the nails I brush along her hip. Then upward.

Her breasts are small, not plump like Cassius prefers. *No.* He isn't here and I cut him out of my skull. I focus on her, her breathing, that delicate little song. I can't hear him.

Good.

Still, I don't touch her. I let my fingers dance in the air just above her skin. I watch her body react more violently than if I had groped her with raking nails and biting teeth. Or perhaps the knife she's used to. Her hips are small, her thighs thin and compact. I want to see what lies between them, but she clamps her knees together. Her hands fly to her chest, then lower. Up again. She's fighting the modest part of herself, screaming that this is wrong.

To let a vamryre drink in her naked body is oh so wrong.

The fact that just looking isn't enough is even worse. I need to touch. Feel. Take. My fingers twitch. I'll go insane without feeling that delicate skin beneath them.

Your debt, Caspian, Cassius warns, his voice blaring as I attempt to shut him out.

My debt. His pleasure.

Don't care. Don't care. I want her. Need to...

Touch. I grip her arms and push her back into the wall so hard she gasps. Terrified. No. She's impatient, lifting her head to bare the throat she teased. *Fuck.* It's like she knows the price I have to pay. She's daring me to gamble what little of my soul I have left. She'll make me offer it up to Cassius piece by piece.

Maybe I will.

The sound she makes when I press my hips into hers is too damn soft. She is too damn soft. Her skin is ivory silk, likely to tear with one wrong move. After all, I've torn her already, those knobby knees. I crane my neck to eye my handiwork—the first of many bloody masterpieces I'll make of her before this all ends...

There is nothing beautiful about the healing scabs. They're too stark against her flesh. I don't like them, and a new word trickles into my skull from some distant memory. *Garish.*

Fuck.

She's messing with my head again. I meet her gaze and silently dare her to continue. Let her think that she can manipulate me. Yet her stare is neither frightened nor defiant.

I look at her and all I see is greedy selfish need. Not for my cock—no, not yet. She is after something else.

"I have what you want, don't I, fae?" I taunt her, bringing my mouth close to her neck. Close enough to bite. I'd be risking Cassius' wrath but I don't care.

I do. I break the rules, and he'll cut my game short. So I'll play for now. I just breathe her in, that strange sweet scent. I brush aside a strand of her hair, thick, boundless ebony. Then I run my tongue over the galloping pulse where I long to bite.

Her whimper isn't what I want to hear. It's excited. Thrilled. Not terrified. So I lick her again. Again. I press my teeth to her flesh and feel her pulse explode. *Thumpthumpthump.* The poor thing might hammer itself from her chest if I'm not careful.

Not that I give a damn. Oh, how I long to see that heart in all its glory. One day...

I'm going to rip it from her chest. My fingers shoot out, finding the spot. However, my thumb slips downwards and captures a nipple instead. I watch it harden and feel her entire spine shake in response. No one has ever touched her like this, not even that stupid, male fae.

Her eyes are wide, horrified and brimming with emotions. She can't reconcile this. Standing still and letting a vamryre defile her.

It's not like anyone else wants to. Except him.

Except me.

I stroke that peak until it's sharp enough to cut. Around and around and around I grind her beneath my thumb until she's choking on a broken sound that can't quite leave her throat. I've made my point. It should be enough.

But it isn't.

I capture her entire breast against my palm. Squeeze. Caress. Crush.

She whimpers again, her face turned away from me, chest heaving. Terror should be the emotion gripping her. Yes, that's what I want. What I crave...

Then I smell her. Her body exudes a newer scent. Instinctive. Hormonal. Arousal.

Fuck.

I can't stop touching her. I can't keep my fingers from seeking out that strip of flesh between her thighs, shrouded by a thatch of dark curls. Damn. The lips of her cleft are soft, so soft I go against my own intentions. I won't rip and claw her here. I prod. I test. I taste. With the tip of one thumb, I tease the inside of the little fae.

She is molten. Too fucking hot to be contained. My fingers will melt if I probe any deeper. Should I try to fuck her, I'll set my cock on fire. The interior of this fae is scorching.

But damn...

It feels good to burn inside her. Too good. Can't stop. I slide a whole finger inside her all at once, and she clutches at my shoulders with tiny, scratching nails. Her voice breaks around a sound. Not a cry. Not a scream. Something else.

A series of rasping syllables that explode over my eardrums and render me deaf to every other sound but her. I need to hear that sound again. I crook my finger through her flesh, trying to coax her into making it again. Fuck, I need that sound.

Another gasp. Another whimper. More. More.

I keep stroking her, and the fire grows hotter. It's like velvet, how tightly she grips me. My finger strokes her again, and she's wet. Damp. Drenched. I can't stop. Not until she goes limp and her knees buckle. Not until she utters a string of noises that echo through my skull. Not until her nails dig at my skin—as if she could ever pierce it. Hurt me. Mark me.

I've already marked her. I'll always be the first man to make her head rear back, and her eyes roll in her skull. The first creature to have her panting and breathless and broken.

The first monster to make her bleed. She's a virgin, so tight she'll rip when I shove my cock into her. So tight she might swallow me whole. So fucking tight, I'll never hear Cassius in my head again...

My cock is throbbing, swollen and needy, but I don't free it yet. I step back and watch her shiver on jellied legs, her hands braced against the stone, dark hair tangled and wild.

More words spill onto my corrupted, broken mind. Cassius'? Mine? A torrent of descriptors. *Rosy nipples. Glistening skin. Taut flesh over incredible bone structure. A work of art. Art...*

It's more than a word to me. Even thinking it makes something rip through my chest, sowing a burning searing pain. What the hell is this feeling? I can't remember.

No one—not since this damned immortal life—has ever made me feel anything. Not once. No matter how many I pleasured for him. No matter how I performed for him.

I never wanted it. Never wanted them. They were all stupid toys.

I can't fucking think around her. There is no desire to fuck her and seduce her into joining the collective. I want to pin her down, slam into her for my own pleasure. Rake my fingers through her hair and grip her skull. I want to mount her. Mate her.

Sink my teeth into her throat and dare her to give me the one thing I never ever gave Cassius...

"Wait." Her voice is a wail trapped between clenched teeth. I assume she means wait. Don't fuck her. Not yet.

Too late. I'm reaching for the buckle of my pants. I undo the clasp. My finger inches back inside her, and even as she shakes her head, I feel her grow wet all over again. Melt. "Wait," she whispers. "Wait. Wait!"

She's warning me of something. Someone. The bastard male fae. I can hear him tiptoeing back toward this corner, oblivious that the one he desires is already mine. I could fuck her in front of him. Make the fool watch. I want to...

"Please," she insists, her hand flat against my chest. She tries to push. I let her, taking a step back. She crouches and scrambles into her robes. Wide and fearful, her eyes meet mine as the idiot draws near. "Please," she whimpers. "Please. Please."

I don't hide, but I let her run, slipping past me to greet *him*. I hear her voice, false and high-pitched.

"Greetings, Day."

Day. That's what they call each other, all the fae. Numbered like the days of the week, or in this case their age. The youngest born are sunrise, then dawn, day, night, elder, whatever-the-fuck. Don't care.

It's not the name that irritates me. It's how she says it. Fearful and worried. Hopeful and afraid.

She's uneasy around this stupid fae, not like how she is around me.

She fears him. I wonder if she even knows it.

CHAPTER 12
Niamh

I am a twisted mess of thoughts. My mind no longer makes sense—it's a once orderly archive that's been raided, every book torn open and burned. Pages ripped out and scattered. The worst part is that the intruder, the culprit, is still there. In my head. In my skull.

He laughs at my attempts to kick him out.

And it isn't fair to me. It isn't fair to poor Day who watches me with a half-frown instead of his half smile. He's spoken words to me that I haven't heard. Make requests I haven't heeded.

The worst part is that Caspian isn't here. He left. I could feel his essence retreat like a dark storm cloud finally rolling past, but it's too late. The damage left by the storm remains and I alone am tasked with repairing it all.

But the truth is, some things are ruined beyond repair. In some intrinsic way I will never be the same again. The vamryre took something from me, but I'm not even sure if it wasn't his to take in the first place.

The book I read on the subject was a lie. It described an act cruel, cold and impersonal. Something like a bodily function, relieving waste or intaking food. Something that didn't matter long after it happened.

But this... Whatever happened in the archive matters in some unknown, sinister way. I can feel his touch long after he's left. Even when Day gives up trying to speak and watches me pensively, I still hear him. Caspian. His voice etches itself into my skull, taunting and inescapable. *Little fae... Little fae...*

I'll never escape that grated rasp. I'll never get his touch out of my skin.

I will never be as I was again.

"You are distracted. Again," Day remarks. The way he drew out that final word makes me swallow hard with guilt. *Again.* He takes time from his studies to visit me and I am distracted. A mortal sin on any other day but today. I need to think—repair my shattered psyche.

"I'm tired," I lie. "I didn't sleep much."

He doesn't accept the excuse and sees it for the fragile lie it is. His eyes gleam.

"Because of the ceremony," he says. "You've heard them talking."

Them. Who? I don't know, but I prefer his happiness to his annoyance. So, I nod.

And he smiles, a real ripe smile. On the surface it's more beautiful than any a vamryre could display. So why do I feel as if he flashed a mouthful of fangs?

Because you're corrupted, a part of me whispers. *Sullied by a night creature.*

"You know the significance now, of what this means." He steps forward, his head held high, his hands tugging his robes into place. Then he does something odd—something he's never done before. He reaches out and brushes his thumb along my cheek. A brief, gentle contact.

But it stings. Burns. It's wrong. He's broken so many rules already just by seeing me in secret. Why risk a greater punishment? He isn't supposed to touch me.

"I'm sorry," I say as I jerk out of his reach. As if I made him do it.

Rather than remember himself, he reaches out for me again. Takes my hand. His are so soft in comparison to mine—ugly and calloused with broken, ragged nails.

Not because I keep them in such a state. But because I dug every last one into the flesh of a vamryre hard enough to hurt another creature. He didn't even flinch.

But Day does as I wrench back. "You shouldn't," I say. It's wrong. I don't want him risking any trouble for me.

"I will," he says, clasping his hands over his front. "One day after the ceremony. No one can stop me then."

I don't know what he's talking about. I don't care to know. I need solace and silence. I need to think.

"You should leave," I say. "You've come here too much already. What if someone sees? What if someone knows?"

I cast a furtive glance to the door of the archives, but Day laughs. Startled, I look back at him, but his gaze is locked up tight. He's smug about something though, which isn't like him. He's gloating over knowing something that I don't.

"Tomorrow," he says, but I stiffen. Shake my head.

"Day, please don't—"

"Tomorrow." He turns and leaves as silently as he came.

And in this solitude I craved so desperately...I break. Tears come too hard and too fast to smother. I have to capture them in both hands as if I can shove them back inside my skull where they belong. Too late. They cascade down and through my upturned fingers. I'd need a wall to ever keep them back.

Creatures like me are not supposed to cry. How dare we? We are sheltered and fed and kept safe from those who would harm us out of rightful disgust. I have no reason to cry.

Even if a vamryre made me feel things I didn't know a body could feel. Dirty things. Sinful things. His memory hurts my soul.

Why?

What did I do to deserve such a villain? Perhaps he is my atonement from all my years of disobeying Lord Master. I can't pretty up the transgressions or lie to myself anymore. I've sinned and sinned and now I'm being punished.

Punishment is meant to serve as a painful reminder, however. A deterrent.

Ideally, one shouldn't want to commit another sin.

CHAPTER 13
Caspian

I am a defiant, devious, and sinful boy. Cassius tells me so but his tone is more amused than angry. Why? It's as if ever since I took more from that fae—increased my debt to him—he's been humming with glee.

I am not so self-centered, however. Something else has his spirits high. Something important enough to distract from me. What is it? What is it?

I want to know. Need to know.

Whatever pleases Cassius means misery for me.

I try to prod his thoughts, but this far from the mansion he can easily swat me away.

I could go back.

No. Don't want to.

I stay near the Citadel and watch her instead. She's infuriating.

Cassius torments me for a night, and I rage for weeks after. Even the thought makes me hiss through clenched teeth.

But her. She's safe inside her skull where I can't follow. There, she's pure and untouched, waltzing around her archive with her head held high.

Like she wasn't writhing for me. Craving it: destruction at my fingertips. Like she wasn't eager for me to do every last thing I've taunted her with. As if she didn't steal an orgasm from me.

Damn the fae. She is good at playing pretend. I almost believe her.

Then I see how she walks. How she winces when she crouches down to tend to her chores. It's not pain that has her biting her lip. It's not fear that has her glancing over her shoulder, searching for me.

Oh yes. I can see it so clearly, what she's desperate to hide. That's the thing, though. She *hides* it. She lies to herself. She denies the obvious.

She'd fuck me even if I didn't deliver information about her precious realm. After all, Caspian the vamryer has never been denied.

Even Cassius can't ignore his attraction to me. Men and women all react the same. This pretty face beckons them. My voice lures them into a false sense of security as I ask them to bare their necks. When I bite, they never see the pain coming.

Attraction is the one skill I've honed as a damn vamryre. I know how to cultivate it. How to wield it like a knife, slipped in the back of an unwitting victim.

Yet she is unaffected. I can admit that. The beauty of my appearance does not appeal to her. Her interest in me only extends to what I can do for her. She's as transactional as a vamryre, craving knowledge instead of blood.

We can go days without the substance. Weeks. Cassius keeps us placated until he decides when and where we can indulge the urge. It's the one grace he gives us, or so he says.

He protects us from hunger.

Not from pain or hate or regret. He lets all three fester in me.

She acts like she's above such base emotions. Above hunger. Above lust.

Lies. Lust is what I tasted in her, deep in those archives. I need to taste it again.

Want to.

For now, I'll stay back. I watch her scurry in and out of her little hiding place. I watch her wait for me.

I don't go to her. Not yet.

I let her squirm. I keep to the shadows and let the hours tick by. Until I can't.

After nightfall, when the other fae have scattered, I corner her. When she's returning some book to a shelf like it's the most important thing in the world. I press into her and feel that slender body shiver.

With no fear, however. She's so damn ready for me. The second I reach for her, she lurches into my touch, but keeps her face averted from me, as if that makes it less sinful. Shameful. I hook my hand through her hair and grip her skull. Then I force her to look at me.

She isn't quivering like a timid little virgin in those stories she likes to read. She meets my gaze dead on. She's ready for any corruption I could deliver.

That makes her braver than I ever was.

It makes me hate her all the more.

"Have you thought about me, little fae?" I ask her. *Me,* not the dare I've proposed to her. Not her obsession with the other realm. Me—my fingers inside her. My cock, eager to claim her.

She shakes her head. Little liar. It is difficult to ignore the clarity in her gaze, however. She probably believes it. If she tells herself that lie enough times it makes it true. She hasn't thought of me.

But I've thought of her. All the things I will do to her. The ways in which I will make her scream. Beg. Whimper. I'm going to have her by the time this is all said and done.

But then I will have you, Cassius murmurs, always listening in.

The moment I kiss her again, he falls silent. Poof. He's gone. There is just her and her skin and her fingers scratching at my chest. She pushes me off and I let her win. I let her think she's in control of this game.

All the better to turn the tables on her later and shatter any hope that she could ever defeat me.

"Tell me," she gasps. I blink. It's not a denial. Not a plea to stop. She merely wants her payment upfront. "Tell me more about the realm—"

"And what good will that do?" I counter. "You'll never see it."

She will never leave this place until the day of the ceremony. Then her corpse will never leave the Citadel.

However, she refuses to follow fate's plan. She bares her teeth defiantly. For a split second, she reminds me of Cassiopeia. Where is she, my sister? My companion? The only one who knows my pain and shares my hate?

Don't think of her, Cassius murmurs. *She is a traitor.*

Was she? I can't remember. He won't let me remember.

"I want to," the fae says, her voice soft, but a broken note gives her fear away. She knows she never will. She hopes in spite of everything—the dank, dark reality around her. How pathetic it is. How sickly sweet.

I should laugh in her face.

"How will you?" I ask. "Can you fly, little fae?"

I've seen her smooth back marred by a tapestry of scars; I know she can't. Her wince confirms that she knows it too. Her limitations are many. After all, she is an abominable creature. She shouldn't exist. No power, no specialization distinguishes her.

However, when she presses her hand against my chest...

Fuck. It's magnetic. Even Cassius' fingers don't hold the same sway. Her hands are so fucking delicate I could break them. I snatch for her wrist and grip it tight. But my eyes are on hers, and I don't look away.

I can't.

"You come in here unnoticed," she murmurs, her voice deadly soft. She knows her words are sinful—so she whispers them as if that makes the rebellion less so. Still, I'm listening. I'm leaning toward her, silly little fae. Damn, I strain to catch every word.

Corruption is fun, but having her hope to dangle on a string? That is an entirely new game.

No, Caspian, Cassius warns. *Betrayal.*

I ignore him. I'll deal with him later. Make a trade. Whatever price is worth this, making her say what I know she will. She wants something from me—in the same way I want her to make new words spill into this chained, slave-mind. She'll ask.

Voice scratching the air, she starts, "You can..."

"Say it," I snarl when she trails off into silence. I run my thumb over her mouth and pry those pink lips apart. "Say it. Tell me what you want, little fae. Ask me."

Her breath coats my fingers as she utters, "You can help me leave."

Her eyes widen. Oh dear. She's said such a dangerous fucking thing. Never ever has she voiced as much out loud. Never has she begged anyone for a damn thing. Not even him. Especially not him, the creeping male fae.

Because she knows he would refuse.

So will I.

As long as she doesn't bite her lip like she does now. If her breathing doesn't hitch. Fuck, until I feel her hands creep up to the bare skin of my throat am I sure that I'll deny her. Silly little fae. Who is she to demand anything of me?

"And what will you give me?" I ask.

"I told you." She swallows. "Anything."

The price, however, is too high. Whatever I take from her, I'll inflict upon myself—a double-edged sword. Things I've denied for centuries or decades. Why the fuck can't I remember? In any case, no. She isn't worth one night of sin with that sick motherfucker.

She isn't worth debasing myself before him.

Good, he murmurs. Spying, jealous Cassius. *I can let you have hundreds of bodies. You can let loose on the city. Have anyone you want.*

For *him*. In the end, anyone I take will always belong to him. But not her. I can own this fae, and he can never, ever touch her. She'll be mine...

Unfortunately, the price is too high.

So, I laugh in her face. "You think you are worth the risk?" I ask her. "To go against the council is to risk prison or worse."

It's clear from her frown that she knows the answer without having to speak. Of course, she isn't worthy. Isn't a prize. She isn't worth the one kiss—*two, three, four*—that I'll have to give Cassius in exchange.

I wait for her to confess as much. Admit it to herself and to me. She's worthless. Even so, she cannot say it. Then I see why—glistening wet drops shining in her eyes. Those tears I've fantasized about causing.

I should grin in triumph.

"Stop." I jab my thumb to the corner of her eye and feel the wet warmth as if force alone can keep any more at bay. Too late. Another falls onto the pad of my finger, and I watch it shimmer there. Then I crush it in a fist. "I said stop it."

I shove her against the wall. The shock alone should shut her up. Make her stop. Those tears... I want them, but not now. Not like this.

"Fucking, stop!" I press my face to hers. I'll glare those tears away. Fear will make her stop. Shut up. I need her to shut the fuck up.

"I..." Her lips quiver. She's still trying to answer my question. Is she worthy? "No. I'm not. I know I'm not—"

"Then why ask?" My voice is a rasp. Curiosity is what roughens it, nothing else. Certainly not concern as those eyes continue to well and more tears fall. "Why?"

She blinks, sending two droplets down those hollow cheeks. "I need to know."

I grip her thin shoulders. Shake her so hard her head rears back. "What?"

She inhales raggedly. Licks those uneven lips. "I... I need to know if there is more out there. More than *this*."

Her words linger in the air, a longing confession. One I should laugh at. Spit at. Taunt. I would do all three if it would make her stop fucking sobbing, silent and frozen. She doesn't even flinch as I lower my mouth near her ear, at the curve of her throat. That racing pulse beckons in an unsteady thumping. I could bite her now, give her something to truly sob over.

Instead...

"A day to think," I hiss into her reddening flesh. She gasps, trying to blink the tears back. Fuck her. She's ruining everything. Her punishment comes swiftly—I step back and force her to meet my gaze. Then I press a finger against the corners of both black eyes and smear any residual tears into nothingness.

"Stop crying. Give me a day to think." I'm a good enough liar that she believes me. She swallows. Gasps for air. Nods.

I can have a day, a reluctant request. A way to stall for time. No way in hell will I help her.

No way in fucking hell.

I shove her back and turn away. No taunting goodbye. No threat to come tomorrow.

Because I won't. This game has gone far enough. I'll see her again at the ceremony when I can bite and tear and take what I'm owed. Not her body, but the next best thing.

The only thing that matters.

I'll have her life in the palm of my hands, and *that* is all I want.

CHAPTER 14
Niamh

I am so very tired. It isn't the natural exhaustion I used to feel after a particularly hard day of chores. No. This is something else. A malaise that drains me every waking moment. It festers and weighs me down until—for only a second—I can breathe again.

It's those moments that I hate the most. They happen in snatches, whenever I feel an icy breath fan against my shoulder and a gruff voice whispers into my ear. Then and there, I suddenly have all of the energy in the world. To run with. Fight with. Die with.

And I'm frozen. Whenever he touches me, I'm frozen. Can't resist. Can't push him off. Can't deny...

But it's the price I'm willing to pay. Corruption I'm willing to endure. Anything. I'll suffer any indiscretion or punishment. My entire life, I've endured worse for far less.

But his cruelty...

It doesn't hurt the way it should. He doesn't feel the way he should. I don't want...

Until I feel his fingers grazing my skin, and I'm greedy again. Too greedy. And I can't remember exactly what I'm after. Can't remember the only thing in the world I desire. To leave. To see. To experience the mortal realm.

Whenever he touches me, I drown.

My only solace is that he won't come back. I know it. I got too greedy. Demanded too much. For the first time in my life, I asked for far too much.

There are some things that a vamryre cannot provide. Some risks are too great, and I alone am not a worthy enough prize. If I knew what he really wanted, I'd scrape and crawl to get it. I'd give him anything. I would.

I can't. And it hurts. It hurts like a gaping wound that won't heal, and for the first time in my life, I can't move like I used to. My chores are a nightmare, tedious and tortuous. I'm sweating before I've finished cleaning the floor. Every book I return to the shelves weighs an almost unliftable amount. I am so heavy and slow and bumbling.

When Day appears, I can't even muster up a greeting or a smile. All I can do is avert my face so he can't see my frown. My disappointment.

For the first time in my life, he isn't the one I need to see standing there.

"The ceremony is nearly upon us," he says, his voice lifting with excitement. He is so very happy. Happy to ignore my rudeness. Happy enough to stalk forward, radiating warmth and light. Happy enough to take my hand without asking.

And I am shameful enough to cringe back and trip over my own feet. Shameful enough to clutch my hand to my wrist as if it burned. Shameful enough to feel—even for one second—unnerved. As if... I don't want him to touch me.

"D-Day, I'm sorry," I say to the floor, struggling to right myself. When I look up, he is no longer smiling. His green eyes are blazing and angry. He almost resembles a vamryre. Almost.

"What is wrong with you?" he asks, voice trembling with derision.

"I... I don't know," I croak back. I don't know. The entire world is shifting and spinning around me. For once, I don't know my place. I've forgotten it. My little hole in the shelf is sealed up and inescapable. Where in the world do I belong?

I don't know. Maybe deep down, I never really knew.

"You've been distracted for days," he continues to rant. "I have tolerated your disrespect, but honestly, sister. Is this how you repay me for all the times I've visited you?"

"I'm sorry," I whisper. But I can't look at him anymore. All I can do is stare at a shadowy corner that remains empty.

Give me a day, he said.

A lie. He will take an eternity and never return. I ruined it—the only chance I'll ever have. I'm so stupid. Stupid.

"Look at me!" Day snatches my shoulder and wrenches me around to face him—but it hurts. His nails scrape at my flesh and sting. There isn't any mocking careful care. He slams me into the wall, his expression furious, teeth bared. "After everything I've done for you! Everything I've been willing to risk. You treat me like some dust beneath your feet."

"I'm sorry," I rasp. Because he is wrong. Day could never be beneath me. I will always be below him. In every aspect. Every way.

I could never see him as my equal. He isn't some unwanted creepy, shadow thing. He isn't a man with white hair and red eyes that peer into my soul and make me quake. Day is no risk to me. He doesn't threaten to shatter my pathetic, imaginary place in the world. He doesn't make me want to sin.

"I think I know why," he snarls, his voice uncharacteristically cold.

My heart stops. Does he?

"Someone else has come in here to see you, haven't they?" His green eyes peer into me, probing and accusatory.

Breathless, all I can do is sway. Can't speak. Can't deny.

"Who is it?" he wonders. "Some nosy lower fae? Tell me!"

Air trickles into my lungs again. He doesn't know. Not truly.

"No one," I whisper. "No other fae."

He isn't appeased. He starts to pace, jaw clenched, hands twitching at his sides. "You're lying to me. You never lie! Not to me!" His voice rings out, far too loud. He'll draw notice. Attention. He'll get himself banned from ever visiting the archives.

Fear is why I do the only thing I can think of to calm him. I sink to my knees, head bowed. "I'm so sorry," I croak to the floor, and I mean it. I am. "I don't deserve your visits, but I cherish them. I do. I'm sorry."

He stops. I look up to see him smoothing his robes with self-assured hands. His head is high again, confidence assured again.

But... Something is wrong with him. It's obvious in the way he holds his head and the way he looks at me. Creeping, glancing looks that travel up and down the length of me.

I stand. Then, I cross my arms over my chest and huddle in my robe. I don't know why. I am dust. He is a Day, a fae, my dearest one of my blood. So why is he staring at me? Watching me?

Why do I press myself into the wall as though I aim to squeeze through every cracked and crumbling bit of stone? My heart races. Something is wrong. Very wrong.

"I am so very sorry, Day," I say, my voice thick. "I didn't mean to upset you. You are right. I have been awful to you. You don't deserve it."

He nods in agreement. I have been awful, treating him in a way he doesn't deserve. But why...

He's still looking at me in that strange, calculating way and I don't know why.

"Tell me what's been distracting you and I may forgive you," he says.

I lower my head in contrite thought. Liar. I'm hiding my face from him. Hiding my shame from him. Hiding how I lie.

"It's just the ceremony," I say, my voice rasping. "I don't want to disappoint the Lord Master."

Even if I don't know what my "role" will be. Even if I haven't thought of it once since the night a monster crept into the courtyard and taunted me with temptation. The ceremony is one of only three important days of the year and I haven't thought of it once.

Day sighs. It isn't like him. He's anxious and on edge, but I am a small part of his irritation. "You don't know, do you?" he says.

I shake my head, my gaze still downcast. "My role? No, I don't."

"Not your role," he snaps. How dare I even assume he meant me. "*Mine.* You really don't understand it, do you? I saw the book and thought you understood. I saw the book and thought you knew what was at stake."

The book. The historical reference on prior battles? No. I know the answer even before I look up and catch him glaring angrily toward that shelf in the middle of the archives. That taboo subject. The one I read only to entertain a price only a vamryre would request from me.

Why does Day care? Because it is sinful of course. Shameful. He's afraid my indiscretion will infect him as well.

"It was just a book," I insist, hoping my voice alone conveys my conviction. Just a book. Just a sinful, dangerous, all-important book. Just a guidebook to my dealings with Caspian. It's all he wanted from me. All I had to offer.

And it still wasn't enough.

"No!" Day snaps, turning on his heel, robes swishing, red hair flying. He's animated today. Tonight. For the first time, I realize it is later than he normally visits. The others are all abed. I am alone, lurking long past the hour I should be in my room asleep. Because I'm waiting for him. Hoping for him.

And hope is such a dirty, sinful thing.

"You have no idea, do you?" Day remarks, spinning to eye me, his expression one of disgust. His upper lip curls, nostrils flare. He has never once been disgusted with me in all the years we've met in secret. What have I done to offend him so?

Or maybe nothing. Perhaps he's finally accepted what we have both known all along?

"You are so naive of the ways of the world." He advances toward me angrily and reaches out, snagging a piece of my hair. He winds it around a pale finger, but it isn't gentle, a harmless touch. He grinds the strands between rubbing fingertips as if chasing out my very essence, spreading corruption all over his fingers. Then he breathes in but it's a long, lingering inhale.

My heart lurches. Skips. My throat feels tight. I feel dizzy and sick. Something is wrong. Very wrong.

"You don't understand, how could you? You have no idea what I mean to offer you."

I can't speak. I have to lick my lips to find enough traction. Once. Twice. When I breathe in again the air is different. Thicker. Heavier. Spicier. I feel a familiar chill and my body comes to life again.

"I think you're beginning to understand," Day says, his smile back. Pulsing. Relieved. I've made him happy but I don't know how. He smiles and runs his finger along my jawline, tracing the shape of my bottom lip. It's curled upwards in a weird shape.

My own imitation of his half-smile? But Day thinks he is the cause of it. He isn't. It's my own greedy selfishness. Maybe...

Maybe I can finally get what I want. The potential deliverer is here, watching and waiting. Impatient. I can tell without even seeing his face. It's like I can hear him, hissing, *Send him away. Away.*

"I hate that I've wasted so much of your time," I tell Day. "You are so very busy with your studies. You don't need to visit me if it is a chore."

A part of me winces. Will I deny myself my only real distraction? Maybe. If. If. If...

If I can attain something else. But poor Day, he is worthy too. Worthy of so much more than chasing hours in a dank crypt with an unworthy abomination.

"You should go," I tell him, moving cautiously as his fingers still trace my lip. Over and over they trace. Too many times they trace.

I step back. "You need rest. I hate to be the cause of distracting you from the ceremony."

He frowns, fingers still hanging in the air. They reach for me again. "Don't you see? You are the only part of the ceremony that matters to me! I can save you," he hisses, gripping my shoulder tight. "I can save you from all of this. I can give you the life you've only dreamed about."

I don't understand. I don't.

"Day, I—"

"Don't you see?" He yanks me closer, bringing his face within a hair's breadth of mine. I've known this face for most of my life. Now, I barely recognize it. "You are my rightful Aurelia. Not the other one. You know your place. You will serve me with modesty and obedience. It will only be you!"

My voice breaks. I try to move away. "Day—"

"No!" He takes my hand again, gripping the fingers so tight it hurts. I gasp. His eyes widen with guilt. Then narrow. His hand clamps down over my own, jarring the very bones.

"You can't deny me," he warns. "I am the only one who has ever cared for you. Who taught you. Look at me!"

I can't. I turn my face away rather than see the look in his eye. Something dangerous and dark buried within that once friendly green.

"Look at me!" He snatches a fistful of my hair—something he has never done. Yanks me toward him. Presses his mouth to mine—

"No!" I push him off. Try to. He is too big. Too strong. He steps into me, lashing at my lower lip harshly. So hard that he bites. Draws blood.

I'm bleeding.

"Day, stop!" I wrench away and stagger into the wall. He's panting, swiping at his mouth. A drop of red gleams there and is instantly chased by his tongue. Gone in a flash. I don't know him, this stranger eyeing me, his chest heaving, eyes blazing.

I want to run from him.

Hide from him.

My foot twitches against the floor, but then I go still. Movement flickers against the wall across from me and a new fear takes over. A living shadow approaches us both, looming above, threatening to descend.

I can feel its dark intentions seep into the air: to kill.

"Don't you see?" Day continues, oblivious to me and the creature creeping toward him. "I can save you from all of this! Your place will be by my side. *That* is where you belong."

"Of course," I say, but I barely hear him or what he says next. All I can see is the pale face creeping closer, fangs bared, eyes blazing.

The longer Day touches me, the more ominous the moment feels. Need to stop it. End this.

So I'll say anything. "Of course. You are right," I tell him, this unfamiliar figure wearing the face of dear Day. "You are always right. I understand now."

"You do?" His voice is so hopeful it hurts. It sounds like my voice. Too close to my voice.

When the vamryre offered me the world, and I begged for a price.

"Yes," I insist. "So please rest. I am sorry. I understand."

"Good." He smiles for real and finally withdraws. My heart pounds as I watch him go. I intend to watch and wait for him to slip out of the main chamber.

Too late. My shadow monster has grown tired of waiting. He latches onto my shoulders and steers me back, back into the most shadowed section of the catacombs. He pins me against the wall there. He steps into me. Slams his mouth to mine. Creeping fingers inch beneath my robe and upward. Then brush past a tender slip of flesh and plunge inside of me.

It hurts, but in a different way than it should. The way it hurts to breathe ice-cold air on a winter day. But you breathe in deeply. It's fresh. It's cold. It's thrilling.

And you need it.

I need this. His touch, stroking from the inside out, sowing friction that makes the world fall away and makes me forget who I am and what I am. I need this.

My teeth clench. A strange sound catches in my throat. A noise he doesn't like. A noise he craves and presses his weight into me until I make it again. Again.

I can't stop making pathetic, tiny, choked sounds.

With a sweep of his tongue, he chases the violence, demanding more. Always more.

I feel him tugging at my robes and scratching the flesh underneath. Steps back. Head bowed and half-cocked he takes me in. Every greedy, selfish inch of me he inhales with glowing red eyes. Grasping the front of his black pants, he approaches. A flicking thumb unhooks a metal clasp. A clenched fist tugs the waistband down.

And my mind is wiped blank.

He is a sinful creature too beautiful to exist. Too beautiful to compare to dull illustrations and diagrams in that hated book. I never knew that beneath heavy fabric and dark trousers, bodies could morph and change. Muscle can strain against flesh in a haunting, lovely refrain.

I never knew that the sight of a vamryre's body could make me hate myself more than I already do.

The way he looks at me, however, is all wrong. As he stares, my eyes burn, sear, and prickle. He doesn't look at me as Day does.

It's as though he's hungry, starving, ravenous, and I'm a thing to be devoured. Not barely palatable sustenance like the bread I eat. He looks at me the way I look at...

The way I look at the sketches in my secret mortal sketchbook.

"Stay there," Caspian snaps. Maybe I tried to move or flinched. Maybe I just needed to say something to fill the silence and regain control again. He steps out of his spilled trousers and advances toward me, naked from the lower half down.

I feel dizzy with relief. Finally. Finally. He's changed his mind. He'll accept my price. Finally.

It will be a painful bargain, but finally, finally...

I'll have what I want, perhaps. Finally.

As his lips brush the crook of my throat, I realize I almost forgot to ask. Almost forgot the entire point of this twisted, filthy game.

"Will you take me there?" I ask him.

"Will I take you?" he echoes, his voice mocking and cold. But his touch is fire, licking a path down my hips, beneath my legs, inching inside me again. "I'll take you," he grates out, but he doesn't mean what I want. He's solely focused on his greedy desire; the game he finds in turning my body into a puppet on a string. "I'll take you to a place you've never been, little fae. I'll make you scream. Make you pay. For this, I will make you pay."

For what? He doesn't say. He doesn't deem me worthy enough to explain. And Day, he can have his secrets. He is special, my dearest, a fae.

But him?

The vamryre can't deny me everything. My hand disobeys the protocol I've always followed. It finds his wrist and grips it tight—flesh over marble. A string wrapped around stone.

He could easily shrug me off, but he stills. Groaning in frustration, he stills.

"What?"

"Tell me that you'll help me." Oh no. I'm saying strange things. Nonsense. Incoherent nonsense.

In any case, he understands me. His eyes flash as he draws back. He bares his fangs. Brings them dangerously close to my mouth. Nips —barely soft enough to avoid breaking skin and drawing blood. Then he hisses a sigh.

"What do you want?"

"The other realm," I say.

He snarls and hisses. Without permission, he strokes my back, sending shockwaves down my spine.

"I can make you feel better than the fucking mortal realm," he snarls into my throat.

I know he can. That's the terrifying part of this exchange. My bargain with a blood devil. He offers a world beyond my wildest dreams. Things someone like me should never ever feel.

But if I lost my one hope, I'd lose me.

"Please."

He growls and staggers back, hands clenching and unclenching. Eyes fiery holes in a perfect skull. "Damn you. You aren't worth it!"

"I know," I say, taking a step toward him. He is my only chance. My only chance. I can't let him escape. I need a promise. I need a plea.

Vamryres are deceitful creatures, but him...

I know he'll keep any promise he agrees to. I know it.

"Just tell me about it," I plead, taking another step. "Please! How to get there. What it's like. I'll settle for that much, I will. Just tell me—"

"No." He lunges for me. Slams me back. Takes my hands in both of his and pins them up, holding me flat. I can't move. Can't breathe. Then he claims my mouth so hard I see stars. His tongue rakes over mine as if in punishment for the words he'll say next. He can't help himself.

Honesty is my virtue, but *he* embodies it.

"Fuck you," he grates, panting against my open, wet mouth. "There is a way. Only the elders know it. A secret path. No approval required. In and out. It's how they sneak in when the folly strikes them. It's how *they* break the rules."

His eyes blaze. It's like he's drunk, the way the workers get on ceremony days. Too intoxicated to care for what leaves his mouth.

To me, each word is gold. Precious.

"More," I beg him, but my body does something I don't tell it to: arch into him, press my chest to the hard expanse of his. My nipples are sharp enough to graze him through the material of my robe. I don't care. With a ragged sigh, I tilt my head and offer up all I have to give. I need more. He'll give me it all.

For a price.

"How can I get there?"

"Not alone," he hisses. Harsh and cold hands slip beneath my skull, angling it away from him. Then back until those eyes are all I can see, and his touch is all I can feel. Care about. Need.

Except...

"How?"

"You'd need protection," he grates out. "It isn't safe. You'll be eaten alive."

He means it as a threat. A deterrent that should silence me. Yet, another request is already poised on the tip of my tongue. "Then... Come with me."

He laughs as those eyes go wide. Then he groans and slips his hand between my legs—but I don't clamp them tight like I should. His touch is sinful, coaxing my knees apart, letting him cup his palm against me. A mass of aching flesh, he has me, putty in his hands. Then he crooks a finger, sliding it inside me. Then another.

My eyelids flutter as I struggle to register the intrusion. He is ice cold. Hard as stone. Disturbingly gentle as he eases those probing digits deeper and deeper. I never knew one could feel so full and yet so empty. My senses scatter. Already, it's getting harder to think. Remember...

Our bargain.

"Tell me," I breathe before I lose my mind completely. Too late. His thumb comes to rest on a bundle of flesh that makes me lurch as if burned. In this moment, pain was expected—not what I feel crawling up my spine in its stead. Pleasure.

If he did so to silence me, the punishing friction does the opposite. My tongue loosens and a command slips out, "*Help* me—"

"No!" He means it, that angry wail. He won't tell me. He can't. He refuses. It's forbidden.

"Please—" I reach for him, pressing a shaking hand to his shoulder. He snatches it and tugs my wrist downward, between us. A firmness brushes my fingertips. Danger. Pulsating. Ice. He wants me to cringe in fear—give him a reason to stop this.

I don't. My fingers flex as if of their own accord. In response, he shudders, teeth grated, eyes blazing.

"I need to fuck you," he rasps against my throat. He isn't asking, yet... He wants an answer from me. Badly enough to wait for it, teeth gnashing, voice guttural. "Tell me I can," he snaps in response to my silence.

I don't know why these words spring from my tongue next, "Promise me first. Promise—"

"No!" Grunting, he bats my hand away and wrenches my thighs further apart. His fingers are then replaced by something thicker. Heavier. Harder. It penetrates my outer folds with menacing pressure. Waits. Then his hand hooks around my backside as he slams into me. Groans. Goes limp.

I'm on fire, impaled, and emboldened all at once. I know without even looking down, what he's initiated. What he's done—taken his price. My body. My soul. All in a brief thrust of fiery pain.

Yet corruption isn't the degrading destruction I thought it would be. I am not fearful and trembling. I feel swollen and needy. Desperate. Demanding. He is inside me and perhaps that is why; I'm infected with his power. His dominance.

How I even manage to speak, I'll never know. Somehow, I plead into his ear, "Please. Promise... Say it—"

"Fuck," he says, grunting out the word as though it was being torn from his throat. His fingers flex, manipulating my waist so that our pelvises collide. Then he bucks his hips, making me empty. Slams forward. I'm full. Again, again and again, until the pain fades away and all I feel is *everything*.

This isn't mating. It is decimation. He rips through old barriers my body had in place and sows chaos in his wake. I whimper and writhe to adjust to the sensation. It is unlike anything else. Burning, aching, fulfilling pain, spreading like wildfire. Beneath the discomfort, I can't deny a sense of relief.

His price has been paid. Our deal is done. But... I can't escape a nagging need for *more*. More secrets. More corruption. More bargains to be struck. My fingers grip his shoulders tight as my vision clears and I catch my breath again. His face is buried against my shoulder now, leaving his ear within reach of my gaping mouth. "Please," I beg of him. "Promise. Promise me—"

"Yes," he hisses, lunging forward, expanding his invasion. Another thrust. "I'll take you. Yes, yes, yes—"

It's all I need to hear. It's all I'll need ever again.

He'll help me. He'll help me.

More relief renders me boneless, held up only by his grip. Undeterred, he grinds himself into me, as hard as he can. Nowhere near hard enough.

My thoughts splinter, and my one and only hope is pushed aside for a brief moment. As far as my body is concerned, it is all sin and fire. Finding relief is vital. I can't think about anything else.

I can't need anything else.

I bend my knees and wrap my legs around his waist, drawing him closer. Deeper. Not enough.

And then a dangerous sound—more alarming than the rest—slips out of my mouth and makes him growl in response. It makes him wild. He hooks his hands beneath me, wrenches me from the floor. Slams me against the wall, pushing into me from a newer angle. Harder. Harder.

Isn't enough.

He takes me back to the floor instead. Grips my thigh and raises it high, his teeth bared, gaze feral. His mind is fixated on one focus. One goal. Something he can't find until he's so deep inside me I cry out, and my head lolls back against the stone. Then he reaches between us, stroking, rubbing, and setting off fireworks.

My lips part. Another dangerous sound trickles out. Another. I hear it this time, echoed back, taunting me.

His name. Over and over, his name leaves my throat. Nothing else.

CHAPTER 15
Caspian

They always climax too soon. Or not soon enough.

The pretty ones I plied for Cassius. I'd touch them with hateful hands and feed them lies. I'd look at them with this pretty face, and they would simper, whimper, and moan. They'd orgasm all at once, or in a drawn-out display.

None of it fucking matters. None of them are memorable.

But she...

I slam my length into that tiny cleft and make every inch fit. Her eyes widen. Then she grips me back, clinging to my body like she has a right to. A need to. Like she can't fucking breathe without me deeper. Harder. So deep it hurts, and she gasps. Then moans and pleads for more.

More more more.

She needs more. More of my cock inside her. More of my mouth on her skin. More of my fingers caressing every fucking inch. It's never enough.

She writhes for more.

The feeling of her orgasm, her body clenching me like a damn fist, isn't enough. Isn't long enough. Intense enough. I make her do it again. Unravel again until her body is drenched, her throat is sore, and she can barely make those noises again.

Then she does. I slam into her for the millionth time, and she moans my name.

Over and over.

And it. Is. Fucking. Never. Enough.

One whimpered, whispered *Caspian* is worth a lifetime with Cassius. Two, and I'd give the bastard my soul. A third time...and she has me, stupid little fae. Beautiful fucking, foolish fae.

She says my name, and I'd give her my heart in a bloodied fist. Don't know why. Don't care to know why.

I'll take every grated, whimpered noise until I silence that voice forever. Until she can't say a fucking word ever again.

Until Cassius chokes on his own twisted jealousy. I feel him. Hear him raging in a wordless howl.

The fae chokes out my name again, and he falls silent. Cassius is dead fucking silent. And it is her doing. Her fucking power.

She makes him disappear. At least until my orgasm steals the last of my strength away, and I go limp, crushing her pale body to the stone floor, devoid of everything.

We're alone in here, but it doesn't fucking sound like it. Her panting breaths echo back to me. Cassius' shouted cries echo back to me. Oh, I've done it now. He is so fucking angry.

Good. He should be.

I never wanted him.

Always hated him.

His anger is now so great that he has decided to put an end to this game. Angry enough to send his army of mindless toys after me. He'll have me dragged back and locked away. Perhaps with Cassiopeia, perhaps without. He'll make me repay my debt to him.

And he'll take my fae toy away.

No. I won't let him.

She stares up at me as I stand and wrench my pants back into place. She watches me, naked and breathless and fucking beautiful—no, she isn't. She isn't.

I snatch her robe and throw it at her. "Get dressed."

We don't have long. Mere minutes before the vamryre hoard descends, and my punishment begins. Oh yes, Cassius, bring them all. It will take all of his collective minds to bring me down. To take me back.

I'd rather die than go back.

She'll die then. He's angry enough to let them do it—rip her to pieces right in front of me. Teach me a lesson that will really sting. That's why he's so angry. So furious. So vengeful.

I wanted to fuck her, and I enjoyed it. More than any other time he made me dance and preen and fuck for him. I enjoyed it. I'll do it again. All over again.

I'll pay her stupid price.

"Something's wrong." Her voice is so hoarse, but it still breaks.

She can sense the tension in the air. Cassius' anger is audible from his damn mansion, even for fae ears to hear.

But no. Her black eyes are focused inward, and she shakes her head, sweat-damp hair clinging to her skull. "Something's wrong. I..." Suddenly, her eyes widen, and she takes my hand. Clings to it. "Day! I hear him!"

"Who?"

The male fae. He never left. He listened at the door and heard her whimper. Heard me claim her. He heard his little piece of prey be fucked by another monster—and enjoy it.

She closes her eyes, her mouth an o of pure pain. "Oh no. Oh no—"

"Hush," I tell her. I need to think. I need to move before the hoard reaches me. I start forward, intending to leave—but my hand is still in hers, only I'm the one gripping tighter. I tug her along, and she scrambles to keep pace.

Right to the door, she struggles. Digs her heels in and tries to resist. "Not that way. I can't—"

But it's the only way. Through the door and past her stupid, male fae. He gapes, wide-eyed, but he's already a shadow, fading in the distance. I need to move. Through the courtyard. Up to the main tower complex.

After that, I should face my punishment. Face my dear brothers and sisters. Rip them to shreds.

I shouldn't keep moving, blowing past the main door. Then, toward a staircase—

"Wait!" She tugs on my hand. Makes me stop. "Please!"

She wants a detour. Down a short hallway paved in stone. Up a rickety set of stairs. Into her little hovel.

My ears twitch, picking up a distant toll. An alarm bell. Oh dear. The little fae are all riled up. Soon they will amass, joining the vamryre already on my heels.

Oh, what fun.

"Come," I snap at her.

She does, shuffling toward me with a bundle under her arm. It's square-shaped, wrapped in a set of torn robes. My nostrils flare, catching the faint, rotting scent of a rose.

"I'm ready," she says, just as shouts rise up in the distance—near the archive. Too many voices. Too many fae to fight off at once.

Don't fight, the monster in my head growls. *Stand and face me, Caspian! Face me! OBEY ME—*

I snatch for the fae and he's gone. Her wrist in my grasp, I head in another direction. Down a dusty, narrow passage that opens onto a larger one with pretty paneled walls and plush green carpeting. I don't recognize it... No, wait, I do.

The ceremonial antechamber. Don't know how I remember that name. Remember this place or the fact that if I open a set of gleaming black doors I will find a forgotten staircase. It leads to a dusty dead end: a landing piled high with crates and cobwebs. A deceitful illusion. If one shoves aside a stack of junk, it reveals an old statue carved into the very wall.

The statue of an old, hunched fae with one staring, carved eye and a space where the other should be. If one sticks his finger in that hole, he'll feel a pinch—the bite of some unseen mechanism. Fed just a mere drop of blood, the sated statue will spin to reveal a doorway. Old. Crumbling.

Behind it lies a space where an indigo light emanates.

A forgotten cavern. Here I need to run, too fast for the lazy guards to catch. Deep down into a tunnel that cuts beneath the earth—beneath the very realm.

"Oh, my..." The fae breathes and her steps falter. She slows me down. Makes me stop. Has me staring as she reaches out a trembling pale finger toward a wall of glistening black stone. Embedded within it are glowing things. Strange things. "Fae stones," she whispers, hesitating before touching one. "Such magic. I never thought—"

"We need to go," I tell her, dragging her along, deeper into this winding space.

A tunnel that Cassius has made me forget. This far from him, I start to remember. It was at his request that I sneaked down this tunnel now and again. A snaking protrusion of stone, embedded with the rocks the fae claim are magic; the same magic that ripped our realm from the mortal one in the first place.

They claim the official portal above is the only way to leave. A lie. There is also this way, discrete enough for a devious vamryre to tiptoe up to the mortal realm and lure any unsuspecting prey back. It's forbidden—not allowed.

Cassius doesn't fucking care. They are fae rules. Fake rules. When he kills the high council, there will be no more rules.

That's why he so flagrantly had me take a mortal here, a mortal there. For years, he's had me creep and take. Some to be bled dry. Some to be fucked and swallowed into the mindless collective.

But I was his only one. His trusted one.

Because as long as he kept Cassiopeia close to him, I would always return for her. My sister. My lone ally in war. My other half. The only one who truly understood what it meant to resist him, and hate him, and endure him.

Until he took her away from me, and he crushed all traces of this tunnel from my memory.

The sick bastard did so out of fear. He knew that without her...

I'd find this tunnel and follow it all the way to the end. I'd climb up the worn metal ladder heading toward a heavy trapdoor made of stone. Once I shrugged off that final barrier, I'd be free from him. I'd run and keep running.

I would never fucking go back.

CHAPTER 16
Niamh

I read a story once of a greedy fae who achieved everything they ever wanted. Power, wealth, and prestige. Yet, they still wanted more. More still.

Then they died alone and unhappy atop their mound of false wealth.

It was a warning. A cautionary tale. A lesson cloaked in drama and prose.

But a lesson all the same, and one I took to heart. To crave something out of greed only leads to disappointment in the end. A selfish creature can never be sated. Never be satisfied. They will always want more.

I believe that, right up until the moment that Caspian grips my hand impossibly tight and pulls me through a dark, dank hole underground. A portal.

I believe in that precious fable right up until the moment I open my eyes and breathe in fresh air. Until I see a blue, blue sky and feel an icy frost against my cheek.

I believe that greed is a sin until I see the mortal realm for myself. Beautiful, barren emptiness.

And a fullness I never knew I was missing made my heart feel heavy. I could die here content and happy. Even with a vamryre looming beside me, angry and scathing, I could die utterly happy.

Either he lets me go, or I wiggle away from him, but suddenly I'm walking freely, my hands outstretched, taking in this clean, fresh air. No stone. No watchful bell tower. No fervent, furtive glances my way that I was supposed to ignore.

The air is so clean. The sun is so bright. Everything smells wonderful. Feels wonderful. I'm running, my bare feet traipsing through grass and muddied earth.

It's beautiful. Everything here is beautiful.

I throw my head back at that perfect, wonderful sky and laugh aloud. Without fear of judgment or derision, I laugh and laugh. I run and laugh. I throw my arms out and spin and spin and giggle with the knowledge that no one or anyone could take this moment away.

Not Lord Master. Not myself. Not Day. Not even the vamryre.

I spin and spin until I grow dizzy and stumble to the hard ground. Still laughing, I look for him. Maybe he's gone, his duty fulfilled?

But he's not. He stands near the hole we crawled up out of, watching me from the shadow of a tree. Coldly and intently, he stares. As if he's never seen another creature remotely like me, he stares.

A silence falls between us, heavy and still. Something changed in our frantic race here. Something is still changing, morphing, and transforming. What is it? What is it?

I doubt I'll ever know. He watches me for so long that the rest of reality fades to a hum. We are the only two souls in this plane of existence. Then, slowly, he inclines his head and says, "Come."

On trembling legs, I stand.

And I obey.

CHAPTER 17

Caspian

I'm starting to remember.

All of the things he made me forget. All of the lies he shoved in their place. All of the rule infractions he had me commit for him.

The bastard is the king of sin, and I am his greatest devil, a monster of his creation. More than once did he send me into the mortal realm for him. More than once. A dozen times. A hundred. A thousand.

To fuck a mortal for him here and there. To lure one or two back. Mainly to kill.

He used me to kill.

Then he made me forget. Dampened my mind and sent me right back to his enclave, a castrated little gelding in his stable of puppets and whores. That's the real reason he deemed her off-limits.

Because he couldn't crawl inside my skin while I was inside her. He was regulated to his own mind then, poor, hateful, devious Cassius. His mind, where the monotonous din of his other spawn both pleases and bores him. He had to watch me enjoy her, knowing all the while that he could never have a taste.

For now, he's far, far away. Too far to hear his screams and commands. So far, the others are a muted little hum. *Caspian... Caspian...*

Without their drone, I can think again. I can feel again—in all of the ways he made me deaf and dumb to what wasn't him. I can feel her hand slip into mine. I can feel her tense with unease. Then I feel her shiver as I grip her back, making my hand a manacle that shackles her to me.

I have her in a way he never could. I'm not in her head, controlling her movements. I've made her stay with words alone. A promise. One I would be foolish and stupid to keep.

Take me to the mortal realm, oh Caspian. Take me there, parade me out among the mortals. Let me sniff their scents and dance under their sky. Let me laugh in a way you will never ever hear me laugh again.

Then take her back—that's the inevitable second step. Return her to the Citadel and watch her die. Be the one to bleed that little body dry.

Yes.

Yes.

But for now, I've done the impossible and stupid thing. I'm holding the fae's hand in the mortal realm.

Far from Cassius' shadow, I'm also realizing that I know the place like the back of my fucking hand. I've been here too many times to count. Too many times for the novelty to affect me like it does her.

Stupid little fae. I know this place well enough to tell her all she wants to know. There is no magic to be found here. Just mundane mortals and their dreary little lives. Sans Cassius, the other realm has...

More. More liveliness. More drama. More death. Everything.

This place is dull and quiet. So fucking quiet.

Then I remember. This is just a sliver of their world—the outskirts of some big city. A giant rat nest of beings. The portal never takes one into the heart of the mortal world. You have to walk down a dark, winding road shrouded by a forest.

Without her, I would run. It would take minutes to reach their little city made of brick buildings stacked like toys. With her...

She's too slow. Too weak. Too tired. Already, she's dragging on me, her weight slowing me down. Even when I take her bundle from her, she can't keep up. Trails behind me. I should shrug her off. Flee. Run.

I fulfilled my promise. I got her here.

And I've got Cassius on my tail. He'll hunt me down with great glee. The bastard.

I will never let him catch me.

She is a drag. An anchor around my neck. I shake her loose and walk away. Run away.

She can take her chances in this realm she craved to see so much.

No longer is she of any use to me.

Let her rot out here.

Let her die out here.

Yes, yes. I keep running until the sound of her heavy breathing is a distant memory. I run until her scent dissipates on the wind. I run and run.

It's only when I near the outskirts of that teeming, filthy mortal city that I remember; I have her bundle. What stupid items would a fae hold dear?

I already know one of them, even before I stop and rip open her bundle to see: a single dying, once-white rose. It rests on top of, of all things, a leather book, worn with age, reeking of must. I assume it's one of her fae stories until I flip it open to a random page. Not words. Drawings are scrawled across these pages. Ugly. Too much color. Too bright.

I want to pitch it into the darkness. Rip it to shreds.

I start to.

As I loosen my grip on the leather object, a new word trips into my skull. Not a color. A feeling. It makes me think of her, my foolish little fae.

Remorse. Disgusting word. Stupid word.

Don't care.

I drop her bundle on the ground and walk away. She doesn't matter. Her ability to inspire words doesn't matter. The past doesn't matter.

Who I was before Cassius *doesn't* matter.

Nothing does.

Not anymore.

But then...

I catch her scent on the air, and it draws me back. Back to that stupid fucking book. Back to her bundle of worthless things—all she has to her fake, stolen name.

Why leave them here for her to find?

I take them, tucking them under my cloak.

A bargaining chip to come in handy for another time, should I see her again.

If I see her again.

CHAPTER 18
Niamh

There is something in my throat I can't swallow down. It's a thick lump that threatens to choke me whenever I breathe. Swallow. Think about him in this wide, waning darkness.

Realize that I am alone. For the first time in my life, truly alone. There are no fervent whispers to haunt my steps. No workers of the Citadel darting in and out of my reach. At least then, I knew I was some kind of being. A live one.

Here I am empty, soundless, nothingness.

It's what I wanted, after all. He gave me what I wanted, and for that...

I watched him go and let him leave. I didn't even say goodbye. I didn't try to follow him.

Even if I tried, I could never follow him. His strength is on display out here, in the wilds beyond our home, where the grass grows tall, and there is nothing around for stretches and stretches. Nothing but looming trees and swaying shadows and...

I am not afraid. I hug myself in my thin robe, easily pierced by a cold, bitter chill, and I tell myself over and over that I am not afraid. I don't need Caspian. I don't want him to return.

I am capable out here where my prior limitations no longer apply to me. In the old realm, I am sickly and weak. Here I am...

So very cold. The wind drives into my lungs, each breath a stabbing knife. My feet are numb, limbs trembling in the rapidly falling darkness. I can't see, even as I keep walking forward through looming, bending, twisting shapes. I'm in a valley of hungry shadow. They howl for blood and reach toward me with grasping, gnawing limbs.

I shiver past them, hunched forward, head down. I struggle forward and I remember what Caspian told me. *"You'd need protection. It isn't safe. You'll be eaten alive."*

Eaten alive by cold and shadows. Eaten alive by fear.

No. I keep moving. Keep walking. One foot in front of the other. I use my sole desire as the driving force to keep me going.

I want to see a museum. I want to see...

Anyone. Anything.

The shadows start to speak, in creaking, crackling mumbles.

I run. Trip. Fall. Crawl upwards, grasping and groping. Pull myself upright. Stagger. Sprint. Run. I run until my lungs ache. Until I can't feel the tears falling down my cheeks. I run and run until the forest gives way to a dark, flat river or stone that cuts a path forward.

And then on that path a light appears, beckoning and glowing. Two lights, a brilliant yellow, like eyes in the dark. I race toward them. Panting and choking, I lunge for them.

After that, the world slams into me and everything falls silent.

Black.

Nothing.

"Holy fuck! She came out of nowhere, I swear!" Someone hisses in alarm, their voice frantic. Panicked. I hear footsteps rushing and hurried. "Oh shit. I think she's dead. Fuck. Fuck! Pulse? You want me to check for a pulse? Ok. Fuck!"

Someone comes closer. I can feel them, so very warm. They pry the hair from my neck and press into the flesh there. They are so very warm.

But their touch hurts. Everything hurts. My legs won't move. I can't open my eyes. I can barely breathe in and out. My chest aches when I do. Everything in me aches.

"God, she is so fucking pale. She has to be dead. Wait! I think I feel a pulse. Fuck, I gotta call for help!" There is a musical sound like the toll of a bell. Then the voice continues, even more frantic. "Hey, yeah. I... This woman came out of nowhere right in front of me. She's hurt badly. We need an ambulance out here on Greyland Way—"

Something new crawls from this forest, advancing on me and the stranger's voice. It's quiet but quick, like a knife cutting through the door.

"What was that? I think someone must be with her. Shit!"

Cold hard hands grab me, ice cold but brutally gentle. They lift me up and I do something I shouldn't be able to. I fly. The wind tears the hair back from my face and then I realize I haven't sprouted wings and taken flight of my own accord. In reality I've never even left the ground. I'm being held.

Strange. I've never felt peace like this. Strength like this. Viewed the world like this. Through one cracked, swollen eye, I can see the rest of the world rushing by. Through throbbing ears, I can hear the low, frantic breaths of my captor.

Only, wait... He doesn't need to breathe, not really. He's growling, whispering angry things as he runs through the night with my body in his arms.

"Stupid...stupid! Don't you die. Don't you DARE die. Stupid, fucking, foolish..."

He's angry with me, not that I can blame him. He brought me here and I already failed in my grand plan. I've been eaten alive by a pair of glowing yellow lights.

But in his arms, I don't feel the pain like I should. It's a quiet thing gnawing at the back of my mind, too weak to fully penetrate. Crushed and cradled against him, all I feel is fresh air and those thrilling hopeful feelings that made me dance dizzy when I first inhaled this perfect mortal air.

He's too dangerous to cling to, I know that. Far too dangerous to trust.

But I want to. My fingers scrape his cold, hard skin, and I want to hold him so tightly he'll never run away again. I want him, and it is a horrible thing to realize. My sole desire has a new vital component part, shoved in like a puzzle piece that can never quite fit.

I don't *just* want to see the mortal realm.

I want this vamryer to show it to me. I want to see it through his unfeeling, red eyes. I want to huddle in his arms, safe and broken but protected.

I don't want anything else, I promise. My greediness will run its course as long as I get to keep him...

I want him.

I'll keep him.

CHAPTER 19
Caspian

Stupid, fucking, stupid fae. Stupid, fucking, stupid Cassius. Stupid, fucking, stupid me. I've let my toy wander by herself for a fucking second.

One second.

And she wandered her way right into danger. Another creature ripped her apart and left her body torn and bleeding. I can feel her dying. Taste her blood, painting the air. There is no Cassius to please anymore, no rules to follow. I could stop running. Set her aside in some dark, dank place and drain her dry. Feast and feast.

I want to.

My steps slow, and I hear her ragged, half-assed breathing. In and out, she sucks in air, but she's running out of time. Her tiny heart is tired of pumping. It starts to stammer and fizzle out. The longer I linger, she'll fizzle out. Already, she's too limp. Too weak. Her voice is a croak, and I can feel her wet, warm blood dripping all over me. Spilling all over me.

Yummy. Delicious.

I only have to lower my mouth to her neck and look past those wide, staring, half-closed eyes. I only have to prod her throat with a hungry tongue. Lap up some of the precious, beautiful red that's already spilled.

I can drink her. Take her. Have her entire essence, then throw away the dried-out husk. I can do it. Oh, how I want to.

Do it. Do it.

I can't. She's too weak. Too pale. One drop could never be enough, and then she'll be dead in a heartbeat. Which is what I want.

Isn't it?

Yes.

No.

Fuck me. Fuck her.

I keep moving, heading down the road the mortals call a highway. They navigated it blindly in little cages of metal and rubber. Cars, they call them. Trucks as well, bigger and longer. One of those infernal contraptions plowed into her. Shattered skin and bone. Her ribs are snapped. I can hear one of the jagged edges scraping into her lungs. Scritch. Scrape.

She should be moaning in agony. Writhing like they all do. The damage caused by the truck was great, but I've done worse to others. Many, many, many before her. I tore them apart with my bare hands while Cassius watched and goaded me on.

Such a good boy, his Caspian was.

He loved to watch me fuck his chosen appetites, but he liked to watch me kill even more. He used me like a rabid dog on a leash. Let me snap bone and chew and gnaw on the gaping, gory pieces.

During the throes of the death rattle, all of his victims loved to beg. They would murmur their final words, like, *"please, don't." "Have mercy." "I have a family."*

Boring, worthless, meaningless lies.

But her... She pries her heavy lips apart, and to nothing and no one, she says, "Beautiful. So beautiful."

We've left the darkness behind for a world of lights. Bright, nonsensical color—that's what the mortals like. They drape their homes in neon and let their world sparkle with nauseating brilliance. Cassius would like to do it, even in our other realm. Perhaps he would if his two elders didn't keep him in line. They made him dim his shine and confine his extravagance to his mansion.

I prefer the dark. The cold. The quiet. Endless misery and stoic silence.

Or I did.

Until I heard a broken, dying, uttered "beautiful," and saw this sickening world in a new light. A new way. She doesn't prize mindless beauty like Cassius. She feasts on the novelty. The brilliance. She sees these twisted lights and towering buildings as though they are the stars in the sky, fallen to her feet, suddenly within her reach.

I hate her. How she looks at this realm, dying and broken, and still praises it. How she clings to me with soft, powerless fingers and struggles to stare. She'll kill herself faster if only to see more of this realm before she goes.

She's so fucking selfish. Out of spite, I can't let her die. Not yet. Not here.

So, I run.

This city unfurls before me, its roads well-tread and buildings changing, but my knowledge of it withstands the test of time. For centuries I've roamed these dirt, stone, now asphalt roads. More memories I wasn't aware of flood back, giving me a clear idea of what to do next.

I take this fae through empty streets and winding alleys. I take her to the one place Cassius had deemed a haven for our kind in this wasteland.

A motel, shaky and crumbling, squeezed in between a laundromat and a deli. I forget its name, something that implies a double entendre in the mortal tongue.

My victims would remark on it more often than not, whenever I brought them here.

"Bleeding Hearts Motel," they'd read, eyeing the flashing lights at the top of the building skeptically. Sometimes, they'd laugh. Sometimes, they'd sneer and beg to go somewhere else.

But there was nowhere else. Because this place was run not by fae or vamryre or lunaria, but half-creatures. Bastard bloodlines long forgotten and left behind. They would let Cassius do his bidding in peace for a price.

They'll let me stay here for a price.

How will I pay it?

Who the hell knows? Who cares? If they keep her alive, I don't fucking care. I'll give them anything.

Except return to Cassius—never that.

But anything else. They won't have a choice. When I enter the ruin, the fae in my arms, a woman at the front desk barely looks up from some tawdry image. A magazine. She sighs and shrugs.

"How can I help you?"

She isn't fae or vamryre or lunaria, but she isn't entirely mortal either. Her eyes sparkle in a way humans don't. Her nostrils flare, picking up a scent they can't. Then she looks up and she sees in a heartbeat what I am and where I am from.

But fear isn't what makes her gasp and stagger forward.

It's recognition.

"What the fuck are you doing here?" she demands, her cheeks splattered with angry red, her pudgy arms crossed over her chest. "Fuck, I thought they'd locked you in some dungeon or whatever the hell it is they do. You aren't allowed in here, bloodsucker. Not anymore. Get the fuck out before I sick my dog on you!"

"No." I dig my heels in. I hold the fae tight. She's running out of time, her breathing frail. But she's watching. Greedy, stupid thing, she's watching and curious and fighting with the last of her strength to take in what little she can of her precious mortal realm. She isn't staring at the woman or the disgusting room with stained floors and shitty music blaring from a metal box. Her gaze is fixed straight ahead. I risk a glance down to watch her. Her one good eye widens with hope and delight.

She's disgusting. This place is disgusting.

Except for a painting hanging on the wall behind the woman's head. She sees it, and she's content enough to die here and now.

Not while I have any say in it. I grip the back of her skull and wrench her head around to face me. Then I eye the woman and say, "Heal her."

"Hell no!" She sputters. Then eyes the fae and her eyes widen with unmistakable interest. She sees what she is. Knows it. Vamryre are a dime a dozen around this place, but not her kind. Not her. Fae—corrupted or not, she is a novelty. A new treat I can exploit.

"Heal her," I snarl. "Then supply me with a room. You don't have a choice, mundane."

That's the term Cassius told me, once upon a time, to refer to these half-immortal kinds. Mundane. Unspecial. Unpretty. Unworthy of entrance to the other realm.

So they live here among mortals and hide their powers and differences. In a way, they live like she did, my fae. Making themselves small by shrinking and hiding.

Their overseers aren't the members of the high council. Just their own disparate set of rules meant to keep mortal fears in check. How silly. How stupid.

Their rules aren't what I fear.

"Heal her, or I will rip you limb from limb," I tell her.

She swallows hard. She knows I mean it.

I will. I would.

But if I set the fae down in order to bite and tear, she'll die faster. Already, I can feel her slipping away. Away from me. Leaving me behind like I left her.

"Do it!" I bellow.

The mundane sighs. "I can't heal her, you idiot. That isn't my skill. Besides, if you lay a hand on me, the boneys will throw you in the pits where you belong."

A refusal. Then I will rip her to pieces. I start to set the fae down.

"But," the woman continues. "I know someone who can help. It will take her a while to make it out this way though. Your girl might be gone by then. Better to just pay off a boney. They'll pay good money for one of them kind, I think. We can split the fee." Split a fee. A price for the dead fae. A price nowhere near high enough to compensate for what I've done. No stupid mortal coin could ever be worth enough.

"Call your healer," I demand. "No one else. If anyone touches her, you die. If she dies...you die."

Her cheeks hollow. She sputters and spins around for a hook on the wall. Several hooks, most sporting keys.

"Fine, you stupid bastard." She snatches a handful of metal and throws it at me. "Last room on the left. a suite for your high and mightiness. I'll call the healer girl, but I've warned you. She won't get it at least until the morning. If that woman dies before then, don't you dare let it stink. We've got other paying customers to tend to. The last time you were here we had to close down for a fucking week to repair the damages."

The last time. When was the last time? I wrack my brain but it's a mess. There are too many new memories to sort. Too many old ones demanding attention. Cassius kept my thoughts neat and orderly, but without him....

It's a chaotic mess. Good. I'd rather be insane than be under his thumb. I'd rather be here with her.

Stupid fae. Dying fae. She struggles in my arms, croaking out her last few breaths.

No. I refuse to let her die here. Not now.

I take the keys the woman threw and go up to the last room on the left. There is only a dank, long hallway and ten rooms in total.

She gave me the suite, or so she claimed.

It's a square box with a bed and a closet holding a porcelain toilet and sink. Mortals. They construct their dwellings in strange, illogical ways. A boxy bed. A narrow window with a view of brick.

And a porcelain tub nowhere near big enough to capture the dripping blood pouring from my fading, dying fae.

I drop her onto the bed instead. Then I watch and wait. I'm wasting time by being here.

All of this is for nothing. Nothing.

I've brought her here for nothing. Wasted my moment to inflict her death sweetly, slowly, for nothing.

She will die for nothing.

No. I won't let her. I crouch onto the bed and hover above her, body braced on both hands planted beside her head.

"Look at me," I command.

She does. With one open, bruised, bleeding eye she looks at me. She's never stopped looking.

And in that eye, my brain goes silent. The anger I've known and craved is snuffed out. Cassius is a forgotten, fading thing on the edges of my psyche.

I look at her, and all I see is her. My fae. Mine.

"Don't you dare die," I tell her.

She swallows and tries to speak.

"Shut up."

Defiant in her final moments, she inhales raggedly. Sucks in as much of a breath as she can. She speaks.

"Thank you."

Thank me. For killing her. For leaving her. For letting another creature rip her apart into broken, bleeding pieces.

Thank me.

No.

"Fuck you," I hiss at her. "Don't die. Not yet. I won't let you die just yet."

My fingers twitch closer to her, coiling in the dark hair that spreads out over a yellow blanket beneath her. I twist those strands around my fingers. Tug until she winces, issuing a pained gasp. Then I stroke and smooth.

Hurting her more will make her die faster. My alternative is to stroke her. Caress her. My hands don't know how—they are tools used for destruction. Bred for destruction.

Still, I stroke her anyway. Pet her. There, there. I'll treat her like glass if it will make her stay.

"Don't die," I command. No, wait... I'm asking. I'll ask. The niceties will keep her here. She won't die then; she's too polite. I'll keep her here in any way I can.

I'll kiss her sweetly, press my lips to her forehead and beg. "Stay with me. Don't die yet. Can't die yet. I need to be the one to kill you."

"Ah..." It's the only sound she can make. *Ah. Ah.* But a new tear forms at the corners of her eyes, both of them, one closed and one open.

Fuck her. Fuck.

"You haven't been to your museum," I say, a cruel taunt. But it's a strong enough motivation to keep her here, I can see that. Her good eye widens. She parts her lips. Tries to speak. Can't.

I press my lips to her skull and murmur another deadly secret just for her. A promise. A threat. I'll keep her here anyway I can. It isn't lying in this case. Not if I intend to keep the promise. Maybe. Never.

Maybe someday.

"I'll take you there," I tell her. "You'll show me one of those stupid paintings. You can't die yet, stupid fae. I want to see the look on your face..."

When she sees her art up close. When she realizes that her hopes and dreams are all an illusion. Nothing is worth anything. There are no hopes in the world worthy of being fulfilled. Everything is a lie.

That's one thing Cassius taught me, the sick fucker.

There is no such thing as perfection. We are all tainted, twisted little lies. Broken dolls, performing for a master desperate to pretend that he matters. That we matter.

That all of this matters before the inevitable end.

But I'll make her believe it too, I have to. I'll feed her that silly, foolish fantasy to keep her here.

"Don't die," I snarl. "Don't fucking die."

And she doesn't. As the seconds tick by, she holds on, my stupid, foolish fae. She holds onto her life with all her might. She's dumb enough to believe me. To think I care about her wish enough to fulfill it.

She thinks I care about her.

Oh, what a fool. What a poor, stupid soul.

But I'll make her believe it.

"You matter," I lie. "Don't die yet. Stay here. Stay with me."

Because one day, I want to be the one to kill her with my own two hands.

It's what I have to do.

What I was born and bred to do.

A killer is all I am, before Cassius, after Cassius.

I can never be anything else.

I can never *want* to be anything else.

And she can never make me be, not her. Not someone so weak and stupid as her.

I can't help her fly and she can't make me feel.

My heart is dead. I am dead.

What makes me so desperate for her?

I don't know.

CHAPTER 20
Niamh

Death hurts. It is slow to arrive, and oh... does it *hurt.* Not in the way I thought it would feel. Blissful and quick and eagerly accepted. I always knew I'd die anyway.

When and where didn't matter, just that it would happen, and I would welcome it. Yes. Then I could be free to dream and be and never have to live by fae rules ever again.

How selfish a thought. How greedy.

Rules provide order. Rules... provide pain and shame and hurt and disgust. The rules that governed my life were killing me anyway, what would real death be in comparison?

Welcome. It would be so very welcome.

Not now. Oh, not now. I struggle and suffer, and everything hurts. I struggle and suffer but I refuse to give in. Not yet.

Caspian made another promise to me—and he has shown an

inability to break his promises, however small. However meaningless and insignificant he finds them.

He promised me one more thing, and I can't let it slip away.

So, I breathe and hurt. Hurt and breathe. I listen to him curse me, and growl and threaten to maim and kill.

"I'm going to kill you one day," he tells me, his voice soft and sweet. His voice loud and angry. "I am going to be the one to kill you, so don't you dare die."

I won't. He makes me resist fate itself, and I hate him for that. If only I knew it was this easy. If only I knew that strength could be found in the voice of a beautiful, broken, twisted male vamryre.

I would have sought him out myself. I would have bared my body to him sooner.

I would have given him any and everything.

But I wouldn't ask for the mortal realm first.

I'd ask for his power. His strength. His ability to make me resist and break the bonds that have bound my life for decades.

But those are selfish thoughts.

For now, I will contend with trying not to die. Holding on. Breathing on. Gasping...

"Niamh!" He flicks his tongue against my forehead. "Stay awake. Don't you dare fall asleep."

Or die. I can't go to sleep or die.

So, I try not to do both. I try even as my lungs fill up and air becomes a rare, valuable thing to get a hold of. I try.

For him, I try...

And he is enough. It's so strange to realize as much. I'm feeding off his energy. His strength. The more he touches me, strokes through my hair, and presses his mouth to my cold flesh.

The easier it is to cling to life. I could outlast death for an eternity like this, with him on top of me. Beside me. Inside me.

I could survive anything.

But then he pulls away, and I struggle to see why. The air becomes too heavy. Impossible to inhale. My vision turns cloudy, tinged with inky black. I'll die if I can't hold on.

If I can't feed off his nearness and resilience, I'll die.

I'm dying...

I'm already dead...

"Heal her, now." Caspian's voice is a frail whisper. A bellowing shout. It echoes all the way back to the other realm, where even the Lord Master can hear it.

I am sure of it.

He speaks as though he intends the entire world to hear it. Death itself.

"Heal her—"

"I'm not sure I can," a new voice cuts in, clashing with his. Soft and sweet and delicate. Such a nice voice. "What the hell did you do to her, vampire? Jesus!"

"Heal her, you foolish mundane," Caspian replies in a heady growl. "Or I will rip out your fucking throat—"

"Save your threats," the second figure replies. A woman, I think.

Her voice is so beautiful. So lilting and strong. Different from the accented speech of the fae. Different.

"I can't do a damn thing to help her with you scowling over me! Wait over there. Now, vampire. Or I will slip a poison into her veins before you could even think to stop me."

"Heal her," Caspian snaps.

"Keep silent and let me think."

I'm drowning again. The soft fingers that prod my forearm don't have the power to yank me back like Caspian's do. Still... they are very gentle. Very kind. Very warm.

"I got here just in time, it looks like," the woman admits, sounding closer. Nearby. Above me. "She's barely hanging on. I'm surprised you didn't drain the last drops out of her. Now move! Let me work in peace."

In peace.

I so very much long for peace.

Or at least I did.

Now, I don't.

I long for chaos and dancing red and clashing ivory. I long for one last glimpse of those fiery, hungry eyes.

I wish I could grant him his only wish.

I'll let him eat me. Gobble up what's left of my soul.

I'd let him be the one to kill me if it was what he wanted...

As long as he stayed.

CHAPTER 21

Caspian

The healer is a mortal. She smells like one, anyway. She resembles one, thin and frail, her blond curls coiled tightly at the nape of her neck. She's pretty. Not pretty enough for Cassius, but pretty all the same. Not furtive and shaking and so damn bold, she makes a vamryre bend to her whim.

I'd kill her if I could. Wouldn't even drink. I'd rip her to shreds.

But only in her hands does the fae stand a chance of surviving. When she crouches near the bed and touches her with doctorly prodding fingers, I can tell. Mortal or not, she can save her.

So why isn't she?

"Heal her!"

"I'm thinking," the woman snaps. She's young, very young. As young as my fae. It's easy to tell from smell alone. The youth have a secret fragrance, a certain tint that Cassius learned to discern as one would fine wine. He liked them aged. Not too young. Not too old.

Thirty was a ripe, perfect age. The best age.

She must be twenty, at least. Too young for his tastes.

Too old for mine. I don't like screaming, flailing youths. I like them at an age that transcends some stupid number of years. A mental age. Old and young alike can fit my criteria.

I like them innocent and hopeful. Young at heart, not in body—children are off limits, even in Cassius' eyes—with naive, wide, innocent eyes. Seventy-years. Twenty. Thirty. Fifty.

Their mental age is all that matters to me. Youthful and young in the soul.

This mortal is too damn old. Her mind reeks, older than other mortals at fifty. A hundred. She has decades of knowledge in her skull, and it's made her weary. Vengeful. She is no innocent.

She sees the world at a glance for what it is: cold and hopeless. She is too old for me.

Too much like me.

"I can't work with you staring at me," she snaps, setting something down at her feet: a slim leather case. She opens it and pulls an array of tools out. Cutting tools. Probing tools.

Tools for healing or killing.

I won't let her out of my sight until I know which.

"If you kill her, I will kill you," I insist. Remind.

She scoffs. "Go do something useful rather than sulk and stare. She needs clothing. Did you forget? We don't wear your fancy robes out here. Get her something clean to wear. You can do that much, can't you?"

Do that much. Because out here in their realm, the mortals have their own particular clothing tastes. Tastes that have changed and waned within the decades. Fashions have fallen out of favor and come back again.

They aren't stagnant like the robes of the other realm are. We are color-coded there by race, given an array of fabric to help us remember our place. Green for fae. Red for vamryre. Blue for lunaria.

Gray for her alone, the meaningless fae.

In the Citadel, her color is meant to be ignored and overlooked. Here, she will draw too much attention. If she lives, she needs to fit in, long enough to outlast Cassius and his ploys. Long enough for me to fulfill my last and final promise to her.

I start to leave. Then I remember.

"If you let her die—"

"I won't," the mortal insists. "Now go!"

Go. I'll go. I'll get her clothing to keep her safe. I'll make sure no agents of the other realm are near.

But I will return. I better find her breathing.

Or...

I will turn this realm upside down in a way Cassius could only dream.

I will raise hell.

CHAPTER 22

Niamh

Time slows to a crawl. My pain fades. Breathing gets easier...

I am still alive, I know that. Mainly because the world is so heavy—a cacophony of noises, smells, and sounds. Slamming doors. Running feet. Voices, so many voices. Shouted, whispered, moaning voices. They sound so close. So far. They sound like the occupants of a million other worlds and realms outside of my own.

They sound free, unlike the murmuring that filled the Citadel. Fearful and hushed and only occasionally giddy.

Mortals are so giddy. They thrive on life and feed off of it.

They don't need a vamryre to show them how to breathe. How to live. How to want to live.

He was gone once, but I can feel him near. His anger is so volatile. His scent is so unique, apart from any other in this entire realm. In the entire world and universe.

Caspian is a creature unto himself, but he lingers near me. Even though he doesn't want to. Even though he doesn't have to.

He lingers within my orbit and for that, I am grateful, so grateful.

I don't know why but I am.

He is near me and for that I am grateful.

However, there is someone else beside him. Someone new and sparkling and clean. She radiates a bubbly warmth and an icy confidence. She won't let anyone stand in her way or dictate to her their rules for life.

She makes her own rules, and they are simple. Keep everything calm. Keep everything clean. Healing is her domain, her purpose for being.

For whatever reason, she is trying to heal me. Trying to because it is harder than she thought. I'm not like the others she's nursed back to health. I am different.

Broken and different. My body doesn't react to her methods like it should. I am too different. Abnormal. Defective.

Frustrated, she sighs. "What is she?"

"A woman," Caspian replies, his tone cold. Cutting. Stone. "Heal her."

"I'm not stupid!" The woman scoffs and a noise trickles out of her that could be a laugh. "Damn you, you idiot. What is her race? She's not vamryre. Not human. Not a mundane. I would assume she is fae but—"

"Fae," Caspian snaps.

"She can't be," the woman insists. "They can't enter this realm—"

"Enough," Caspian growls. "Try harder."

"I am trying! Um... There is one last method. You stay there. Even if she screams you don't touch me, or her. Understand?"

Silence. Then a harshly uttered, "If you kill her—"

"You'll kill me," the woman replies. "Whatever. But if I don't do this she will die and none of your threats will matter one damn bit! Do you understand me? But... What I must do, it could heal her. Maybe."

"It better."

"But..." The woman sucks in a breath, and I feel her hands on my skull. "It's going to hurt."

And it does.

Whatever she does to me it hurts.

It hurts.

CHAPTER 23
Caspian

Stay back. Stay back. Stay back!

The fae will die if I kill the mortal. I could hear the truth in the woman's voice.

But then she reaches toward the fae with grasping hands. Fingers full of tainted, dirty, black magic. Wrong magic.

It seeps into the fae's pale skin and she screams. Throat rasping, limbs jerking, she screams and screams.

But I can't help her. To do so will be to let her die—or so the mortal claims. So she says.

Regardless, I take a step. Another. The screaming is too loud. This alone is killing her.

"Stay back!" the blond mortal hisses, her brows furrowed in concentration, hands moving, sowing her twisted magic.

So, she isn't a mundane. She isn't vamryre. She is something else.

Some kind of defective being. Her kind of magic shouldn't exist. It isn't clean. Isn't nice and neat like the spells of the fae.

It is messy and painful and it...

Repairs. I can hear it. Her magic rips the fae apart piece by broken piece and puts her back together. Painfully. Slowly.

But it mends. She can breathe again. Move again without wincing. She can open her eyes and gape at the ceiling. She can work that throat and say my name.

"Caspian?" Afraid.

"Caspian." Worried.

No one has ever said my name so damn worried. Except for, maybe...

Cassiopeia. She said it that way once, when we both went too far against our master. We wanted to kill him. Tried to kill him.

Together, we almost killed him. Something went wrong, ruining our plan. I was meant to do something. Something important. Find...

"Colleen?" The fat mortal raps on the door. I can hear her jowls jiggling and stubby fingers thumping. "What the hell is all this ruckus? I'm gonna lose business if people think this is some kind of torture house!"

The mortal woman winces, still spewing her dark magic. A few more seconds. Then she lets her hands fall and nearly collapses onto the floor completely. Sweat drips down her pale forehead, pungent and sweet.

"I... I'm sorry, Mo," she says in between pants. "I'll keep it down from here on out."

"Good," the fat woman replies. "Oh no, Mr. Morris, don't you worry. We assure discretion here for any sort of kink. Come downstairs, and we can discuss a discount on your next stay, eh?"

This place is a den of debauchery. A haven for sin, mortal and immortal alike.

Cassius has never come here, but he knew of it. He used me as his mule to lure victims here for him. To drink. To puppet. To play with.

It was never my choice. I can see them clearly again. Remember some of their faces. So many frightened, desperate, greedy faces. Happy in the beginning...

In the beginning, when they thought I was a savior. A protector from boredom. From a loveless future. From ugliness.

But, oh, I never protected them.

I'd give my soul for her. Gave it up already. But why? Why?

Because she asked. I look at her, breathing easy, body limp. I look at her pale, gangly limbs. My limbs. Mine. All of her is mine to have. To take.

But only if she asks me to.

Why? Why?

"Did you hear me?" the blond mortal asks, having regained some energy. Colleen, the other one, called her. She is pale and thin with coils of blond hair threatening to burst from that bundle at the nape of her neck. Pretty, but not enough for Cassius. Young, but with a mind too old for me. She seems older than I am, as if she's lived centuries. Lifetimes.

"I asked you what her name is?" the woman retorts, eyeing me from over her shoulder. Her hands are trembling, her brow still coated in sweat. It dampens her blue sweater and makes the wool cling to her flesh. Pink flesh, brimming with blood. "Can you not speak English?"

"Name?" I snap. "She doesn't have one."

Then I remember. Spit it out, "Niamh."

"Oh, that's pretty," the mortal whispers, eyeing the fae once more. "It's Irish in origin, isn't it? I thought your kind didn't have names like ours."

Like them. Disgusting, vermin names. Humans have too many to keep track of. They name their children with whatever folly enters their minds at the time.

Stupid.

Foolish.

We are named for a God, our maker. Our master. I am a proud spawn of Cassius, one of the elder three—

No. I shake my head and grit out a hiss. Even here, he creeps into my thoughts if I'm not careful. Even here, the bastard still seeks to infect me.

Because of her. I'm not near her. I creep closer from the corner the mortal banished me to. Crouch on the other end of the bed, too close to the fae. Nowhere near close enough.

I run my thumb along her throat. There. Like magic, the world is silent again. Only annoying blond mortals can penetrate with wary gasps and uneasy swallows.

"What is your relationship to her, vampire?" she wonders. "She isn't a mortal, but she isn't one of your kind either. Did you steal her from somewhere? Take her? Aim to sell her on the black market?"

"Yes," I reply. "I took her."

The truth.

A lie.

She followed me willingly. Followed me as a means to her end. Followed me to achieve her real aim.

But still. There was no Cassius prodding my every movement. No motel to drag her to.

She followed me out of that forsaken realm. She wanted to follow me.

"I don't know what Mo lets your kind get away with, but I am not one for bribes, vampire," the mortal hisses, her pink cheeks flushed, blue eyes angry. "If you have harmed her, I will report you to the authorities. Slavers are not tolerated here. The boneys will throw you right into the pits if—"

I laugh, and the mortal jumps. So I bare my fangs and laugh again. Words aren't necessary. Just this. As if any authority could maintain a hold over me.

The only authority I fear is Cassius.

Wait. No. Don't fear him. Hate. Hate. Hate—

"I mean it. Now, where are the clothes I sent you for?"

I growl but gesture to a pile by the door. Garments stolen from some place. A store. The humans display their clothing rather than have it assigned. They pick their status, either honestly or dishonestly. They wear their wealth on display.

"Good," the mortal says, rubbing her hands. Slowly, she stands, barely as tall as my shoulder. Those curls threaten to explode as she reaches back to cup the mass in the palm of her hand. Then she sighs. "I'll help her get dressed."

She says those words as if they mean something. A command.

One I don't understand. Don't care to process.

"Dress her," I say.

She flinches, a blush creeping across those pretty cheeks. "You should leave. Offer her some dignity, at least!"

Dignity. As if the fae deserves it. As if I haven't offered her everything and anything.

However, this mortal... She is dangerous. That corrupted magic leeches from her, tainting the air. If she touches me, she might rip and tear. How fun. How irritating.

She'll cost me more time.

After looking at Niamh, I step back.

Her eyes are on me, sparkling and alert. Alive and pleading. She wants me on my best behavior. She wants me on her leash.

But...

For now, I'll play along. Cassius is waiting and lurking. He'll be here soon. So soon.

It will be then that I will have the bloodshed that I crave.

CHAPTER 24
Niamh

I have never seen magic being worked up close. Even Day would never break that rule by showing me. I wouldn't expect him to.

A vamryrer's skill works in far different ways, more obvious ways. They can manipulate and convince. They can soften the hardest of hearts and charm the un-charmable.

Perhaps that explains his hold over me? I want it to. I crave a simple answer for the way my heart races around him and strains without him.

I am alive and breathing, my pain gone. But I don't feel right. At peace. I keep staring at the door he's disappeared through.

I keep waiting for this dream to end and the nightmare of reality to descend.

"Are you okay, honey?"

That's right. I am not alone. A beautiful woman crouches on the floor beside me, her smile wary, her eyes kind. But she is also uneasy, as she should be. She sees the danger lurking in Caspian's gaze.

She saw the damaged pieces of me.

She assumed he was the cause. He wasn't.

I try to say as much. "I..."

"Oh, don't try to speak yet." She winces, guilty. "My magic... How I healed you, it can be pretty intense. Your windpipe was broken and I, um, had to fix it." She wrings her fingers together as she lurches upright and begins to pace.

Watching her move, I am struck dumb by recognition. She isn't wearing robes. Not green or red, white or gray. She wears a brilliant blue tunic paired with blue pants. *Pants.*

She is wearing mortal clothing.

After noticing my stare, she stops short. She tugs at the sleeve of her tunic and frowns. "Well, let's get you out of those bloody clothes, hm? Then I can at least begin to explain. My name is Colleen, by the way."

She extends her hand and then awkwardly lowers it. "Ah, right. Let's get started."

Her name is Colleen. Not Day, Dawn, or Night. Not Caspian or a name that denotes a follower of another vamryrer master. Do the lunaria even have names? I'm not sure. If they do, they are monickers derived from their own language, older than the moon itself.

Her name is a mortal name, chosen for her specifically at birth. Colleen. So pretty. So foreign.

I am jealous.

She helps me stand and into a narrow closet. A bathroom, far different from the ones in the Citadel—not that I was ever allowed to use them. I had to relieve myself in a corner of the courtyard, but I didn't mind.

I didn't know what I was missing. Warm water on aching skin. A sweet-smelling liquid that seeps into my hair and makes it shiny and clean.

There is also the most magical novelty of all, a sheet of flat silver that changes color before my eyes. I step in front of it, and it displays the image of a woman with a familiar visage and dark eyes. She looks nothing like Day or Lord Master. Nothing like flawless Caspian.

But... when I raise my hand toward her, she copies me. Blinks alongside me. Gasps with shock at the same moment I do. Then another figure appears—the blond woman. But she's behind me as well, her lips forming a soft smile.

"I guess they don't have mirrors in the other realm, do they?"

I shake my head. Then nod. The mirror woman does the same. No... I do. My reflection.

"They do," I whisper, breaking her rule. It feels important to speak. To hear my own words in order to know that this moment is real. Real. "I've just never seen one."

"What a shame," Colleen says. "You're so pretty. But please, no speaking. I mean it. I would hate it if something went wrong with your healing, and I'd have to do it all over again."

She laughs.

I shiver at the memory of that pain. Her magic. A strange, fiery magic that tore me apart and then stitched me back together. I could feel it, like an uncertain hand testing various bones and tissues to see how to repair what.

"Thank you," I whisper.

She shakes her head. "Enough. Now, let's get you out of these filthy clothes."

She helps me strip my bloodstained robe. She then offers me new clothes, but they are not made of stiff material like I'm used to. There is a short tunic like hers, but of a heavier material and bright yellow—a *sweatshirt*, she calls it. Paired with it are *sweatpants*, also yellow.

I pull them on reverently and watch my reflection in the mirror. Objectively, they are the most beautiful garments I have ever seen, incomparable to Day's ceremonial robes, even. I can't stop fingering the hem of my shirt. Any high elder would be lucky to wear clothing such as these.

"The idiot vampire could have gotten you something flattering," Colleen mutters. She doesn't approve. "This will have to do for now. Maybe I can bring you some of my old things? You look to be about my size."

I can't contain my shock. And gratitude.

"Thank..." I swallow hard and then nod.

Frowning, Colleen holds up another object, left behind at the bottom of my pile of new clothing. It is small and made of black fabric with a long strap. A bag of some sort.

"I guess the vampire thinks you need a backpack?" She wrinkles her nose in disapproval and tosses the bag aside. "What an idiot!"

But he isn't. I lunge for the container and cradle it to my chest. Then I inch back into the room, searching, hunting for... I find it on a small table by the bed: a bundle of gray fabric, muddied and tattered, containing a single wilting rose and a sketchbook. Gingerly, I place the items inside the new bag and close it.

Instantly, my gratitude toward Caspian grows.

"Let's get you back to bed. I changed the sheets by the way," Colleen says from behind me. She gestures to the square surface I woke up on. It is small with a bed with sheets the color of sunlight. So beautiful.

I lay down tentatively. Luxuriously. Never could I have dreamt of such a bed. Such a place to rest in.

"I'll let you get some sleep," Colleen says, heading for a white door. "Goodnight."

Goodnight.

No one has ever wished me as much before.

No one.

CHAPTER 25
Caspian

I sit in a bar on the motel's first floor. Noisy. Half-empty. Chaotic. Mortals crave enclosed, dank spaces, like rodents. They obscure their boring surroundings with cigarette smoke and drink liquid until they vomit.

Disgusting creatures.

Lonely creatures.

How I used to hunt them with excitement and glee. I used to enjoy those brief moments off my leash doing my master's bidding. Like a good dog.

I remember more now. Things I don't want in my skull. Memories of all the people I hurt and plied and seduced for him.

Recalling those memories isn't so fun in this realm. It's not so fun to remember what a monster I can be. The monster I am.

How greedy and desperate I was for a chance to run. Slip away. Bleed and bite.

I used to think I was being rewarded for being such a good boy for him.

Now I can see: I was being played with, like a toy within a game of *many* dancing toys.

Even now, with her…

She was another game for him. Another prey at my disposal for good old Cassius. I should go up there and kill her now. Kill her far away from the ceremony, where it will matter to no one but me.

No, I swear I can hear my old master shriek. *No. No. You'll ruin everything.*

I should ruin everything for him.

I stand, and as if to aid my plan the blond mortal comes skipping past, down the hall out of sight. I don't care where she's going or why she came here. I only care that she's gone.

No one to witness. No one to see. No one who matters anyway to watch as I creep up those stairs and toward the last room on the left. I grip the doorknob and breathe.

I can smell her in there, alone. Niamh. My Niamh.

No—his. She is his cog in a grand scheme. The object of his devious plans. What? I don't remember. Don't care to remember.

Something about the ceremony and the fae and rules. Something about control. Something…

Killing her will be within my control. I twist the knob and push the door open. I watch her there, thin and frail, curled up on her side, dark hair spilling out around her. She has a black pouch cradled against her chest and I know her bundle of things is inside of it.

I step inside. Close the door behind me—quietly. Not slam it like I want to. Like I should.

I move quietly. Inhale quietly. I watch her. I swallow. Observe her.

She remains lying still, deeply asleep. Not the fake, fitful slumber she struggled through in that shitty room atop the bell tower.

Her chest rises and falls, her dark eyes closed, her injuries faded to mere bruises.

I want to touch her. Rip. Tear.

Touch. I run a finger along her shoulder and grit my teeth.

Damn. She's so soft. Too soft. I finger a thick coil of dark hair. Lower myself to the mattress and inhale. So sweet. Sweeter than she was in that dank, dusty archive. It's as if the mortal air has stripped some of the stifling sadness on her away.

That stifling stillness.

Even mortal clothing cannot hide what she is. Pale skin. Magic sparkling in her flesh. Corrupted fae but fae all the same.

She stirs. Falls silent again. Still alive, her heart still beating.

Because I haven't killed her. Not yet.

I'll wait.

Another day to play my own game. Another day to stall going back. Cassius will come soon. I know he will.

I can give her one more day, though. Just one.

And she will give me more...

All that's left of her.

THE BLONDE MORTAL COMES BACK ONCE, TIPTOEING down the hall and peeking inside. Her eyes are bloodshot with exhaustion, her hair a wild, coiled mess. She eyes me like I'm a dangerous creature crouched on the mattress. A monster, hungrily drooling over a fresh, willing fae.

I am.

She breathes a little sigh of relief when she sees the woman unharmed.

Her anger then rises to the surface as she glares at me. "I'll be nearby, vampire," she snarls in a whisper. "If anything happens to her, you will be reported. Your council has no sway out here, but we make our own rules."

She believes the threat will intimidate me.

Fuck her. It doesn't. Out here I can kill as I please. Take what I please.

She is already mine, mine, mine. I look down at her, my fae prize. All mine. My fingers are still in her hair and I coil the curl around and around. Let it fall. Slip my fingers beneath the hem of her stolen borrowed shirt. She's so damn soft, and she jerks at my touch, her eyelids fluttering.

I withdraw. Touching her is a new, wonderful, delicious game.

For now, it's better to watch her sleep. She enters a world I cannot follow. However, I am the one who shapes it. Twist and corrupt what she sees. I lower my mouth to her ear and whisper a command she'll have no choice but to heed.

"I want you to dream of me, little fae," I tell her. "Dream of me inside you. Fucking you. Wringing those little noises from your throat."

She shudders and whimpers, still asleep. Her pulse drums, her exhaustion heavy enough to outweigh any other emotion.

For now.

I lie there beside her, my mouth at her ear, and I watch her sleep. I listen. I chase her into that dream realm the only way I can.

But as the night goes on and the noise of fucking, drinking mortals ebbs and flows around us...

I don't wake her up. I let her sleep.

Jealously, I let her sleep until morning comes and her black eyes blink awake.

She watches me, our gazes locked, bodies parallel. Confusion dawns over her face, then she frowns as she remembers.

The mortal realm. I brought her here. I left her here. She nearly died here.

It's not anger or sadness that flashes across those dark, haunting eyes. Giddiness. Happiness.

Disgusting relief.

"You're here," she says, pulling herself upright slowly, as if afraid to shatter the moment. Wake up in a nightmare, back in that cold, dank crypt. Warily, she stretches out her limbs. Looks back at me.

Smiles.

I glare. She smiles. I glower. She smiles. Nothing I do can shake that expression: pink plump lips, upturned, bringing light to those fucking dark eyes. At least until I snatch her wrist. Pull her down to me where she belongs. Beneath me where she belongs.

Her body is healed, so when she shudders as I grip her waist it isn't out of pain. When she bites her lower lip to trap a sound low in her throat, it isn't one of agony.

Fuck her. I've thought about killing her with these very hands. I will kill her...

In spite of that fact, she lurches into these fingertips. Greedily, she chases my touch. Lets me peel the clothing from her flesh and gape and stare.

Because I own it, every inch. I own her, I do...

I don't.

She inhales and I go still, hand on her thigh, mouth near her throat. I know that sound. That noise.

Uncertainty. Regret.

"I gave you what you wanted," she says, her voice small. Pathetic. Sad? "I know you owe me nothing. I don't have anything else to bargain with. But..."

She lets that word hang in the air. But. But. It seems as though she has nothing left, yet she's willing to ask for more. To get me to stay. Desperation is evident in those dark eyes—desperation I created.

In spite of myself, I grind my teeth. Drive my fangs into my own flesh. Curse her.

Damn her. Fuck her.

Grabbing her hair, I make her face me to better interpret the look in those eyes.

Shame. She paid me her due. She gave me all she had. There is nothing left for me to take. She thinks the debt incurred is hers alone.

Stupid fae. Silly, stupid fae.

I press my fangs into her throat, almost biting. Not quite.

"I want more," I tell her. More. More of my mouth on her skin. More of her heat at my fingertips. "You haven't given me everything. Not yet."

Another valuable prize is locked inside that pretty head. In search of it, my hand ghosts over that slender belly, plunging between those thighs. She's bare there, with nothing to shield her from the finger I slip inside her. As she quakes at the intrusion, I add another. Another.

Yet I still want more.

A sound rips from her throat, in between a moan and a gasp. She doesn't understand. Considers the sex a one-time affair. Satisfied with having had her once, I should demand her blood next. Make her pay me day by day. Her body. Then her skin. Then her eyes. Blood. Bones. Soul.

I'll chew all of her up and swallow every last bit whole.

However, I'm not interested in sex alone. I need the one power she possesses—the ability to dispel Cassius. I can hear him still, gnawing away on my psyche.

Come back to me, Caspian! Caspian! COME TO ME—

"Say my name," I tell her, once she's wet. A slavish, stupid fool, I've given her more than I've taken already. Using my thumb, I tap the bundle of nerves relied on by women to find pleasure. Her lips are bitten and her eyes are wild as she writhes. Her arousal is evident, dripping onto my fingers and the sheets beneath. "Say my name. Say it!"

She inhales raggedly, her gaze unfocused.

More convincing is necessary to entice her to make this trade. So I free my cock and thrust inside her. *There.* Her head falls back and her fingers fly to my shoulders, pulling tight. Pulling me close. Closer still. She's begging for destruction, grinding her hips into mine.

But she lied, the stupid, devious little fae.

She has what I want, but she refuses to give it. Not until I fuck her hard. Pin her body to the thin mattress as if I aim to shove her through it. Push us both through it.

There is no creepy male fae to watch. No master looming overhead. Here in the mortal realm, there is just my body and hers.

Even without Cassius' rage to tempt me, she feels so damn good. More than ever, I want her. Harder. Harder. Deeper. More. I take her until I see stars. Until her body clenches around me like a fist, squeezing out all I fucking have.

It's not enough.

I push deeper into her. When I put my mouth to her throat, I can taste the pulse that surges beneath the surface of her skin. I want so badly to bite.

But I can't.

She doesn't want me to. I can feel her intentions coil through me, snaking along my mind as if they were my own. Touching is important to her. She longs for me to caress her. Cradle her like the mortals Cassius plied would want me to.

Don't want to.

I must, if I'm going to get what I crave from her: another dose of her twisted, sinful magic.

I drive her into me by hooking my hands beneath her waist. Press my mouth to hers and kiss her deep. Only then, broken and hoarse, does she give me my payment.

"Caspian..." She whimpers against my lips. "Oh, Caspian."

She goes limp, her eyes closed, chest heaving.

But I'm the one grinning now. Grinning in triumph. Grinning in fucking hatred.

Now she may have some power, but one day I'll take it back. I'll make her as desperate to hear her name leave my mouth as I am for mine to leave hers.

Only I'll never give it.

She will never fucking hear it.

Never.

CHAPTER 26
Niamh

I wake up in his arms, at peace when I should be afraid. It's terrifying, this unnerving, persistent feeling. Like I'm standing on the end of a precipice, and he is below.

Jump, he says.

My body still remembers the first time he issued such a dare. He let me fall.

Let me hurt.

Then he left me again.

Now he's inside me again, and all those aches and pains feel as though they never happened. He can get inside my skin so easily. It must be a vamryre skill.

You let them inside your body, and they crawl into your head. They whisper secret desires you weren't aware of. Start fires in your soul.

It hurts, and it burns to feel parts of you that you thought you knew turn to ash and fade away.

But left in their place are new spaces, aching to be filled. Demanding to be filled.

I'll let him break me if he wants to. I'll give him my pain if only it means that...

He won't lose interest. He'll stay near. Won't leave me again.

He can't leave me again.

Because that hurt. Worse than any fire or glowing orbs with the power to break bone. He left me and for a moment, I'd forgotten myself.

So I burrow my face into his shoulder now. I let him claim me as deeply as he wants to. I let him think...

I let him think that I'm his to corrupt. This game was always his from the start, not mine.

I'm not really the one in control.

But I am. I *have* to be. I can't let him leave me. At least not until...

I fulfill my heart's desire, then he can go. Maybe. Maybe then he can go.

"Where are we?" I ask him, if only to distract from the cacophony of chaos playing out in my mind. Oh, how greedy I am in this open, mortal air. I don't shy from him like I would in our old realm.

I hook my fingers around the back of his neck. Gently. Trembling, interlocking fingers—an embrace he could easily break without a second thought. I stare up at him, into those festering red eyes. I watch them glow as he feasts on me.

But then the flames fizzle out. He's empty, staring down on me. Remembering what we are and where we are. It's my fault.

I asked the wrong thing.

"Where you wanted to be," he hisses, drawing away from me, lunging upright. His body is perfection, even in this room with peeling, yellow walls and beige flooring. Even here he is so beautiful. So dangerous. So deadly. The look in his eye claims as much. With one question, I have him enraged. "Get your fill of it, fae," he snarls, fists clenched, eyes downcast. "You are in the mortal realm. Prepare to live out your pathetic hopes and dreams."

He means those words to sting—and they do, but not for the reason he intends them too. It's a reminder that this moment has a time limit. An end point.

I get what I want. He's gotten what he craves.

The end. There isn't any more to this sordid tale.

But I don't want it to end. Not yet.

"Wait," I tell him, my voice tight, throat heavy. "You have to take me to a museum."

He has to. He has to. Then our deal will be sealed and done. Then...

Only then can he leave again.

Angling his head, he rakes a hand through his pale hair. Still glowering. Growling. But I can tell from how his shoulders tense and then relax that he's sated, for now. I paid the toll for another day. He will stay. To get me to my desired destination, he will stay.

"I'll get dressed," I say, scrambling upright. Only my knees don't work right. My legs threaten to collapse beneath me, and then they do, pitching me to the hard floor.

But I don't fall, because Caspian comes from nowhere to catch me, arm hooked around my waist, body pressed tightly to his.

He hisses in annoyance. He inhales with greed.

I shiver. It feels so wrong to be in his embrace. Wrong because I crave it. I don't endure his touch like I would Day's wandering glances and accidental touches. Contact wasn't needed with him. Wanted?

With Caspian there is only want. Only need. Only hungry, vicious feelings.

"You'll get dressed," he grates out, teeth clenched, icy breath on my shoulder. "I'll get you dressed."

He takes me into that closet bathroom and sets me on the end of the basin Colleen helped me wash in. A sink, she called it. He stares at the empty basin. I reach behind me and turn one of the round knobs meant to trigger a flow of running water.

Like magic. Only it isn't magic. Mortals have their own ways of making the world conform to their will. Like by conjuring light to illuminate their homes with, via stagnant, tiny bulbs that glow. Each room is flooded with warmth that creeps through the walls and foundation.

Most intriguing of all are their mirrors. They show the world reflected back as it truly is. In this moment, I can see Caspian from the corner of my eye: looming over me, watching me. His jaw is clenched, gaze reluctant.

He watches me like he could stare for a century. An eternity of gazing at me in silence.

But never, not once, would I ever be able to know what he is thinking.

What is he thinking? I wish I knew. Which is a dumb thought. Vamryres have a hive mind. A collective mind. The man before me is one of many. Perhaps... He has never acted on his own volition but with the permission of his master.

I think it. Then I look forward into that burning, icy gaze and I remember.

A price, he told me. Hissed at me. I was worth it. Then not. Worth it. Not.

I press my fingers to his lips unbidden as if I can make him tell me the truth. Am I worth this elusive price now? Is this all just a puppet show at my expense? Does he really even feel of his own accord?

Of course not. He can't. There are rules that govern this world, and we all have no choice but to live by them. Die by them. Thrive by them.

As he remains silent, I lean forward and press my lips against his jawline. Oh no. I'm a pathetic begging thing, but I need to know. Have to.

"Is it you that wants me?" I ask him, my Caspian. I have to know. Have to hear it.

"No," he says. "Of course I don't." He holds my chin in a stone grip and makes me stare at him. I couldn't turn away if I tried. If I wanted to.

I don't want to.

"Cassius wants you dead," he tells me, voice harsh and mocking. "He wants you bleeding out over their ceremonial floor. From the start that was my goal. Kill you. Gut you."

Nothing else.

I feel my heart sink in my chest, like a heavy weight. I can't seem to breathe anymore. All of the work poor Colleen put into this worthless body is wasted. I'm dying all over again, my injuries numerous and invisible. Fatal.

"Don't," he snarls, scraping the pad of his thumb below my left eye. "Don't. Don't. Don't cry."

Cry. He makes it sound like more of a sin than the Lord Master ever did. To cry in the old realm was to believe, even for a moment, that I deserved more than I had. More than my lot.

I didn't. Therefore... crying was greedy and shameful. Stupid, ungrateful girl.

With him, crying is to sin against him. Irritate him, my Caspian. Make him feel as though he isn't enough. But he is enough.

I want *more*.

"Stop it," he hisses, still swiping. "Shut up. Shut up! Fine—" He leans in and brings his mouth to my ear, teeth nipping dangerously close. "I wanted you, foolish fae. From the start, I wanted you. I took you. I have you. You are mine."

He laughs. *Hahaha.* He won this game.

Nevertheless, I am glad. I need him to win me, have me. I'm his to take. His to have.

"Yes," I whisper to him, closing my eyes to guard against his reaction. "Yours. Yours."

He groans. It's an angry sound, not quite pleased. Still, the trickle of running water nearly drowns him out. Icy fingers grip my legs, prying them apart. I hear him grapple for something nearby. Feel cold, damp fabric lap at my skin.

He's washing me. Slowly and carefully, Caspian washes me with water that isn't too warm nor too cold. Then he sets the rag aside —I hear the damp, heavy plop of it hit the floor. His fingers tease through my hair next, gathering it in a single fist. Then he grips it like a rope and coils it around and around. When he finally steps back, I open my eyes again. I crane my neck and look back.

The figure staring back doesn't look like the blurred, scattered images of the Niamh I knew in the Citadel. She is paler here. Her eyes are brighter here. Coiled at the nape of her neck meticulously by a vamryre, her hair shines here.

Reflected not just in the mirror, but in his eyes, she is beautiful.

"Thank you," I say to her. To him.

He says nothing. His mouth finds its home near my ear, his inhalations loud and slow. He doesn't need to breathe—at least I don't think so—but he does around me. He feasts on the air around me. Then he inches closer and presses his lips to my throat. Against the skin, he hisses, "Don't."

Don't thank him.

I must.

"Thank you. Thank you." I lean into him. Practically throw myself into him. He catches me, gripping my body tight while the water still runs behind us. As long as he catches me, I will be fine.

It's all worth it as long as he catches me.

As long as he catches me.

"Hello?" A knock rattles the door to the main room. *Bang. Bang.* "Are you awake?"

"Stupid mortal," Caspian growls. He steps back and lunges inside the main room. Throws the door open. I can hear it thud against the wall and I race to the doorway just in time to catch the woman lurking behind it before she steps inside. Head held high, blond curls tied back. She smiles and beams, bringing light into this room, like a living sun.

"Good morning, vampire," she says, her tone cold. Then she spies me and her smile widens. "Ah, good morning, Niamh! You look so much better." She carries something on her back—a leather case with straps that she shrugs off one by one. "I'll just check some of your vital signs. Vampire—" She doesn't even look at him. "You can square your debt with Mo, downstairs. Cash only, or a fair exchange. I'm sure you know the drill anyway."

The drill. Caspian does know it, apparently. He narrows his eyes and stalks into the hall, slamming the door behind him. But then he lingers. Waits.

"I won't hurt her," Colleen calls back, sensing him as well. "Idiot," she mumbles under her breath, arms crossed, blue eyes glinting with irritation and confusion.

The vamryre's care confuses her. Confounds.

But it thrills me. *Yes.*

If I can't make him stay with a good enough trade, then I will take anything. Concern. Pity. Guilt.

Anything.

CHAPTER 27

Caspian

"Your tab's been closed, I'll have you know," the fat woman snarls as I approach. "Ironically, your visa's still active until Sunday. I don't even want to know what you've been up to for an entire year. I can't call the boneys on you for illegal entry, though." She shuffles papers at her desk. Pretends to be oh so busy.

It's a lie. She isn't busy, she is worried. Worried because of me. She hides behind her strip of wood and yards of space between us. Her throat is jiggling, pulse trembling.

"And don't think you can start a new line of credit, either," she spits. "Not after the last time."

Last time. I stare at her, waiting for the memories to appear. They don't. Cassius must have locked those up extra tight. Even out here I can't access them, far away from him.

Yet, he hasn't come for me yet. Why? Good. But why?

"Well," the mortal sniffs, still uneasy. Her eyes dart to a circle hammered onto the opposite wall. Moving appendages contort to point to different symbols. Numbers. A clock it's called. I remember that much.

She eyes her clock and becomes more uneasy with every passing second. She's waiting for something. Something that will come when the number she has in mind is struck. Tik. Tok.

"Don't think you can run out on your bill, neither," she huffs. "We ain't special like you all, but we do have our ways. I'll have the boneys after you in a heartbeat, vampire. They know how to deal with your kind. Imprison your kind."

Because these "boneys" have talents. Magical unworthy talents. Or so she thinks. Out here, they are tricks and illusions. Fake spells. Fake magic.

Except for the mortal upstairs. Her magic is real.

"Anyways, you can square your tab with me another way," the fat human squeals. Mo is her name, or so the other one claimed. A fake name. These vermin hide their deceit with false fake names.

She needs one too, perhaps. Niamh. To keep her hidden safely. To keep her mine a little longer. Then I remember that her name is already fake. Already a secret. Already mine.

Because I know without asking that she hasn't told anyone else. She didn't dare to. It's my name that should change. Something other than Caspian.

As if that will ever be enough to erase Cassius' hold over me. I am Caspian. In spite of him, I am Caspian and it is my name. Wasn't always, but it is now. Mine. Mine.

Won't change it out of spite, not even to outrun him.

"You can do me a favor," the fat woman drones on and on. "I need you to deliver something for me. Then bring the payment for it back. It's nothing you vamps from there will want to steal. Take the package. Bring the payment back here, and we'll be square. The doctor will get her cut from me, so you don't even have to worry about squaring up with her. All good?"

"Good," I hiss, watching her scurry and jump. She's antsy, this one. More anxious than I have ever seen her.

Because I have seen her before. For years. Decades. I've seen her when she was a young, gangly teenager lurking in the shadow of another older, fatter woman. I've seen her deflate of any beauty she once had and become a hunched, shallow wretch. I've seen the light and joy leave her eyes and she's seen me parade victim after victim before her.

Victim after victim she smiled at, sniffed at, ignored. Victim after victim whose blood she had to clean out of the floors. Not in the room Niamh is in now, but another one. A designated one. There were two, I remember as much now. I would ask for them on cue, one or the other depending on Cassius' specifications.

One room to fuck in. To ply the stupid mortal in tow with enough wine and drink to make them slumber. To make them stupid. What happened to them after that?

I don't recall. But I would see them again, in the mansion, hair white and eyes empty, one of Cassius' new dolls.

There was another room, however, that was more fun. My favorite.

I got to kill in that one. Bleed those victims dry and rip them limb from limb.

Only I didn't want to. Didn't always want to. Sometimes he made me. Told me it was what I wanted.

You are my monster, Caspian. A killer. A murderer. For me, you'll do it. For me, you will do anything—

No! I shake my head to block out the memories. It is those remnants of this life that I do not want. They're not what I want to see. Stupid, stupid Cassius.

He ruins everything. Even death and violence which I love and crave. He taints everything with his stupid lies.

"You alright?" The fat mortal Mo has shied further away from me. Her back is to the opposite wall, a pile of papers clutched to her chest like a pathetic makeshift shield. "Don't forget why you got banned the last time, eh?" She leans in and whispers loudly, "We just got one rule in here for your kind. Keep it in the room, on the clock, and pay in advance. Don't you go feeding on anyone indiscriminately. I got a business to keep and clientele to protect."

Clientele. Because I am hungry. That is why I'm leaning forward, hands braced over her little wooden desk. That is why her jowls jiggle as she swallows a nervous gasp. I frighten her.

Because I am hungry—but I don't recall this feeling. It isn't familiar. Cassius always kept us well-fed, on his lies. He blotted the hunger from our little brains unless he could use it against us.

Out here, there is no master. No leash. I laugh. Laugh again.

The fat Mo turns pale. "You should go now, before I change my mind." She waddles close enough to drop something within my reach before darting back. "Do the delivery and we're square."

Square. I do the delivery and my debt is paid. I do the delivery and there is one less step tying me to the mortal realm. One less day with her.

We are square, me and Niamh. But no, she still wants something from me after all. I should draw it out. Keep her here for more days. Weeks. Years even.

Keep her. Keep her. Let her block out Cassius forever.

"Fine," I tell the mortal, snatching up her little box, wrapped in brown paper. "I will do the delivery."

She cringes at my tone. Nice. Sweet. Fake. "Just go."

I'll go. But not without my toy. My Niamh. I head upstairs to that room at the back of the hall. I wait, ears straining for her voice, which I easily pick up.

She's speaking to the mortal, animated and lively. Not in those stilted fucking one-word, yes-word sentences she fed that male fae.

This is her, truly speaking.

I should enter the room and silence her.

I don't.

I listen and drink in her voice. I listen and wait. Listen to her...

The world goes fucking still.

CHAPTER 28
Niamh

The other fae would never acknowledge me. They didn't have to. Didn't need to. I respected their silence and never held it against them. At least consciously… I never held it against them.

Colleen, however, dwells in the mortal realm and she speaks to me. Whenever I answer back, she doesn't cringe away in disgust. Spew rules and decorum. Remind me to be proper.

She responds. Happily, excitedly, and giddy, her mind full of topics and things so foreign to me. She speaks not of the ceremony but "classes."

"I'm in general anatomy now," she explains, her body curled on the floor, chin perched on her raised knees. "It's a bore, the lecture part, I mean. But we get to dissect cadavers so I can't complain."

"Cadavers," I echo. The word is strange and unfamiliar.

"Bodies," she elaborates, her eyes alight with a mixture of disgust and curiosity. "Gross work, but one can't understand how the body works without seeing it up close in gory detail. It's what my professor says, anyway."

A professor. Like a master, only, she doesn't refer to them in the same awed reverence that I do the Lord Master. Not with fear.

Excitement. This professor feeds her new information, and they have her full respect.

"I can't wait until cell biology next term. In that one, we get to use microscopes. That's what I want to do by the end of it. Be a microbiologist. Study bacteria and viruses. I'd like to get a job at the CDC like my dad... Oh, look at me, talking you to death." She giggles and shrugs. Her supposed indiscretion doesn't make her shrink with shame. She laughs it off. It's a topic she likes to speak about and so she will, her subject's opinions unheeded.

"I don't mind," I say. My body is hunched toward her, my fingers trembling as they press against the mattress on either side of me. I love hearing her talk.

I wish I could make Caspian talk. I'd make him tell me about all the things he knows that I don't. Dark things. Dangerous things.

But I can't forget; he is one of a collective. His mind isn't his own. His thoughts aren't his own. Even when he touches me... The will isn't his own.

"What about you?" Colleen asks me, her head cocked to the side, gaze wistful. "I don't even know if your kind have a university or the like over there. Do you study for degrees, or do you just conjure them up?" She laughs again. The idea thrills her.

I feel my lips curl into a frown. Because I don't know. She's given me so much, but I can't repay her. My topics are small and little. In terms of knowledge, I don't have much.

“I’m not sure,” I admit.

Her eyes widen. “Ah. I take it you aren’t like that vamp. Are you a fae? I’ve never seen one of you in person before.”

Her wide gaze drinks me in even as I try to speak. No, I should say. Not fae. Something else. Some dirty, broken, in-between creature.

But I can’t speak.

And she has already flitted to another topic that interests her. “What’s the deal with that vampire?”

“Vamryre?” I say, confused by her phrasing.

She laughs and shakes her head. “We just call them plain ol’ vamps out here. No matter the name, they’re dangerous creatures all the same. Did he hurt you?” Her tone turns cutting at the thought.

Did he hurt me? Yes and no. He has, but it’s a price I would pay over and over again in exchange for him existing near me. Staying near me.

Pretending to be mine.

“He is Caspian,” I say.

“Caspian?” She sneers at the name. “I’ve heard of him, a right prick! I’m surprised old Mo even let him back in here after the mess he made the last time.”

My interest is piqued. “Mess?”

Colleen grits her teeth, her lips pursed in anger. “He went fucking mad last year and drained no less than ten people dry downstairs. Right in view of everyone! It was a right fucking mess, it was. Mo nearly went bankrupt bribing the uppers to keep quiet, and I had to—” She breaks off, arms crossed, chest heaving. “It doesn’t matter. But you let me know if he’s threatened you or hurting you…" Her voice turns soft, her pale hands curled into fists. "I'll make him pay. Has he? You can tell me."

Tell her. Tell her the truth.

"He hasn't hurt me," I say. "He saved me—"

The door flies open and Caspian himself appears. He crosses to the bed and snatches up my bag of things. Slings it over his shoulder. Turns to face me once more. "Come," he says to me, ignoring Colleen completely. There is another parcel in his hands. He holds it awkwardly as if it is a dirty thing. I want to reach for it. Carry it for him, whatever it is.

Then I hear Colleen's voice in my head warning, *"He went fucking mad. Drained no less than ten people dry."*

I know enough to read between the lines and decipher her true meaning. Caspian killed ten people. One right after the other.

"I should head back before my dad gets up," Colleen says, lurching to her feet. She grabs her leather case and slings it over her shoulder. Then she sizes up Caspian in a glance, and marches past him. "Make sure you square up with Mo, vamp," she snarls over her shoulder. "If I'm not squared up for my payment there will be hell to pay. For *you*. Not her. See ya around, Niamh. I love your name, by the way." She speaks on her way down the stairs, right up until she opens the main door and steps out into a bright, brimming daylight.

We've followed her, Caspian and I, side-by-side, hand-in-hand. I think I reached for him first. Maybe I didn't. His touch is possessive, radiating ownership.

My touch is greedy, radiating ownership. I don't care about the reason for his nearness. I'll take it.

I'll take it.

"Come," he hisses, pulling me along down the stairs and to the door. He reaches for a battered metal handle and then hesitates. I watch bright, yellow sunlight lick at his fingers and paint them red.

"You forgot your limitations or something?" A woman calls out.

I turn to her and gape. She is wide and round with jiggling brown curls and sad brown eyes. Her pink dress is too tight, fighting to conform her shape to a smaller size. But her body is too big and round. Beautiful. It strains at the material disobediently, but she doesn't care. Conformity doesn't matter to her one bit. She glowers at Caspian, her face handsome, her eyes furtive and shrouded with secrets. She reaches for something behind her counter and throws it at him. "One of your kind left this here. You bring it back along with my payment."

Caspian says nothing, draping the material around him. A black coat with a hood long enough to shroud his face and wide sleeves to protect his hands. At his hip is my new black bag, inside of which he stows his parcel.

He reaches for the door again, but I touch it first. The daylight doesn't harm me. As long as he's beneath his hood, it doesn't harm him either.

The door slams behind us with a clinking sound—the tolling of a tiny bell attached to the top of it, sounding a hello and goodbye with every opening and closing.

Goodbye, it tells us now.

Hello, it trills.

For we are in the mortal realm.

I've fulfilled part of my only wish at last.

At last...

So why do I still feel so greedy?

PART TWO

The Mortal Realm

CHAPTER 29
Niamh

The mortal world smells. Oh, how it smells, like things I didn't even know had a scent. Loud and bustling, brimming with life. It teems with nasty smells, and beautiful smells. I take a step, and I am bombarded. Overrun. Overwhelmed.

My senses are at critical mass, and it feels utterly amazing.

I keep my hand in Caspian's as we walk down a stone path past the tall building we came out of. A peeling red sign reads: *Bleeding Hearts Motel.* A perfect name. A beautiful name.

Everything we pass is perfectly beautiful. There are smelly puddles in the streets that blot the landscape like lovely, little flaws. Clouds of steam waft up around my feet, sour-smelling and warm to the touch. The sky is a puzzle piece overhead, squeezing to fit in around tall square buildings that somehow seem more plain than the ones in the Citadel and yet more grand.

More perfect.

Oh my, everything here is perfect!

I need to know what everything is. What everything does. I'm so wrapped up in curiosity that I make a mistake.

I tighten my grip on the cold fingers entwined with mine, and I say, "What is this? What is this?"

And he says... Nothing. Not at first. He doesn't want to. His eyes darken, and his upper lip curls in abject disgust. Then, a big, rolling square of metal shoots past us and draws my attention.

"Truck," Caspian says bitterly and reluctantly. "Do not stand in front of them. Not again. You'll be killed."

Again. It must have been a truck that I encountered, with glowing, yellow eyes that blazed through the dark.

"I won't," I say. I promise him. He won't have to rescue me again. Pay for me again. I'm the reason for the package hidden in my newly purchased bag. The reason why he hisses beneath his hood, his head bowed low.

But then I spy something that distracts from my guilt for a moment. "Oh! What is that?"

He looks up. Hisses. "School bus." A yellow truck, brighter than the sun.

"And that?" My eyes have darted to something else. Another marvel.

"A dog," he says. A beautiful creature tethered to its owner by a colorful bit of red string. I know of dogs and wolves and animalistic creatures. I've read about them.

Never have I seen one.

Nor a "cat" that darts across the street next, as if to flaunt its newness before me.

"Oh," I utter again and again as Caspian dutifully and angrily explains the world to me.

Cars. Honking horns. Street lights. Stop lights. So many different lights.

Like the mortals and their clothing. Bright. Dark. Colorful. Vibrant. Muted. They cram so much color into these small places in between their enormous buildings. I will never learn enough. Discover enough. One day will never be enough.

Then we pass a "park." A place with lush, green, wide open spaces, and I get greedy. I grip the hand in my grasp tighter. I lick my lips and ask, "Can we see it up close? Please?"

He stiffens. Grunts. Groans. Drags me forward across the busy street to the park I long to see. We step beyond a gap in two curling metal gates. A stone path unfurls to a world of wild imagery beyond.

"Oh! Oh! Oh!" That sound becomes the only noise I can make. The only word I can speak.

And one that Caspian translates with persistent irritation.

Oh!

"Garden," he explains, referring to a wealth of beautiful flowers.

Oh!

"Pond."

Oh! Oh! Oh!

"Tram. Frisbee. Food stall."

A few minutes in this corner of the mortal realm, and I am exhausted already. Satisfied already. So very pleased already.

There is still more to see. The realization dawns on me as we turn down another bustling street. Then another. Another. Amid a sea of new sights is one I recognize instantly.

A building perched atop a series of marble steps. Marble columns frame the entrance. It is a museum.

The museum.

Caspian tugs on my arm as I stare and stare. Angrily, he snaps, "What is it?"

Then he looks over and sees. Scoffs. "Been here before. Nothing special."

He's been here before, and it is nothing special.

When it is everything.

"Please," I tell him, my voice broken and hoarse.

His teeth grind together. "Where the hell do you think we're going?"

To deliver his package. To square his debt.

But he has chosen to put me first. My desire comes first. A quick stop. A quick trip. Perhaps he intends to leave me here.

Alright, then. I will accept. He can leave me to die here, and I will accept.

But he doesn't wrestle his hand away from mine. Instead, we keep walking through a sea of sleepy mortals, unaware of how beautiful their realm is. How beautiful this city is. They march past the building before us, yawning and heads bowed low.

As if it doesn't matter. It's as dreary a view to them as the Citadel bell tower is to me. Mundane. Unimpressive.

However, I stare. The closer we come, I gape. My mouth falls open, eyes get wider. Wider. Wider. I could swallow up the entire world if I'm not careful. Swallow up Caspian, who glances back at me, his eyes blazing and draped in shadow. He glances. Looks ahead. Looks back. Stares back. Stops moving.

Oh no. With my face—this hopeful pleading expression—I have offended him. Or at least I think so. He inhales raggedly. Runs his tongue along his upper lip. Bares the teasing hint of a fang.

"I'd give anything to bite you now," he murmurs. Hisses.

I take in those words with my hopeful heart, and I don't react to them like I should. I don't shiver and shudder in disgust. I don't rush to deny his request. A sinful request. Forbidden.

Because I know him, this creature, Caspian. When my heart is happy, it makes me smile. Until my mouth hurts, I smile.

When he sees me or any other creature happy, it makes him violent. Hungry. Impatient. It makes him reckless.

He drained ten people dry, Colleen warned me.

It is fine as long as he is only hungry for me.

I owe him my life already.

"Maybe," I say, my tongue heavy, lips tight. "Maybe I will let you."

No. No. I decide here and now.

"Before we return... I will let you."

He doesn't look satisfied. Gratified. Happy.

He scowls and glowers and tugs me along. "Come."

I follow him again eagerly. Too eagerly. Something strange happens. His steps are too slow for me. I start to outpace him. Slip past him. Soon I am the one dragging him along.

"Wait," he commands me. "Wait. Wait!"

"Hurry," I choke back as he tightens his grip. "Hurry! Please." My eyes are on the building ahead of me—so much closer but still so far away. I need to get there quickly. Before this dream fades and becomes a nightmare, I must get there.

He slows at first, impossible to pull. Then he surges, dragging me behind him again through a sea of mortals and right up to those marble steps.

I am here. My heart breaks with joy as I look up and see those familiar, foreign entrances. I am here. But as Caspian steers me inside, I realize something else.

He has fulfilled his purpose to me. His only purpose.

Then he'll go. Leave.

There is no reason for him to stay.

CHAPTER 30
Caspian

I have been here before. Once. Twice. Many times. Under Cassius? I think.

No.

Before Cassius...

My skull aches. I can't remember. I hold her hand, and I can't remember. Good or bad. The past means nothing. I hold her hand, my stupid, foolish, smiling, little fae...

And her reality is all I give a damn about remembering. Ensuring. Protecting.

She wants her paintings, so I take her down a winding hall and shove her before one.

Oh. She should say. Then, we move on to the next. Done. Her will is fulfilled.

And she will smile that stupid smile again.

I wait for her sound of awe. That gasped *Oh.*

She says nothing. She stares at the portrait on the wall before us and says nothing. She stares. Wide, black eyes fixate on canvas and splatters of paint as though they are the most beautiful things in existence. The way Cassius would never look upon his horde—he never cherished us anyway. Not all of us.

Just me. She looks at this wall the way Cassius would look at me. But her obsession doesn't irritate. Doesn't disgust and make me want to rip out her fucking throat.

I want her to look at *me* the same way. The way she looks at this piece of canvas and oil and pigment is the way I want her to look at me.

In silence. In terrible, woeful awe. As though it holds her entire soul within its woven threads, and after just one look... She will never be the same again.

"Speak," I hiss at her. Scattered mortals flinch and stare. They, too, strive to create silence in this place by staring at images of blocky, distorted paint and perspective. I look where she looks. I see nothing. Color and ugliness and nothing.

"It's..." She trails off. Her eyes water, and my entire body is repelled. More tears from her. Tears not caused by me. But these are different. Not of pain or utter disappointment.

These ones... I reach out and brush one along her cheek and watch it disintegrate. These ones can stay, even though I don't understand their purpose. Their cause. They can stay and speckle her pretty, pale, hollow skin.

One by one, they fall. They adorn her face like diamonds and gold. They drip, drip down. But I need to know why.

“Speak,” I demand, low enough for only her to hear.

She sucks in a ragged breath. Sighs. “It’s so beautiful. Art… is so beautiful.”

Beautiful. She says it with the breathless awe of some precious, incredible thing. I look, and I see ugly smears and meaningless marks.

“Show me,” I demand, stepping closer, insisting upon it. “Tell me how to see what you see.”

She swallows, her eyes still fixed on her painting. She shakes her head. Then takes our combined hands and presses them to her chest, right over her beating, thumping heart. “It’s in here,” she murmurs. “You see it with this.”

With this. A beating heart. But mine doesn’t pump and churn hot, flowing blood. It hasn’t for a long while. Not since the night Cassius crept in…

Did he creep? I can’t remember. That’s the funny part. I can’t remember one damn thing about the night he took me. Made me. Turned me into this.

“Tell me what you see,” I snarl at her. “Tell me. Show me.”

She takes my hand in both of hers and stares forward, fixated on her own painted world.

“The color is so beautiful,” she says. Then hesitates. She’s used to shutting up. Her stupid male fae would shut her up. I should shut her up.

“Tell me.” I step into her, crowding her little body closer to the wall. With my lips near her ear, I stare forward and try to see what she sees. I want to see what she sees.

How better to destroy it. Embody it. Make her look at me and see the same stupid view she sees now.

"Tell me more."

"You can see the brush strokes," she says, my hand still clutched to her breast. Every breath she takes, I feel. In and out. Out and in. "You can tell what the artist was thinking, what he was feeling. You can see everything he was feeling."

But how? I look at the canvas and see colorless, formless shapes. Then I blink. Look again. Faces appear in the blurred, painted mess. Shapes. Structures. People on a lawn of green. I think.

Fuck. I can't remember how to interpret these strokes and blotches and colorful things.

Because Cassius made me forget how. I remember, I think... Art. Museum. I remember.

He made me forget. For the same reason he wants to erase her, he made me forget.

"Tell me more," I snarl, commanding her.

In a soft, halting whisper, she complies. "You can see the sunlight there." She points, her voice so fragile. I have to strain to hear her —*me*, with superior hearing. I have to strain to hear her. "If you look closely enough, it's like you can feel it, on your skin. You can hear their laughter, their chattering. This is magic."

Her eyes water again and more tears spill, glistening glass from this angle. My fangs ache and tease my lower lip painfully. I'd bite her to get her to stop. I'd bite her to make those tears continue to fall.

Beautiful things. No, ugly. No... beautiful. Raw and real. I see her tears, and I remember what it feels like to feel. Something other than hate and rage. Something softer than lust. What? What?

I look at her, and smell her scent, and it's closer, just within my reach.

What? What?

"Tell me," I beg of her. As if a vamryre could ever beg. But it's my voice I hear echoing back. *Tell me. Tell me.*

My old master would relish in my desperation. He would draw it out. Make me dance for him. Perform for him. Kill for him.

There was a prize at the end of those murders. I think. I wanted something. I think. Something badly enough to kill for it. To kill and kill.

I didn't want to. That's the lie he made me accept. Believe. Internalize.

I didn't want to kill for him. I never did.

My free hand is in her hair, my fae's, tangling and coiling the strands together, creating a makeshift leash to tether her to me with. Prevent any escape. "Tell me more."

She does. Gentle and soft, her voice is a salve on old wounds. Festering bleeding wounds that Cassius made me ignore.

Art means something to me. Meant something. Once...

I don't care, the monster in me hisses. *The past. Old mortal bastard. Don't care!*

But that doesn't mean I don't want to remember.

So, I let her speak. I let her sing to me, my little fae bird.

And in her voice, I start to recall something fractured, fragile, and forgotten.

Humanity, I think.

Whatever it is, I hate it. Loathe it. Despise it in me.

Whatever it is, she has it in spades. If I can't remember, I can drain it from her.

Drain her dry.

CHAPTER 31
Niamh

In my wildest dreams, I used to imagine what this would be like. To stand in a museum and stare at a painting in person. It would be a wonderful experience, I thought. It would inspire enough joy to last a lifetime, and I could return to the other realm, content.

At peace.

Staring at a painting inspires everything *but* peace. I am angry. I am so happy my heart feels swollen, and it hurts. I am so tired. So desperately sad. So angry.

It wasn't supposed to be this way. A happy moment. A grateful moment that I would accept in a moment of greediness.

But one viewing of a painting isn't enough. I move from the first to the next, Caspian at my side, his questions hot against my ear. The man himself is cold, but his curiosity is molten.

"Tell me more," he demands. Insists. Pleads.

I nearly bite my own tongue in my rush to. "This is a beautiful use of color," I say, eyeing a sky made up of a million different colors. Blues and yellows and reds all smashed together and yet the image they create is simple and recognizable: a sky. "You can see the artist's vision," I say. "You can see things as they see them."

"As they see them?" Caspian echoes. "How?"

I can't say. I don't know how to form the proper words to even begin to describe it. So, I take his hands and manipulate his pale, slim fingers into the air before me. I trace the white nails and silken skin. I feel the strength coiled in every single digit. I try to make him understand.

I use his fingers to paint the air. To view the world as he sees it. Cold, brutal motions. Jabbing motions. Then I curl his fingers inward toward me and press them to my chest, making the contact as gentle as I possibly can. Let him feel my heartbeat hammering.

"Look," I say. "I see endless color and beautiful sky. I see hope and light. Oh... It's so beautiful. So beautiful."

My words are greeted with a grunt from him. He doesn't see. Even so, he steers me to another painting. Looms behind me. Commands, "Tell me what you see."

So, I do. I tell him until my voice grows hoarse, and I can barely see through tears. I'm crying openly, but he doesn't chase these tears away. He's so gentle in his touch, steering me along from painting to painting.

But his voice is grating and violent. "Tell me! Tell me!"

He doesn't understand. He looks at the painted canvas and he doesn't see. It frustrates him. It angers him. It thrills me.

Because I can see for him. I explain, and he grunts in acknowledgement. It's not a full picture—he doesn't truly view it in full. But he can get a glimpse through me. He needs me.

He stays with me. He looks at paintings over my shoulder and stays with me. Has need of me. Demands more of me.

I thought this experience would be fun. Greedy fun. A devious, rebellious memory to hoard later. To store away in my skull long after the misery of my old life swept any other joy away.

In that world, I could leave this realm and go back again. There would be something left of me to go back.

But now...

I curl my fingers around a vamryre's hands and grip him so tight. I want him to stay. I want to stay.

I want to stay.

"The gallery closes in ten minutes." The voice comes from a man dressed in black. He stands near the door, radiating authority.

"Okay," I whisper to no one. Okay. I will leave...

But I could come again. Another day. Another trip.

I have to come here again.

CHAPTER 32
Caspian

A debt repaid. A day wasted. A simple fucking exchange.

I should leave her there at the mouth of her precious museum, her precious art gallery. Leave her there to be gobbled up by hungry shadows and struck by another bus. I should leave her there.

Because bringing her back would be a reward for Cassius. He would get his initial quest fulfilled. Killing her would no longer be the most fun part of this game.

No. I grip her hand so tightly she couldn't pull away if she tried. I lead her from the gallery, though her eyes linger, and she cranes her neck back for one final look. But still, she follows.

She doesn't resist the hand I have clenching her tightly. She follows me. Wants to follow me.

She has to follow me.

Because I have a debt to repay. Because of her. The fat mortal gave me a package to deliver like some kind of fucking messenger boy.

Messenger boy. An image comes to mind: running, chasing down minutes and hours. Parcels in hand, running and chasing.

Me?

I can't remember. Won't remember. The past is in the past. The past is dead.

I am dead. I am Caspian.

A vamryer, the pinnacle of all beings. Unaffected by time. Unable to age. Unable to feel any emotion but greedy, gnawing, thirsty hunger.

But she...

My little fae is hungry. Her steps falter. She winces as her belly rumbles, unused to the sensation. Although she was hidden, shamed, and shunned, she never went hungry. Not for long. Not for days.

Don't care. I try to ignore her. Ignore the growling howls of her stomach. Ignore her dry, longing swallows. Ignore. Ignore. It will take her body days to die from hunger. Days she doesn't have.

Cassius will come. An army will come. The fae, though they hate her and hide her, they will come...

I stop. Fragrance rides a cold wind that whips past and makes her inhale raggedly. Her stomach grumbles. There is food. Mortal food, greasy and nutrient-less. There is a stand on the corner of the nearby street where a man hands out steaming slabs of meat on buns. Rolls, they are called. Sausage rolls.

She wants one, even though she's never tasted it. Never even tasted meat—just lived on gruel and bread. She wants one.

I don't care. I pull her forward and keep walking. There is a debt to be repaid. A balance to right. She owes me enough already. I've given her enough already.

I stop. A mortal stares at me in confusion, a slab of steaming meat raised.

"Give it to me," I say, but my voice is cool, pretty, and sweet.

He smiles. I smile.

He gives me the greasy, disgusting thing.

I give it to her. She swallows. "Thank you. But they pay for things here," she says as I pull her along, leaving the mortal and his meat stand behind. "I read that custom in the archives. We should pay for it. With money."

"Don't have any," I growl at her. It's not like I need it anyway. Whenever I came here on Cassius' accord, he never once supplied me with money. It isn't necessary. I look at mortals in their empty, dull eyes. I smile and make a request. Give me. Give now. Give it all, no questions asked.

They give. They go about their meaningless lives. Money or words are all the same. Only in the other realm does money matter. We can only pay for things with silver there and adhere to the rules. Cassius supplies us with all the money we could ever need.

Because everything we buy is always for him.

Except the day I took his silver and bought a rose. I pretended like giving it to her was on behalf of him—but it wasn't. It never was. I gave it to her because I wanted to...

I wanted to.

"Eat," I snap at her now, shaking my head to clear it. Stupid memories. Pointless memories.

She hesitates. It's stolen goods, and in her worthless, sheltered not-fae life, she's never had to contend with stealing. Just hoping—a greater mortal sin in their world. So what is this in comparison?

"Eat." I pull her aside into the mouth of an alley and make her face me. I snatch the sausage roll from her grasp. Rip off a piece of it. Greasy, disgusting morsel. I shove it against her lips. She bites. Her eyes widen as she bites once more. Chews. Swallows.

"It's good," she whispers, as if she's never understood the concept before. Good food. Better than just palatable food. Like a rich, delicious bloodstream spilling from a gaping neck. A willing neck. Willing blood tastes the sweetest, and she has promised me hers.

That is why I feed her every last bite. I want that heart pumping freely. I want her blood to taste oh, so sweet. Sated and full, she'll taste better than she would starving and frail.

I need to feed her more. She is different than I. Not a flawless, peerless vamryre, but a weak, nearly-mortal fae. Her body will disintegrate into dust and bones if I'm not careful. I've let her be broken beyond repair once already.

I take her hand and pull her into me—protection from the shadows. She is a creature desiring protection. The world looks at her and looms. It doesn't shy away like the pathetic fae and the others in our old realm.

The mortals look at her here, and they don't see an ugly thing. Their eyes linger on her—more than they even linger on me. They watch her swallow. Watched her smile in that gallery. Watched her laugh and spin so freely the first moment she set foot here.

She is pretty to them—no, beyond pretty. She is an otherworldly being, shiny and new in their eyes. She is valuable in their eyes. I will have to protect her here. Guard her here.

She is shiny and valuable, and I can see that so very many want to steal her.

But she is mine.

"Is this the place?" she wonders, her lips soft and shiny with grease, her eyes wide and questioning. She sees a building straight ahead. A building we've been standing in front of for maybe a minute or more. A building I don't want to enter.

I can smell that something is off with it. It reeks of deadly, corrupted magic.

The fat mortal can deliver her parcel herself. I won't.

My little fae catches my attention. I see her, black eyes innocently staring. Heart so innocently pumping. Skin so innocently glistening.

She's drawn several eyes our way without even trying. Without even realizing it. She's used to hateful, furtive glances, but these are lingering and wistful. Men here long for her. They rake their gazes over her body with hungry, groping eyes.

And women want her too. They want to coddle her, hold her, and protect her from the dark, wicked things. Too many people are watching her. Staring.

"Come." I snatch for her wrist and tug her along, closer to that infernal, unwelcoming building. The address on the parcel is the same as the numbers gleaming above a set of main doors in a rusting metal script.

It feels familiar. At the same time, it doesn't. What is this place, and what use could a mortal mundane have for sending me here?

A distraction, a part of me warns. *You know that all of this is a distraction. A lie.*

Because Cassius is coming—*and you want to see him, you sick fuck. You'll lead your little fae into a trap just to see him. Smell him. Kill him.*

Enough. I banish the thoughts and step inside the building, with the fae at my heels. She watches and stares as we traverse a narrow hallway, black with soot and age and the stink from decades of mortals who have lived here throughout the ages.

But mortals no longer live here now. They have been banished by another type of creature. One more sneaking and insidious. It set up shop in this mortal realm, but it doesn't belong.

Like me and the fae, the inhabitants of this dwelling do not belong.

Our quarry lives behind a battered black door. I knock. Slam. Rattle the damn thing in its hinges.

"Coming," a voice replies, sickly sweet and chillingly familiar.

"We're going," I tell the fae, but she blinks at me, confused. She doesn't understand what kind of place this is. Doesn't recognize the light tones coming from the other end of that door.

The creatures living here are not mundane, or corrupted, strange mortals like the blond Colleen.

They are vamryre. All, full-blooded vamryre, hiding in the mortal realm like wayward children. Fugitives. Outlaws.

"I said I'm coming!" The dwelling creature snaps.

It's because I knocked again. Slammed on the door, threatening to break it with every pounding, thudding smash. I should run and get the fae away, but I can't.

I need to see. Need to smell.

I need to look into the eyes of these creatures and see who they belong to. How they escaped. How. How? How!

The door opens and a creature appears on the other end, garish and glaring and dressed in vibrant purple silk. It is a man. Or a woman. A creature beyond such limitations. It, whatever it is, leans against a doorframe, dressed in silk, its hair dark, blacker than midnight, eyes a piercing green.

This creature did not belong to Cassius. A brother or sister from another master. Another slaver. Another collection of broken doll-toys.

"From which corner of bloody hell did Mo find you?" He-she-it, murmurs, their eyes gleaming, fingers clenching the doorframe. Then they see my fae, and greedy hunger flashes across their gaze. No fear. Utter terror. They see her and shy back, hissing through glossy, perfect teeth. They see her, and their fangs spring from their sheaths, cutting the air.

Not to bite with.

To kill.

They see her, my pretty fae thing, and they want to destroy her. Crush her.

They fear her.

"Step toward me, brother," they say, their voice gentle and fake. "Leave it behind. Yes, that is the way. Come toward me."

Their green eyes beckon. Their voice beckons. For they are older than I am. Wiser. A brother in blood and knowledge. I should listen. Need to listen.

A new master. A better master than Cassius...

I let go of her, my greedy, corrupted fae. I let go of her, and the cold reality comes rushing back. I let go of her, and I remember all of the things I don't want to. Don't need to. I let go of her, and the world loses its pretty fucking sheen.

I snatch her again. Grip her again so hard she winces.

But all is well again. I can think like myself again. I can glare at the other vamryre and tell it to go to hell.

"She is mine," I say.

The figure shudders. "Well, darling, I certainly am not one to judge another for their choice of kink. To each their own, I say. Just leave it over there in the doorway—no, not the package, the dirty thing. Yes. Leave it there—"

He means my fae. He doesn't want her in his pretty house, near his pretty, fake collection of sparkly, shiny things.

Too late. I drag her toward me. Bring her with me.

He doesn't want her here, but whatever is in this package, he needs. He needs me to carry it deeper within this maze of rooms and set it on the floor before a closed door. There is something behind this door. Something I want. Need.

Something I have forgotten but desperately need.

Can't remember now. Don't care. I look at my fae toy, and I don't care.

"Well, that is done," the fugitive vamryre remarks. He hasn't followed us here. He lingers paces away at the end of the hall. He watches, his nostrils flared, eyes fearful and furtive. They dart to my fae, then to me, and back again.

He fears her, this corrupted being. He eyes her as if she's the broken one. The lying one. The fearful one.

But he is here, and so am I.

"Who do you belong to?" I ask.

"No one," he replies, chin in the air, throat gripping around a hard swallow. "Out here, I belong to myself, as I assume you do. But don't think you can sow any trouble here, vampire. I know what you are. I know which master you belong to—"

He uses present tense, not past.

"Don't think you can bring your troubles here. I know of your kind. I know of you, boy."

"Caspian," I correct with a cold smile. "I am Caspian."

"You are one of Cassius' toys," he counters as a hint of power radiates through those dark eyes. He dresses like a woman and wears their perfume. He carries himself with the air of a man. He is deceitful but not weak. I can feel his control wash over me and threaten. *Watch yourself, boy.* "It isn't like your master to let your kind wander too far off your leash. Now go!" He beckons us forward and then wills us away with waving hands and delicate fingers. "Get out. You've done your duty. Get out."

I want to. Gladly, I will leave.

"Wait," the creature commands as we near the door, my fae and I. "Make it wait outside. I need to speak with you, boy."

I look at her. I look at my fingers gripping tightly to the little fae. Her hands are pink from the pressure. Pink from the blood flow necessary to supply those tiny, grasping fingers. Blood flow stilted from how tightly I grip her. How hard. I let her go, and the world will fall away.

I let her go, and she might slip away. No. Never.

I keep her close. Keep her near me. Always, I will keep her near me.

"I don't think this is a conversation you want it to hear," the vamryre warns.

Don't care to listen. Don't care to hear his lies.

I start to leave.

"Wait! Just hear me out. Oh, well fine then, have it your way. Do you know what that thing beside you even is? Because I do. I can smell its gross corruption. Its corrupted you already, you do realize? Broken thing. Disturbing thing." It eyes my fae and sighs in pity. It eyes me and sighs in disgust.

Stupid, arrogant vamryre. It thinks it knows everything. It thinks it knows what my fae is.

But he doesn't.

I do.

"She is... freedom," I say in a rush, spinning to face him fully. Growling to prove a point. "She is freedom from him, and she is mine. Touch her and I will kill you. Touch her and I will rip you limb from limb—"

"I know," the other vamryre says softly. "I know, because that is what it does. Corrupts and bends others to its will. Don't you see?

You mean nothing to it. To this creature you are a means to an end. It already has you under her spell."

Under her spell. Where I would rather be than anywhere else. Under her spell, away from Cassius. Under her spell, and able to feel. To fuck and taste and enjoy and *feel.*

Under her spell...

Where I need to be. Where I will stay.

Under her spell?

"So be it," I say. Then I drag her away, my fearful, startled fae. She heard every word that worthless creature said. She isn't smart enough, like me, to discount it. She took in his lies, and they fester in her mind. They toy with her. Corrupt her sense of self.

That stupid vamryre will ruin everything. Everything.

He'll make her think she is dirty and unworthy, and she will hide from me.

She will leave me.

Only I can leave her—not the other way around.

She can never leave me.

I will never let her leave me.

CHAPTER 33
Niamh

For every crime, there is a punishment, whether you intend to sin or not. For every transgression, a price must be paid in return. Retribution. A sin for a sin.

It seems only fitting that in exchange for one day—one beautiful, flawless, perfect, incredible day—I must suffer the ultimate price. The ultimate pain.

Retribution at its most extreme.

Caspian is turning against me. My savior. Mine. The only one to take a price from me and give what I wanted in exchange. He'll leave me, I know he will.

He'll listen to every word that vamryre said. He can hide it. Deny it.

Despite clutching me tight and tugging me along through the twisting streets, he cringes. He will hate me. He does hate me.

I don't know why.

I know why.

I was never good enough to keep him, not always. I was never good enough. I am not good.

Enough.

"I am sorry," I tell him. Maybe that will make him stay? If I plead and beg and grovel. "I am sorry. I am sorry. Don't—"

Leave me, I want to say. Want to scream. *Don't leave me!*

He snarls, "Shut up. Shut up."

"Don't leave me."

"Shut up! I need to listen. Need to hear."

Hear what exactly? We are nearing a familiar building—the motel. The sky is darkening, with heavy purple clouds rolling in. A storm is coming, both literally and figuratively.

The world is gearing up for one hell of a storm, and Caspian is gearing up for one hell of a fight. His posture changes, eyes glow and alight with excitement. In the short time I've known him, only a few things get him excited like this.

Violence and bloodshed.

Something is coming. Whatever it is, he knew it was coming. He is so eager for it. Eager for violence and bloodshed.

But I want to run. I want to claw my fingers from his and run. Run and run and run.

But he won't let me. If he stays, then so will I. As long as he fights, so will I. My heart aches as I look up at him, my Caspian. Mine. I want him. I'll keep him. I'll stay, just as long as he...

"Don't leave me," I whisper. I beg. I plead.

He hisses and snarls in irritation, "Get ready."

Get ready.

Because a trap has been set and laid for us. All day it has been waiting to spring. The trip to the secret vamryre was a trap. A way to waste time.

Because reinforcements are here. The mortal set us up. She turned us in to the authorities that matter—not their fake ones, but the elder council. The elder council is here.

For him.

For me.

But why?

Why?

You know why, a part of me murmurs, dripping with glee. *You are a corrupted creature who stole him away. You are evil. Dirty. Broken.*

You deserve to die and so you will.

You sinned too greatly. Wanted too much.

You will die, Niamh.

And so will he, the creature who led you here like a lamb to the slaughter.

But death doesn't scare me. It can't scare me. Nothing does but him.

I can't lose him. I won't lose him. I dig my fingers into his and beg him. Over and over, I beg and beg.

"Don't leave me! Please don't leave me! Please, Caspian—"

"Shut up," he hisses, still dragging us closer to that damned motel. He can't help himself. He can smell it too. Taste it too. His master is near and all his brethren.

They are here to take him back.

To take him away.

To kill me and take him away.

"Don't leave me," I tell him, but the words aren't strong enough. "Caspian, please. Stay with me. I need you here. I need you with me. I. NEED. YOU!"

He stiffens and goes still, his arm outstretched behind him, his hand still in my grasp. He looks back at me, my beautiful stolen being and he drills his gaze into mine.

"I won't leave you," he says.

And my heart sings. My heart breaks.

Because is it his will or mine?

I don't know.

I don't know.

I don't want to know.

CHAPTER 34
Caspian

They've sent them all; my most cherished and trusted brothers and sisters. He sent them to come for me. His favorite four. His most braindead four. Their minds and will have been snuffed out eons ago. Ages ago. Centuries.

They live as one with him now. A perfect, creepy union.

They are waiting for me, standing in the hallway of that cramped, dingy motel. I can hear them. I can smell them.

But in my brain, the world is silent. I can only hear her, my frantic, terrified little fae. I hear her frantic, hurried breathing. I hear her begging in a broken, scratchy voice. I hear her plead.

"Don't leave me, Caspian! Please, don't leave..."

As if I could. As if I could ever want to leave her. As if I could ever let her leave me.

"I won't," I say to her.

I can't.

She is mine, and mine, and mine. She is mine and no one will take her from me. She is mine and no one will take me from her.

So I pull her forward and enter that dingy, cramped trap house. I once craved to visit this den of debauchery. *Oh, please.* I would beg him like she is now. *Please, Lord Cassius, please. Let me play. Let me run. Let me away from you. Away from you...*

Let me run away to the mortal realm. I will return.

I won't. I wouldn't want to return. He would make me. Compel me.

Even now, he tries to compel me. But he can't.

Because of her.

I laugh out loud as I hear him, a tiny, pathetic whispering beyond my skull. On the *outside* of it. He can't get in now. Can't get inside me and scrape around and issue commands.

He is shut out of me. Forever. For good.

He can never hurt me again.

And neither can they, his toys, my brethren. They stand before the desk of the motel, hands clasped, eyes glowing. Angry, red eyes.

"You have been naughty, Caspian, brother," they say in unison. "Return with us, and you may find mercy yet."

Mercy when he kisses me in repayment for the debt I still owe. Mercy when he pins me down and fucks out the retribution I still owe. Mercy still, when he locks me away and keeps me from the sister whose punishment is for my benefit.

I remember now. I am starting to remember. Cassiopea wasn't the one who sinned. I did. I ruined everything.

And she was taken to punish me.

I look at them now, these smiling, empty reflections of him. Reflections of the master I loathe and the mortal lives he's stolen away. He wouldn't come himself. No, I am not worthy of that.

But this, he can send them. Four messengers. Four protectors. Four punishers to drag me back to him.

That was their plan all along—him, them, and the fat mortal Mo. She hates me, oh yes, she does. She planned to set me up from the start.

I don't blame her.

But I will punish her—not now, because she and the other mortals are gone in hiding. They've left this building empty. Cassius plied them with more than enough silver and gold to make it empty. A perfect mouse trap sprung to catch a stupid, mousey Caspian.

But I am no longer his Caspian. I am hers...

And she needs me. She needs me. She needs me to stay. She needs me near, and so she needs me.

And I will stay for her.

I will fight them all for her.

I will kill them all for her.

Because she wills me to stay.

And I would rather die than go back.

Red robes. Bloodied walls. Gore and violence and bloodshed.

My favorite things. Such pretty things.

Such bleeding, messy things.

Oh dear, have I done a bad thing. The baddest of all, short of killing Cassius like I long to, like I crave. I have done the next best, and worst thing.

I look upon my four brothers and sisters sent to rescue me from the mortal realm. Sent to save me from my naughtiness.

I look at them. Smile at them. Let go of my fae and leave her to watch.

Watch me rip them all to pieces.

Watch me tear them all to shreds.

She's coiled up now in a corner of the hall, trembling with fear at what she's witnessed. Drenched in blood, she is. Beautiful, perfect, and mine to steal.

But I am too dirty to touch her. My hands are too red and blood-stained. Cassius' voice is a whisper. Too weak. A thready, broken whisper, beyond my reach forever.

Caspian, he hisses and rages. *You have—*

What? What have I done?

I wait but he can't finish it. He doesn't finish it, his final threat.

Because I have finally snuffed him out. Poof. He is gone. He and the others are gone. Gone for good—like the make-believe I pretended until now. I had my figurative fingers in my imaginary ears before. I could hear the hum and cacophony they made but I could tune them out. Shut them out.

As long as I touched and soiled my delicious, dear, little fae one, they went silent. Quiet.

But I have sinned too greatly, and now they are gone. All gone.

All.

Gone.

Done.

Silence.

I laugh and laugh and wait. I laugh and laugh and hear no one laughing back. I eye the bloodied mess I've made. The limbs scattered at my feet.

They will heal one day, maybe. Maybe not.

But I am not in their head anymore and they are not in mine.

The world is quiet, utter bliss.

And it hurts me.

It burns me.

I laugh and laugh just to hear a sound. Something. Anything.

I laugh and laugh and laugh.

I LAUGH AND LAUGH AND LAUGH.

Nothing.

Silence alone is what greets me.

My head is empty again. Broken again. The collective is gone, I have been shut out.

I have been severed like dear Cassiopea was.

Whatever happened to her, my sister, my ally, my dear one?

She is dead and gone.

And so am I.

CHAPTER 35

Niamh

I can't interpret violence. It is inherent disorder. It goes against the very laws and nature of the fae. It is violence.

The vamryre's realm of expertise, not my own...

No. I have left that world of old rules behind, and now I must plunge into another. I must weigh the pros and cons of the violence inflicted before me in the same way I would weigh the risks of reading a book in secret or begging for help from a vamryre.

He helped me.

He needs me now.

He needs me now to take his hand gently in my own. He needs me to lead him away. Away from his crouched position on the floor, holding broken limbs like the remains of four broken dolls. He gapes at them. Talks to them. Shouts at them.

"Why can't I hear you? Answer me! ANSWER ME!"

"Caspian," I whisper to him. But he doesn't hear. He can't hear me beyond the realm of his shattered, fractured mind. He can't hear me.

So I touch him. I stroke the blood-soaked hair from his face and crouch down, my voice gentle and broken. Tears fall from my eyes and spill and spill. They're falling from his too. Beautiful, lost, broken tears of a poor, broken, shattered mind.

"Caspian. Oh, Caspian." I stroke him. Pet him. I try to meet those wide, empty, red eyes. He stares right through me. "Come with me. Come with me."

Somewhere safe. Away. We can't stay here.

Because they will come for him again.

They will try to take him from me again.

"Caspian," I tell him. "Come with me please."

He looks up at me, but he isn't here. His eyes are far, far away, pursuing the twisted wreckage of his mind. His poor, broken mind.

"We need to leave," I whisper, tugging him upright. He follows me, but not with the assured, confident steps I am used to. He is weak and tired like a lost lamb, following the first shepherd to come across it.

And I am worried. So very worried.

I have seen the violence he is capable of. Heard it: he drained ten people dry one after the other. He just ripped four vamryre apart, one after the other.

He could rip me apart. Good. I don't care. I would rather he rip into me. Feed from me. Devour me.

Anything to keep him safe. Anything to make him whole again.

So I tug him out into the street and away from that horrible place. I tug him into an alley, my lost, poor one. My Caspian.

I spin around to face him and offer my throat. “You are weak.” I tug on his limp, lifeless hand. Somehow, after being so very strong just minutes earlier, he is so very weak. He’ll fade to dust before me if I am not careful. He will fade away and leave me in another, more permanent way than he has before.

“Feed from me,” I tell him, throat bared, veins straining. “Bite me!”

He doesn’t. He can’t.

He is too far away to hear me. Lost inside his own head, he is so very far away. Too lost to ever return. Come back to me.

If I don’t help him, he will never come back to me.

So I take his hand and pull him along. I race. I run. I go to the only place I can think of to help him.

Not back to the portal. Not back to our realm.

I take him to a dank place on the other side of the city. I drag him —suddenly so very heavy—into a black building with rusted letters spelling out a name and number. A silly name I don’t bother to read.

I’m too busy running, panting, and pulling Caspian along to a door with a golden metal eye.

I pound on it. I beg.

“Please! Please help me! Please!”

Silence answers back. Silence and a weighty presence tinged with sweet perfume who hisses at me in utter disgust. "Go away," he commands from behind the closed door. "You aren't welcome here. Go!"

Go.

"No!" I form a fist and bang and bang like Caspian did upon the same door earlier. I pound and pound and pound away. I beg. I scream.

"Help me! PLEASE! Please help me!"

Because I can feel him slipping away. I can feel his mind shattering and hear the pieces scattering all around us. I will never find them all if I don't help him. I can never put him back together again.

"Help me!" I pound and pound and pound.

BANG! BANG! BANG!

Finally, the door opens, and the strange male vamryre appears. "Will you stop with the ruckus? What on earth is wrong with you?"

"Caspian is wrong with me," I blurt out, my hands sore and throbbing. Bleeding. I've left bloody marks on his door. Bloody marks he eyes in disgust. "He's dying. Help me help him!"

He's standing behind me in the shadow of the hall. His head is bowed, his expression vacant, pink lips silent, eyes far away. Gone. He is nearly gone.

"I can't help him," I sob. Tears spill down my face, but they don't affect this vamryre the way they do Caspian. He is unmoved, watching me with cold, unfeeling eyes. "Please help me help him. I can't lose him. I can't."

Because whatever Caspian is suffering from now, this vamryre has at one point. An affliction that must affect them all—those who dare to run away to the mortal realm.

The man looks at the vamryre behind me and sniffs. "Oh dear. Did you really walk all this way looking like that? Bloody hell! If the boneys aren't on your tail already, they're probably about to bust in my goddamn door. Poppy! Scythe!"

Two figures appear as if from nowhere behind him. But not nowhere. Somewhere deeper in this home, this huge, winding home. I can sense them all. Others, some awake and some not, lurking out of sight and out of reach. In fear, they hide behind this tall, dark-haired monster, only emerging when he calls them.

But now two snap to attention: a girl with bright red hair and a boy with blue.

"Yes?" they question in a disjointed unison. Not quite the way the other vamryre in the motel spoke. As though they have practiced to stay in sync but can't. Not quite. They are the same yet apart. Not one and the same as they should be.

"Scythe, you take this one inside. Show him to a room." He points to Caspian. My Caspian. "Poppy, you take this one—" He grimaces at me. "Take this one and clean up their mess. They tracked blood and gore all the way here, to our door. Ruffians! Clean their messes up, my darling. With gentle words and kind smiles, before the boneys come a calling. Go."

Poppy, the red-haired one, steps forward, her smile sickeningly sweet. "Come with me, dear one," she trills, a hand outstretched.

Any other time, I would. I'd rush to grab her hand. I would relish any hint of kindness.

But now...

They aim to take my Caspian away. Away from me. To help him. Heal him.

But I can't. I can't...

"I can't leave him," I rasp. "I won't leave him alone."

The tall one scoffs, his irritation exaggerated. "Well, you should have thought of that before, darling. Before you cut a bloody fucking trail to my door. Go with Poppy to clean up your mess while I take care of the other one. Go!"

I stare at Poppy's outstretched hand.

"I can't leave him," I croak. "I can't." Then. "What's happening to him? What is wrong with him?"

"Wrong?" The man frowns as if offended by my term. "Nothing is wrong. He has been severed from the collective is all. His mind has been made whole again."

Made whole. A good thing. A good thing?

But then why is he staring so blankly and empty? Why is he so far beyond my reach? Why doesn't he look at me when I say his name?

"Caspian? Caspian?"

Nothing.

"His mind is in shock," the man explains, his tone irritated. "He needs rest and quiet. He needs to repair his thoughts without your wailing and whining. Leave him to us. You leave."

With Poppy. Who will lead me away somewhere and never let me find my way back. They will hide him from me. Shield him from me.

Protect him from me.

"I can't leave him," I rasp. "I need him."

And he needs me.

"Oh, damn you! We've wasted too much time with this already. Poppy, go. Use your senses to track their trail and clean it up the best you can. Scythe, help this one to a room."

Scythe steps forward, tall and wiry. He reaches for Caspian. Touches him.

I wince. "Don't hurt him."

"We won't, darling," the tall one hisses. "But if you want him to get through this with some semblance of his psyche intact, you must let him go to a quiet space, away from this racket. Understood?"

I do. Deep down in the pit of my stomach, I do. My voice alone isn't enough to bring him back from that lost place inside of him. No matter how much I beg or plead it will never be enough.

I can't help him here.

I can only be patient and wait.

"Okay."

I watch Scythe take Caspian and lead his shell to some hidden, quiet room. This house must be full of them, some locked and boarded up. Some are open. There are many creatures living here. Dwelling here. Hiding here.

They trust him, the tall vamryre with dark hair and flashing green eyes.

"Do you call yourself something?" he wonders, an eyebrow raised. "Something other than 'it.'"

"I am Niamh," I snap. The air is different here. Frustrating and charged. I can't focus. I can't be nice, sweet, demure Niamh. I need my Caspian. I need to see him. Save him.

I need to protect him.

"Niamh, I am Altaris," the tall man explains. "This here is my domain. Our domain. The Safe House."

A safe house. But not safe for all creatures, just for them. A safe house for vamryre.

Because they lied to us in the other realm. Their rules claimed that a vamryre can never leave their collective. That a fae can never be born as one of three. That unwanted creatures are dirty and corrupted. That our laws are the only laws worth heeding.

Altaris has created his own realm here, in this house. What are his rules I wonder? Will he bully and command like Caspian's old master? Will he take him away from me?

"We choose to be here," he says, as if reading my mind. Has he? "All vamryre are welcome here. All shapes and forms. You are not—but," he adds before I can throw myself at him with grasping hands, nails drawn.

"But you may stay if you earn your keep. This isn't a hotel like that horrible place. I assume that's where you've come from. Where the cause of this took place..." He wiggles his slim fingers in my direction, his eyes on my chest, on my borrowed mortal clothes.

Clothing that is now red with blood. Vamryre blood.

"The Bleeding Heart Motel," I choke out.

Altaris sighs. "That place. Always causing trouble. A den of sin, it is. In any case, come closer, you. Come in."

He sniffs as I inch forward, leaving the narrow hall by the doorway for a wider room packed to the brim with shiny, dusty, gleaming things.

"You can stay here, for a price," Altaris repeats, eyeing me warily.

I just nod.

Any price, I will pay it. Anything.

For Caspian, I will give anything.

CHAPTER 36
Niamh

This corner of the realm is so strange. So different from what I imagined, and so different from the empty field I first glimpsed the second I came here.

The Bleeding Hearts Motel was loud and violent.

Life here...

Is quiet. Silent. These vamryre are all broken, lost souls that scurry and scatter at the slightest glance. Like me. Like I did in the Citadel.

Like they fear attention or the slightest touch. They fear their own shadow.

Will Caspian become like them? A broken, hollow thing. I hope not. Oh, please... I hope not.

I need him angry and bitter and full of sin. I need him bloody and thirsty and violent. I need him exactly as he was, no more, no less.

It is important to me that he remains Caspian. He can't change too greatly.

He can never lose his spark.

Because without his fire, I will fade out, a dying ember devoid of a flame. I will die out. Here in this perfect mortal realm…

Without Caspian, I will die out.

So, I wait for him. I wait impatiently, but I wait.

I let Altaris show me into another room cramped with bright furniture and paintings and too much to think clearly. A busy, noisy room, though silent if I keep my eyes closed.

"Let your boy rest for a night or two," he says. "His mind has been damaged. For decades. For years. From being one of the collective, to one alone… It is as though one has lost all of their limbs. Their eyes. Their tongue." He releases another wistful, heavy sigh. Whatever Caspian is experiencing, he too has been through it. Once.

How long ago?

I can't tell.

But I am not hopeful as I stare into his haunting green eyes. He keeps his thoughts locked up tight, more tightly than even Day did.

"I want to be with him," I say. Want to, because it may not be necessary. I would rather stay away from him than cause him any further pain. I would rather stay away from him than hurt him anymore.

"I suppose if you are silent and calm," Altaris stresses, "You may see him once he is settled in. Once we have settled upon a strategy for repayment."

"Caspian delivered your payment," I say.

He shrugs. "That was Mo's pay, for the stay in that dreary little shack. Here the rules are different and my prices vary. For succor here, it will cost you. The vamryre will stay free of charge, but not you." He sniffs at me and frowns. "You will upset my darlings, and for that you must pay."

I swallow hard and wrack my mind for anything of value. He is a vamryre. Perhaps blood is what he wants? Or my body, Like Caspian...

No, not like Caspian. Out of duty, I lied and pretended to give him what he wanted. A price was paid.

There was another reason, though. The real reason. One I shy away from admitting, even in my own mind. Maybe I wanted him, this beautiful, wounded, broken soul. Maybe from the start, it was always him that I wanted...

"I don't like your vapid little expression," Altaris sniffs. "Whatever you are thinking—utterly disgusting. You shall repay me with *labor*. My darlings are skittish when it comes to dealing with customers, and I cannot be in the shop at all times. You will work with Poppy in the main shop, starting tomorrow. Understood?"

I nod, even though I don't understand at all. Main shop? A place to sell things? If so, he obviously isn't selling well. His home is full to bursting with so many things.

"When can I see him?"

"Soon," he snaps. "Our payment is agreed. You may stay. For now. I can shield you from the collective, but only for so long. As for the fae... They have no domain here, but I cannot shield you from them. Should they ask, I must deliver you to keep my own darlings safe. Understood?"

I nod. If they asked, but they won't. They should be glad I am gone. Happy to be rid of me. Never will they have to look upon me and see their shame again.

"I understand," I say. "Just help Caspian."

"I will," he replies. "Ah, Scythe," he says, referring to the blue-haired man who silently enters the room alone. "I take it you squared our newest guest away?"

The man, Scythe, nods.

"I suppose you could see him now but be quiet and be patient. You will further damage his mind with your shouting and screaming."

I nod, my throat tight. Then I stand and start to follow Scythe into another cramped, tiny room.

"Oh, and you will begin your work tomorrow. Nine sharp. I do not tolerate tardiness. Poppy will assist you and show you the ropes. You can be as loud and irritating as you want in the storefront but, in here, you will be silent and respectful of my tenants. I will make sure Poppy sends you something decent to wear. And you may wash up in the bathroom near your room. Now go, please."

He waves me off and I follow Scythe, eagerly, impatiently. The need to see Caspian is all-encompassing. More than my wish to visit the mortal realm.

It was possible for me to die without achieving that wish. It would not have been my choice, but I could have.

There is no dying without seeing Caspian. I must see him, I must! Even if it means traipsing through a crowded hallway cluttered with beautiful, shining, porcelain things. He hoards things in the absence of a hive mind, this Altaris. He fills the rooms of his massive home full to bursting as if any ounce of empty space may make him remember...

What it is like to have an empty skull, apart from his master.

Poor Caspian. My sympathy for him only grows as Scythe silently leads me to a room past a winding staircase left partially ajar.

He sits on a bed draped in emerald sheets. The walls are colorful and vibrant: dark green leaves over black. Heavy black curtains shroud what must be two windows. A single lamp illuminates the space, hanging from the ceiling.

But Caspian stares blankly at the opposite wall. He sits and stares and wanders in the chaos of his mind.

I tiptoe toward him and sink to my knees beside him. I take his hand in mine and press it to my cheek. I whisper to him.

"Caspian."

He doesn't respond.

Maybe he will never respond.

Maybe he will never be the same again.

CHAPTER 37

Niamh

I don't sleep. I watch over him, my Caspian. I hold his hand, speak to him, and tell him a million whispered things.

Things I have never told anyone. Things I had no one to tell them to.

He doesn't react. Doesn't respond. His red eyes blaze, still angry but vacant. Even empty, he is still so very angry. Raging with sorrow and utterly blank.

He is a painting with no color. No reason behind it. No artful strokes.

He just exists.

But I stay with him. For however long it will take, I will stay with him.

"Hello?" A gentle knock sounds at the door, followed by another furtive, whispered greeting.

I stand and shake. I'm exhausted. I haven't slept. I'm hungry again. Dizzy again.

I feel like I have been hit by a truck again.

"I'm coming," I say to no one. Then I open the door and find the girl with glaring red hair. Poppy. She shifts awkwardly from foot to foot as if—unlike the quiet Altaris insists upon—she longs to run and bounce. Longs to skip and sing. Like a bird, she is quivering with life.

"Hello," she says, eyeing me warily from beneath a fringe of bright hair. "I am to bring you downstairs and show you the ropes. Around the shop I mean. Mortal slang is so strange, but I love it. Love it!"

"Poppy," comes a scolding tone. A reminder. "Beauty rest is important for all, please."

She nods. Bounces and nods. Her green eyes gleam as she looks at me. Then she shoves something into my hands. "You should get dressed first. Clean up, too. Bathroom is there." She points to a closed door down the hall and then darts away, bounding loudly down the stairs.

"Poppy," another voice calls in a hushed tone. "Quiet, please!"

"Sorry!" Her apology is even louder, ricocheting off the walls. But she doesn't mean to be defiant. Her rule-breaking is innocent, and here...

The others merely grumble in their rooms without punishing her transgression. They won't hold it against her, I can tell. There is a rehearsed quality to their complaints—the ones that come from silent, closed doors.

As if every morning, Poppy runs and shouts. Every morning, they scold her. Every morning.

It is their routine.

But I am lost in this unnatural play. I don't know what to do next. I peek into the room Poppy indicated. Then I drift back into my room. Caspian's room. I strip my clothing, crusty and coated with dried vamryre blood, and then I fold them neatly at his feet. Why? I don't know.

Maybe the smell will bring him back. Maybe the violence will...

It doesn't. He sits and stares and frowns in perpetuity.

I stand there naked and unsure. I miss his hungry gaze on my skin. I miss his hungry touch. Miss the way those eyes would devour and the way his voice would deepen when he...

Did things to me that were payment. Nothing less, nothing more.

No.

When he touched me. Made love to me—the way they called it in that forbidden book. I want him back.

Need him to touch me again.

So, for now, I touch him. I stroke the white hair from his face and press my lips to his cheek. Then I slip into the clothing Poppy supplied. Not a robe in plain shades of gray. Not the thick mortal clothing. This item is a longer tunic with no counterpart. The color is bright, like the hue of a budding red rose with speckles of lighter pink all over. The skirt of it swishes around when I walk.

Any other day, it would be such a beautiful dress to wear. A beautiful dress to borrow, even for a day.

But as I stand and watch Caspian stare into nothing, I don't know how I feel. Beautiful? No. Empty? Perhaps.

As empty as he looks.

Still, there is a debt to be repaid. To stay with him, I must work in exchange. Quietly, I enter the hall and close the door behind me. Then, I begin to navigate the wild maze of the upper floor of Altaris' home. There are several doorways I pass on my way to the stairs. Silence seeps from behind some of them. Murmuring voices from behind others. Apart from Scythe and Poppy, the other creatures in this dwelling don't seem eager to leave their rooms. They huddle and whisper.

But as Poppy bounds to greet me at the bottom of the stairs and shouts, "Morning! Are you ready to begin?"

A chorus of *shushes* slithers from nearly every corner to stun her into silence.

"Damn it, Poppy," an unfamiliar man hisses from behind a closed blue door. "Hush!"

"Sorry," she murmurs, her eyes bright, smile wry. Still smiling, she extends her hand for me, pale but with the nails a garish, glaring pink. "Come," she whispers. Barely whispers.

I take her hand, surprised by how cold she is. In contrast to her bubbly warm expressions, she is ice cold to the touch. I shiver as she leads me along through a set of cluttered rooms and into a strangely bare hallway.

"You should put on some boots," Poppy declares, eyeing my bare feet. She disappears and reappears with a set of leather shoes with long, reaching sides. Boots. "I got these for Daisy, but she hasn't worn them yet. You can borrow them if you'd like!"

She drops them at my feet, and one by one, I pull them on. They are sturdier than the sandals I wore in the other realm. More comfortable than Colleen's borrowed shoes. When I take a step, the soles thud, giving weight and noise to every movement.

"Thank you," I say to Poppy.

She beams and clasps her hands together. "Oh, it's so nice having someone to talk to. Who talks normally…" She casts a wary glance over her shoulder. "The others are so boring and silent. Oh, please come. Let's talk some more."

She babbles on as she opens a heavy, black door and ushers me into the room beyond.

"This is the storefront," she explains. "We sell everything and anything under the sun! Our prices are a bargain with the Altaris' guarantee. He likes it if we say that to customers." She giggles and eyes me from over her shoulder. "Well, not really, but I like to say it. The Altaris guarantee! We are here to please. Over there is the register. It's mainly for show. Here—" She flits behind the counter, and tugs open a cupboard door. "This is where we put the payment. Altaris will go through it later. We never take money here, only a fair exchange. I will show you! In the meantime, we can clean and dust. Altaris likes the dust, but it makes me sneeze." She races to a dustpan and broom and hands them to me. Then she changes her mind and uses both to clean the already gleaming floor. This room, at least, is sparklingly clean and as orderly as one could order a multitude of things.

There are books and gages, bottles of colorful liquid, stacks of fabric, and boxes upon boxes of gems and jewels.

"The shop is normally my job," Poppy chatters on happily, sweeping a pile of nonexistent dust. "I'm in charge here, because none of the others will come out this far. Sometimes Scythe but he prefers the other line of work—" She lowers her voice and raises a reddish eyebrow. "I hate it, so I stay in here. I was going to see if Daisy would help out, but she's still too sad. Poor Daisy."

"Who is Daisy?" I ask, if only out of politeness.

I suspect Poppy would tell me anyway, invited to or not.

She perches her chin on the top of her broom and grins, dancing on the tips of her toes. "Daisy is my new friend. The only other girl to leave the collective. A girl like us, I mean." She gestures to her slender frame. From appearance alone one would guess that she was no older than I am. Twenty-four, twenty-five at the latest.

Her eyes vibrate with youth exuberance, conveying an even younger age.

But there are some things that appearances cannot hide. Though she dances with the excitement and joy of a child, she carries herself with the grace of someone much, much older. Older than Caspian, even. Certainly older than me.

But then she flits about with all of the poise of a fae.

"Young at heart, I mean," she explains with an exaggerated sigh. "The others are so boring. So stuffy. But Daisy is nice. She'll like you, I bet. Even if you aren't a vamp, you seem nice."

"How many people...vamryre are here?" I ask.

She shrugs her thin shoulders and continues to sweep. "Don't know. Some have been here for ages and haven't woken up. Some wake up and never come back out again. Altaris says that we must let everyone grow 'accustomed' at their own pace. Daisy has been here for a year already and she only started to come around last month..." She trails off, biting her lip. "By 'come around,' I mean... She leaves her room, sometimes! I've seen her do it, and she's nice to me. She lets me dress her and do her hair. We will be the best of friends soon, I know it!"

Something in my heart aches as I watch her skip around the store-front and sweep. She seems so happy, but it is a mask she wears to disguise the pain lurking underneath. Underneath it all, she is so desperately lonely.

I know that feeling. I still remember how happy I was to see Day when he visited me. Speak to me. Acknowledge me.

"I like your tunic, Poppy," I say.

Her eyes sparkle. "Oh really?" She tugs at the hem of her brilliant green shirt and spins in a giddy circle. "Oh, thank you. Altaris says it's garish, but what does he know? I like you. Let me show you the ropes!"

She darts behind the counter and beckons me closer. There is a rope hanging on the wall. She pulls it, and on the other end of the room, a curtain is drawn back, revealing a gleaming door, wide windows, and brilliant yellow sunlight streaming in.

"I don't know why Altaris calls it that," Poppy admits, wrinkling her nose. "'The ropes,' but it sounds nice, doesn't it? Now, a customer should be coming soon. Just watch me."

As if on cue, a "customer" appears at the door, peering warily into the glass. They open the door and step inside; a man with red hair and a long, gray coat drawn tight up to his chin. He approaches the counter and gives Poppy a furtive glance.

"Order for 'J. Bim,'" he says.

"J. Bim," Poppy repeats with a nod. Then she yanks open the cupboard beside the one she showed me before. She rummages inside it, though over her shoulder, all I can see are dozens and dozens of brown paper sacks of varying sizes and shapes. With a grunt of triumph, Poppy seizes one and sets it on the counter.

"Order for Mr. Bim," she says, shoving the sack toward the man in question. Then she extends her hand, her smile dazzling. "Payment please."

"Ah, right. Payment." Mr. Bim glances over his shoulder as if expecting someone to descend from the shadows and strike him down. When no assailant appears, he snatches the paper bag to his chest and reaches into his pocket for a small metal trinket. Not money, I don't think. It is round and silver, with three holes drilled into the center. A small, round button.

"Pleasure doing business," Poppy trills, watching him go.

Then, she crouches and tucks the button carefully into the first cabinet. "There," she murmurs, bounding back upright. "All done. It is easy. The only real rule really is that payment must be given in exchange for every order."

"What do you sell here, exactly?" I ask, curious. Unnerved. Those brown parcels are unsettling, but in the way the dusty books at the back of the archives were. Not offensive per se. Just...

Ominous. Secret. Unusual.

"I don't know," Poppy declares with a blissful smile and a happy shrug. "But I like the work in the shop rather than doing the other chores. Labeling is boring and I hate the dank basement. So, I work in here."

She dashes to her broom again and pretends to sweep. When another customer enters, she performs the same awkward, strange exchange she did with the first.

A mysterious bag for a mysterious payment—a crumpled piece of paper in this case, which she treats with no less care than the silver button. Within hours, ten customers have come and gone, and ten strange objects now litter the bottom of the cupboard.

Suddenly, a heavy, tolling sound comes from behind us—a big, square box mounted onto the wall. It tolls, heavy and ringing like the bells back home. Ding. Dong. Ding.

"Lunchtime," Poppy declares happily while shimmying from behind the counter. "This is my break. Altaris says that everyone, every day, deserves a break now and again. I like to do some *calisthenics.*" As she skips to the door, she stretches her willowy limbs above her head. "Want to come with me? It's very fun, I promise. Very invigorating."

"She can't," Altaris replies from the mouth of the little hall leading to the main area of his "home." I didn't even notice him standing there. It's as if he appeared from thin air. Maybe he did. "This one is bound by biology in a way we are not, my darling. She must eat at lunchtime, not run around the city. You go on, my dear. Have fun."

"Okay!" Poppy slips from the main door and dances onto the street, her hair flying out behind her, blazing in the afternoon sun.

"Well, I can see she hasn't eaten you alive, at least," Altaris remarks with a small, cold smile. He doesn't intend to be nice. He is wary of me. More wary than I ever was with Caspian.

As though I am the one with fangs that snap and bite. As though I am the one with a reputation for drinking blood and draining victims dry.

"I think we've gotten off to the wrong start, you and I," the vamryre says, stalking forward. His hands are outstretched before him, a tray balanced on top. There is food on top of that. Steaming, warm, delicious-smelling food.

"It's been a while since we have a guest with your peculiar appetites," the man remarks, setting the tray onto the counter, within my reach—but not close enough for him to touch me. Or me, him.

"I admit my culinary skills are rather rusty, but I suppose that it is the thought that counts."

The thought that counts. I stare at the tray, my mouth watering, gaze still wary. This man despises me—I can see that. He doesn't even try to hide that. Yet...

The food he supplied for me is more than I've seen in one place, all at once. More variety than I've ever had. Soft, pillowy bread, not crusted and stale. Warm milk mixed with a delicious liquid that smells like earth. Yellow, sweet, fluffy eggs. Greasy strips of meat.

It is so much, yet it doesn't seem enough once I swallow down the last piece. In a way, I am still hungry—not physically. But... I want to taste other things. Eat other things. Find other things denied to me. Things I never knew one could want.

"It seems that you've gotten on with that well enough," Altaris says as I wipe my mouth with a white napkin supplied on the tray. He's been watching me from his corner near the little hall. Watching me the way I watched Caspian rip his brothers and sisters limb from limb.

Confused but not alarmed. Surprised but not entirely disgusted.

"Now that is out of the way, we can talk business, you and I," the vamryre claims, crossing his arms over his chest. "Your boy, the one of Cassius'."

I swallow again and nod. My Caspian. Mine.

"How ever did you come across him? I know little of that realm, but I am aware that intermingling is frowned upon."

"You had to..." I start to say. He had to be there. Everyone comes from the other realm. For a thousand years at least. Could he, perhaps, be from before that time? I don't know. For some reason, I suspect he wouldn't tell me, even if I asked. So, I don't. "He found me," I say.

"Ah." Altaris nods. "No doubt to stir up trouble. Cassius and his lot cause their fair share of damage, even out here. But the fact that now *you* are here..." He frowns and runs a pale finger along his chin. "That is the strange part, my darling. Something you must explain."

"I went through the portal," I say. A lie. The tunnel Caspian led me through was not the original portal written about in the official texts that litter the archives. It was a dirty place, forgotten and damp, yet festooned with fae magic. Fae stones.

"No, that is not what I am referring to. How did you make it through in one piece? Fae are not allowed to leave that little stables, that much I know. They forbid it."

"No," I say. "Fae can leave. Through the portal."

If they request to. If they want to. But who would? Surrounded by the beauty and safety of the Citadel, no full-blooded fae would want to leave.

"A lie I'm sure they feed your kind," Altaris remarks with a smile. "It's in the magic that created that place. Something the fae did to seal it away and sever their hiding place from this one. But it traps them there. Full-bloods at least. You, my dear, are a very interesting anomaly."

Anomaly. The term stings, seeming more insulting than *abomination*. It smarts, searing harsher than any wound ever inflicted by the Lord Master's punishments.

"Caspian," I say. "You said you can help him."

"Ah, yes. Frankly, I'm surprised that Cassius let him loose off his leash. He's been so very protective of that particular toy. He must be seething." He smiles as if he knows of him, this Cassius.

But how? If he has never been to the other realm, then how?

"His poor mind is a right sort of damaged," Altaris continues with a laugh. Then a sigh. He is puzzled by the damage of this so-called Cassius' mind. Puzzled and intrigued. Maybe a little excited.

Like me, he loves a mystery, though for very different reasons. I liked the challenge and the risk. He prefers the thrill, and he very much enjoys never solving his mystery in the end. It's the unraveling he enjoys.

"Typically, I would assume it would take him a few decades to come around again."

"Decades?" My heart hammers. I feel so heavy. Decades to a vamryre is mere seconds in mortal life. But fae, as long-lived as they are, still live mortal lives. I am mortal. For me a decade is not measured in seconds. Ten years. Ten agonizing years. Several stretches of ten agonizing years.

Could I wait for him so long?

This mystery doesn't require any solving on my part: *yes*. Even if it took a thousand years, I would wait for him.

"There is a way to speed up the process, I suspect," Altaris adds.

I brace my hands on the counter to keep from lunging across it. From grabbing the front of his pretty purple clothing and demanding an answer.

"Really? Tell me!"

He laughs and unfurls his arms to lace all ten of his tall fingers together. "An experimental option to be sure," he admits—but there is something he is hiding beneath those words. A threat. A dare. "You would have to put your trust in him, and I would have to put my trust in you."

"How?" I demand, impatient. Desperate. "Tell me!"

"For starters, you brought something with you. I can smell it, bundled in ragged cloth and decaying floral. Tell me what it is. Do not lie."

I hesitate. For so long, the sketchbook was my secret to hold. To protect. I can't risk losing it.

Then I think of Caspian, poor Caspian.

"A sketchbook," I say. "I took it from the archives, but it didn't belong."

"Oh my." Altaris tilts his head back, his gaze reflective. "Interesting. Interesting..."

He trails off, thinking whatever dark thoughts a vamryre might think.

I fidget. "Caspian—"

"Helping him will take time. You would need to wait for the moment to present itself," Altaris says. "But you will also need to submit to... Well, let's just call it an examination. You are a strange creature, you do realize. I am sure, as naive as you are, even you do realize that?"

I do. Don't care. My nature is dirty and unwelcome, but it doesn't matter. Caspian is all that matters. For him, I will submit to anything.

"Just tell me what to do."

"For a start you can tell me what you are," Altaris counters, leaning in closer. His curiosity is evident. Draining. It's as though he prefers to sink his fangs into the mind of his prey rather than their throat. He aims to drink their knowledge. He aims to drain their very essence dry. "Tell me where you are from and start from the beginning. Should you lie to me, even once, I shall send you away and you can wait for your boy on the street. Understand?"

"Ask me," I croak. Even if he bleeds me dry, I have to submit.

He sighs and raises a black eyebrow in my direction. The glance he shoots me next is unreadable. In an instant, he transforms from strange, willowy stranger, to a hint of ancient vamryre. A creature that transcends all time. Decades to him are mere seconds. A handful of rocks in a desert of sand.

"Though you came through the portal, you were born of fae, were you not?"

I nod. "One of three." It stings to say as much out loud. One of three. A sinful burden. An admission of my abominable nature.

But the vamryre doesn't hiss and exclaim, "Impossible!" He nods. His eyes gleam. Licking his lips, he waits for more. He may have fed me, but this sates him more than a tray full of food ever could. A tray full of blood, even.

"Three?"

"A girl. A boy. Another girl," I rasp. "A shame upon house Aurelius. Punishment for my sins. I am a shameful thing. A dirty thing."

Altaris laughs. "Oh, my dear, I think that shame is reserved for your mother. My, my, what I wouldn't give to know what she'd gotten up to."

My mother? I frown and shake my head to clear it. Their mother—the rightful Day and Dawn. To me, she is a stranger. A remnant spoken about only in harsh whispers. I've never seen her. Never looked upon her face.

Day has never mentioned her once.

"Night Aurelia gave birth to me," I say. "But she is not my mother. I am a dirty shameful thing—"

"Aurelia, you say." Altaris' eyes widen with greedy, giddy glee. He rubs his hands together and rushes toward me all at once. His aim is a bookshelf crammed onto the wall behind me. He licks the tip of his finger and traces it along a row of gleaming leather spines. Then he tugs on one and flips it open.

Triumphant, he lets out a roar of a laugh. "Ah, I knew it. House Aurelius, oh dear, have they done it now. Lord of all lords. Paragons of all houses of the fae. Oh yes, this is rich." He looks over his shoulder at me and chuckles. "Oh, this is so *very* rich. What I wouldn't give to know who your father is."

The question confuses me. "My father is Night Aurelius." Not really, but correcting the context now doesn't feel important. Altaris is not one for decorum, and I am too tired to care. Suddenly, I feel so very tired.

"Oh no," Altaris replies, slamming his book closed. "The sire of the other two in your litter, maybe. But of you? No. Your father is another creature. A forbidden creature. Oh yes, but who? That is the question." He flits to another bookshelf, tapping his chin, his eyes blazing with churning, inescapable interest.

I watch him tear through book after book. I watch him murmur to himself and practically squeal with glee. I grow more confused with every passing moment. More confused. More unwanted. More hopelessly lost.

"My father is from house Aurelius," I say as Altaris turns his back to me, hunched over another book. "I am a dirty shameful thing. A disgrace. I do not reflect upon those who bore me—"

"Oh, poppycock!" Altaris growls at what he reads in his current book and then tosses it. He snatches another and flies through the pages. It's as if he isn't really reading. Just glancing at each page and remembering the wealth of knowledge already stored in his skull. "They may have brainwashed you and fed you their lies, but you, my darling, are not fae. You are a half breed of some kind. A hybrid of some kind. But of what?"

Half breed. Hybrid.

"I am a stain on house Aurelius," I say, my voice faint and weak. The highest house of all the fae. The only house I have ever known. The only identity I have ever known: broken one, unwanted one, but still fae...

I am still fae.

Yet, I always knew I wasn't. Something else. Unknown. Corrupted.

"Oh, look at you!" Altaris glares at me in utter contempt. "Carrying on like that you'll scare the customers."

Customers. A new one arrives amid the jiggling of a tiny bell affixed to the door. They enter in a hurry, nose buried in an open leather case balanced on a slender hip. "Hey Altaris, I've got a job to get to, so I'll pick it up later... Oh!" The figure looks up, their blue eyes wide. "It's you! Niamh. What are you doing here?"

"Ah, Colleen, darling," Altaris drawls, stalking toward her. In comparison with her slight frame, he is a giant, yet undeniably graceful as he extends a hand toward her.

Rather than take it in greeting, Colleen fishes an item from her bag and carefully places it on the vamryre's palm: a silver comb, far grander than the wooden one the Citadel Mother provided for me to use.

"I'll be back at six sharp for it," she says. Then she looks at me and flashes a sheepish grin. "I heard about the mess that happened at Mo's—"

"And you won't tell her a thing about my new guests, I am sure," Altaris remarks while drifting past me to stand behind the counter.

"Of course not!" Colleen shrugs to sling the strap of her case over one shoulder. "Our relationship is strictly a working one. I don't get paid, it isn't my business. I'm glad to see you're okay, though. Where is the vamp? He get sent back?"

"Why don't you run along, dear?" Altaris smiles, but the expression doesn't reach his eyes. "I'll have your item ready. Six sharp."

Colleen nods and heads for the door. Then she looks back at me. "I'll come visit you another day, if you're still here. A lot of my clients live out this way anyway. Bye!"

The door jiggles to mark her departure, and Altaris sighs.

"Go!" He flicks his fingers dismissively in my direction. "I will tend the shop from here. Go! Let me have some time to think. Oh, but one last thing my dear..."

His voice calls me back before I can run into the main house and out of his sight. I suddenly, so very badly, need to be out of anyone's sight. I can't stand the sunlight on my face. Altaris' gleeful, judging, curious looks. Collen's wary, pitying glances. I can't stand for anyone to look at me and not see what I've always been told.

A dirty fae, but fae. A dirty thing, but still fae.

What am I if I'm not even fae?

A nothing. A disgrace. An empty, nothing being.

"Give me your word that you will let me attempt to bring your boy back with my own methods, hmm? Even at risk to yourself? You will let me try?"

Will I let him? For Caspian, the only one to ever look at me and see a dirty fae creature but want me anyway. Would I risk myself for him?

"Of course," I rasp before darting into the safety of the main house and its towering piles of stuff.

Of course, I'd do this for him.

Of course, I would do anything to bring him back.

Because if I have to wait decades, I may die before then. If I am not fae, but something else... I may not survive.

CHAPTER 38
Caspian

I can smell her. That sweet thing.

I can't remember what she is or what she wants. What she looks like. Why she's here, always near. I can't even touch her—reach out and grip and grasp.

The smell of her is enough for me. Beautiful, terrible, lingering little scent. All mine to breathe in. The world's to take.

She isn't mine, not really.

But...

More than Cassius ever was. More than anyone I have ever tasted or tormented or fucked. More than any other soul I may have killed...

This one, I want. I want it so badly I'll kill to have it. Bite and tear.

I want it so badly I will remember...

All of the bad things.

The many, many, many, MANY times I have sinned.

Mainly for him, but not always. Cassius wound up the key in my back, but I would dance like a little windup doll in their direction with glee. My many victims. Their cries are numerous, scratching and clawing, and scraping at my skull.

There is no collective to shut them out. No Cassius to keep their souls at bay. They haunt me: in memories and images and violent sounds and smells.

Oh fuck, I remember everything.

And her…

She is a light dancing in the darkness. She wandered to me willingly. Came to me willingly. Danced with my dangerous heart out of her own accord.

We will kill her, a part of me hisses and murmurs with joy. *Kill her. Rip her. Taste her. Eat her.*

However, there is another part of me. A forgotten part. It doesn't know what it wants or why it even exists. I barely remember it.

Maybe I do.

A name. A life. A purpose. A meaning.

He existed once. What was his name? I can't remember. I can't remember.

Can't…

Then I smell sweet air on soft skin and I do remember.

Collin. Someone named Collin. I was him once. Once.

No more. Never can I ever be him again.

But he existed once, a part of me that Cassius will never touch. After all these years, he hasn't snuffed him out. Collin. He is who I cling to in this torment of mindless thought.

He is my anchor without my master, Cassius.

Collin. Someone named Collin. I was him once.

I have no choice but to be him again—an amalgamation of him and who I am now. Caspian.

I am Caspian.

Was Caspian.

Still am Caspian.

I want to remain as Caspian until the day I fucking die.

CHAPTER 39

Niamh

I lie beside my Caspian and stroke my fingers through his hair. I speak to his unyielding, emotionless face.

I tell him all about the dark, wicked things in my heart and mind.

"How can I not be fae?" I ask him.

Easy, the silence replies. *You knew you were a corrupted thing. A dirty, unwanted thing.*

You knew.

You knew!

How dare you take offense now.

But that is the thing...

"I was something," I say to the darkness, shrouding us both. Me and my Caspian. "I was something, even if it was dirty and broken. I was something. How can I be nothing? If I am not fae... I am nothing."

I bore my abominable nature with shame and pain, but also pride. I lived among the fae, even if I wasn't fully one of them. In some small way, I was still a part of them.

But now?

"I am worthless," I tell him, my Caspian. "I am nothing. If I am not even a tiny bit fae, then I am nothing."

Caspian doesn't reply. He sits and stares in silence. Even as tears roll down my face and wet his lap, he doesn't react with violence or annoyance. He doesn't react at all.

Not even as I sob in the heavy dark and mourn the life I took for granted.

I thought by leaving the other realm behind, I could fulfill my selfish wish. My only desire.

But in the end...

I left myself behind. There is no unwanted fae creature out here. No Niamh.

Just a thing with no face and no name. No soul.

A truly unwanted thing.

I WASTE THE SECONDS AWAY, WISHING THEY WERE decades. I changed my mind. I could spend centuries here alone with him. Centuries of waiting. Centuries upon centuries of lying against his cold, hard skin and trying to find warmth in it.

Centuries of waiting for him to come back, my Caspian.

He would scoff at me were he here fully. Hiss and laugh at my tears and my pain.

You foolish fae, he'd snarl. *You are a foolish, stupid fae.*

And it would be enough. To hear him declare me as such would be enough. Enough to silence Altaris and the Lord Master and everyone.

What he deemed me as would be enough. I would become it.

Fae.

Not-fae.

Niamh.

Someone else.

I would become whatever he wanted if…

No. Because that is the thing about my Caspian. He would scoff at any attempt to change what I am. Any attempts to erase my pain and shame. He saw me as an unwanted creature, first and foremost.

A creature to kill.

One to destroy.

He saw those things in me and wanted those pieces of a corrupted soul anyway. He wanted me. Niamh. At least, he thought he wanted Niamh.

Was it Niamh he ever truly wanted?

Or merely to rebel. To shun his master and needle him with the thought of me. The image of me. His master wanted him so very badly. Badly enough to give a toy he could never rightfully claim. Badly enough to send his siblings to fetch him.

Badly enough to keep him whole, even if his mind is in ruins.

His master wanted him, oh so very badly.

So, I will have to fix him. I will have to shove his pieces back together and remind him of who and what he is.

"You are Caspian," I tell him softly. "You drained ten people dry in the Bleeding Hearts Motel. You ripped people apart limb from limb. I watched you do it. You frighten me. You thrill me. Oh, how you thrill me... You are Caspian and I want you as you are. Come back. Come back!"

He doesn't. Even as the seconds drip into minutes, then hours, he never comes back.

I am alone again.

Even when Poppy knocks on my door and declares, "Morning!" I am alone.

I wallow in this loneliness. If I am to have no race or identity, then this is who I shall be. A shell of a shell of a shell. I will wear a bright pink dress and let my hair hang limply. I will walk like a ghost and stare at nothing.

Be nothing.

I will let myself fade entirely into nothing.

But I can't. Caspian needs me. Caspian. Caspian.

So I will be this dirty, broken thing. I will remain standing with my head high. I will be, even if it means losing the part of me that was always fae. Not fae.

In a sense, perhaps I am still fae.

But something else. Mixed with something else.

My head spins as I linger in the storefront while Poppy tends to every guest. When lunchtime comes, she skips outside while Altaris brings me another tray of food.

I eat woodenly, tasting nothing. For Caspian, I eat, tasting nothing. For me—whoever that is—I eat, tasting nothing. I eat and eat until I can't swallow another bite.

"Good girl," Altaris remarks as he takes my empty tray away. His tone is softer today. His gaze is different. Pitying. Worried.

Whatever he planned, will he do it now? Wake up my Caspian?

No.

"I don't appreciate your pouting," he says with a sniff. He raises a wrist to his mouth and buries his nose in the silken purple sleeve. "It's crowding the air around here. Making it sullen. I think, however, I have found something that will cheer you up."

My heart races and sputters. "C-Caspian—"

"No," he says over me. He lowers his arm and flounces over to a shelf crammed with books. Having worked here for a day, I'm not even sure what the purpose of these items are. They don't seem to be for sale—the customers seem to request only what has already been prepared for them, in those brown paper bags. None of them felt heavy enough to be a book.

Even so, Altaris tuts under his teeth while running his finger along the spine of a book. With a grunt of triumph, he frees it and offers it to me.

"Some reading material to pique your interest," he explains before dropping the volume onto the counter. It lands with a soft thud and sends up a choking cloud of dust. I cough, my eyes watering, as I warily inspect the cover.

It isn't bound in leather and embossed with gold like the books in the archives. Instead, a scratchy black material forms the cover, and the title is stamped into the fabric in peeling silver paint: *The Other Realms; a history.*

"Other realms?" I say, skeptical already. This must be a fiction novel, for there are only two realms. The mortal world and the other realm.

"Read it," Altaris says. He watches me carefully while stroking his chin. I can't read his expression. It isn't cold like before. Perhaps, questioning. He isn't commanding me to read as much as he's... daring me to. "Or don't. In any case, it's yours. Now take it up to your room and come down with a better attitude, tomorrow. Off with you, now. Go!"

I take his book and return to the green room with it tucked under my arm. Even as I crouch beside Caspian, I don't read it yet. Instead, I lay my head on his lap and wait.

Two Days.

Two decades.

I'm not even sure which timespan feels longer.

CHAPTER 40

Niamh

On the third day, Colleen returns. She arrives just after lunchtime when Poppy has already gone for her walk and Altaris left me a tray of food. She enters the shop, unbothered by the dusty air or the piles of pointless things. She navigates them as though she could do so with her eyes closed.

She knows this place.

Likes this place.

A dreamy expression comes over her as she leans against the counter. She shoves aside a crate of glass bottles filled with colorful, mysterious liquid and sets her case down gingerly in its stead.

"Well, you seem right at home here," she declares while eyeing me from head to toe. "I'm so used to seeing Poppy here, I had a right fright when I came in the other day. How have you been?"

My heart aches. I don't know how to answer the question. Mortal customs are all so strange. Though I haven't left the safe house in three days, I can hear the chatter from the street seep in through the walls, both in here and upstairs. Good day, they say. How are you? The answer is always the same, whether or not there is pain in their voice as they reply. Whether or not they sound tired or frail or in utter despair.

Perhaps, it is their custom. To lie.

"I am fine," I say.

Colleen nods. "Yeah fucking right. You look pale as a ghost and exhausted, to say the least. Is the old vamp overworking you? If so, you just say the word and I'll—" She flexes her fingers menacingly. "Give him the old zap!"

My eyes widen. "No, I am fine!" As surly and abrasive as he is, Altaris is the only one who can bring back Caspian. He promised to.

Colleen throws her head back and laughs, sending her blond curls bouncing wildly. "Don't worry! I won't go after him. I doubt my magic would work on him, anyway. That old vamp is a mystery unto himself. Da says he's been here since the dawn of time, the grumpy old fart."

"How do you know him?" Beside me, Colleen seems so much like the other mortals who pass by the windows of this shop. Radiating life in her green tunic and blue pants. Vibrant. Youthful.

The polar opposite of a home for discarded, empty vamryre.

It seems like a logical question.

Colleen's eyes turn downcast, and she wrinkles her mouth. "My Da used to bring me here. A long time ago."

She doesn't want to say more. I regret even asking in the first place. There are so many rules here—though they vary from the other realm in scope and function. There, the rules are to maintain order. Give purpose.

In this realm, the rules are to respect invisible, unspoken boundaries. It's much like navigating a new language. Learning to read without a stern, persistent Day to teach me.

It's daunting. Yet I want to learn more.

"Besides, it's close to the action, where the boneys patrol," Colleen says, smiling once more. "That means plenty of grifters and scum getting injured. Plenty of wounds to heal for pay."

"Boney?" She isn't the only one who's used that term. Altaris has as well.

"Think of them as the police. They govern us mundane and keep any stragglers from the other realms in check. Keep the order, so to speak. We call them boneys because if you break the rules, they break your bones. Or even take a few as a warning. Fingers. Toes. Brutal as hell, but it's necessary." She glances toward the door leading deeper inside the safe house. "Some of them vamps like to come here and run amok. So do the other kind, lunaria. I've never seen a fae before. To be fair, I haven't met many of you other realm folk at all. Except Slyvie, but she's been out on her own for years—"

"A fae?" I question, my eyes wide. Altaris was wrong. Full-blooded fae can leave through the portal. He was wrong. Very wrong.

"Oh, no." Colleen shakes her head. "She's lunaria, through and through. Moonlights, pun intended, as a bounty hunter for the boneys. Tough as nails but with a heart of gold. She's my best client. In fact, I'm starting to think she likes the pain of the process more than anything."

I wince at the reminder of her healing magic.

"How can you do that?" I ask her.

She raises a slim hand and inspects it in the sunlight filtering in through the main windows. "Don't know really. Not all mundane can do tricks. The ones that can try to trace it back through their lineage. Some even claim to be descendants of fae or the like. In any case, I am what I am and it helps me make a living."

She smooths her hands down the front of her shirt.

"I should really get back to class before another customer comes," she says, reaching for her case. "It's so awkward running into one. It's a small world, n' all. Imagine going to the post office and seeing another Altaris regular working the counter."

She laughs, but the sound doesn't quite seem to match her expression.

"What is a regular?" I ask. Once again, I'm toeing some invisible boundary. Colleen raises an eyebrow, but unlike the previous question, this one she doesn't mind.

"You don't know what people come here for, do you?" She leans toward me and makes a show of glancing over her shoulder as if to check for a vamryre lurking in the shadows. Not that it matters. They can hear us through walls and floors and yards of space. "It's for mementos. Things you don't want to forget. Feelings you can't find anymore." Her voice softens. "Good luck charms. Love spells and trinkets. Silly stuff like that. Not everyone believes the hogwash, but they show up regularly enough."

They do. Every day, though not many, a steady stream of customers arrive and leave.

"Speak of the devil," Colleen says as the doorbell chimes and a slender woman shuffles inside. "See you around, Niamh!"

"Bye," I tell her as she skips out into the sun.

Then I turn my attention to the woman. By now, I've seen enough of the furtive figures come in and out to know my role. Stand here. Smile. Wait for them to give me a name.

She doesn't. Huddled in a brown coat, she twists her fingers around her graying black hair. Her dark eyes dart to and fro. Almost tentatively, she finally approaches the counter. Rather than speak, she eyes the surface of the counter and waits.

"I... Name please?" My voice sounds so high-pitched. Despite two days of serving customers, I've rarely spoken to anyone. Anyone but the Lord Master, Day, the inhabitants of the safe house and Colleen.

The woman doesn't seem to hear me. She continues to twirl her hair around and around. Then, she places a trembling hand on the counter. Cupped against the palm is a tiny object that she leaves behind, her gaze glued to it, hollow cheeks gaunt with tension.

"I need that fixed," she says in a thready whisper. She nods to the object: beautiful and small. A bright blue bulb affixed to a slender white handle. "Now, please."

I stammer. "Um, name please?"

She barely looks up from the object. "J. Green."

I crouch below the counter and open the cupboard. Reach inside and scan the brown bags piled inside. *J. Green. J. Green.*

I look and look.

"I'm sorry," I say, rising to my feet. "I don't see anything for that name—"

"I need you to fix it!" The woman lunges for my arm. "Please! It's just a small little rattle. I need to feel the happiness again. Please!"

"That is enough!" The bellowing voice comes from the doorway connecting the shop to the safe house. Altaris stands there, but suddenly his green eyes aren't charming, neither is his voice. "You were warned," he says while advancing on the woman.

She snatches her rattle from the counter and huddles in his shadow.

"Three times is the limit. You have exceeded it. You need to go." He snaps his fingers, startling the woman into looking up. Their eyes meet—his vibrant and piercing, hers sad and bloodshot with unspent tears.

I watch in morbid fascination. It feels wrong. Yet I can't turn away.

Something is happening to both Altaris and the woman. He looms larger while she seems to deflate. Her hands fall limply to her sides. The tension leaves her small body, making her stand taller. The haggard, pained expression on her face is replaced by a blank, empty smile.

And Altaris lords over her, speaking in a voice that resonates with more power than the Lord Master themself. "You lost your way," he tells her. "You are lost. Turn around and leave. You will never return to this place again."

"Yes," the woman says with her dreamy smile. Then she turns and leaves, her rattle clutched limply in one hand.

"What did you do to her?" I ask as the bell above the door tolls. The sound is mockingly cheerful in contrast to how I feel. Cold all over.

Altaris shrugs and runs his hands along the front of his purple jacket. "That was me taking care of a pesky repeat customer. Next time anyone comes in without an order to pick up, you call for me or Poppy. Now where on earth has that girl gone?"

He storms off, flicking imaginary lint from his clothing.

Another customer arrives, but they follow the same unspoken script the others had. After they leave, another enters. As I fish their order from the cupboard, the door swings open and Poppy rushes in.

"I'm so sorry!" she exclaims, her red hair covered by a bright green hood. "I didn't mean to be late. I had an unexpected detour to make—oh, Daisy, this way, darling!" She waves frantically to beckon another figure who stands resolutely in the doorway.

Slight and petite, the woman wears a similar jacket to Poppy's but in bright pink with the hood drawn haphazardly over her long, straggly hair. It too is also a shade of pink, but the color is patchy. Unnatural. Swatches of white-blond hair peek through, every bit as brilliant as Caspian's.

But, if possible, her eyes are even emptier. Unchecked, her hood slips even further back from her face. As a result, a sizzling sound emanates from her, reminiscent of the sound a log would make when tossed onto a roaring fire. Caught in a strip of sunlight, the tip of her button nose is quickly turning red.

"Oh dear!" Poppy rushes toward her and gently steers her inside.

Unbothered, the customer before me places their payment on the counter, takes their paper bag and leaves.

"Poppy, what on earth?" Altaris' voice rings out from the hallway though he doesn't appear.

"I'm sorry! Daisy got out again. Luckily Scythe tracked me down and we were able to bring her back without another...*incident.*" She herds Daisy forward toward the safe house entrance. "Go inside, darling. Back to the basement with Ginni. That's where your duties are, remember?"

"Well thank heavens for small miracles," Altaris remarks sardonically. "I'll try to have Ginni keep a better eye on her. The last thing we need is another incident. Those damn boneys are still breathing down my neck about the last one."

"I know, Altaris!" Poppy chirps, once Daisy is safely beyond the narrow hall. "No more incidents! No more accidents!" She claps her hands and spins to face me. "I apologize for my lateness. Shall we get back to work?"

Radiating boundless energy, Poppy takes care of the next few customers before flitting around the storefront, sweeping up her imaginary dirt. It's the dust in this place that could use cleaning. I find a rag and help her, wiping down the forgotten items, left abandoned on their various pedestals and shelves.

It's only when an impatient Altaris appears and loudly clears his throat that I realize it's nighttime and Poppy is gone.

"Poppy has requested the rest of the evening off tomorrow," Altaris explains, "so you will tend to the store alone. We will stay open a little later than normal. Do you understand?"

I nod. I understand.

"Good. Now go."

I return to my room and find Caspian unchanged, staring at nothing. I sit by his side and close my eyes. Open them. Carefully, I reach down to the floor and find the book Altaris gave me.

Huddled under the sole lamp in the ceiling, I open it.

Then I read to him.

The tale unfolding in these pages is a strange one. Not fiction—yet it must be. The recollections are too dryly written however, with every air of the historical texts in the archives.

Only wrong.

All, all wrong.

It tells of a time before the Citadel. Before the other realm, even.

It tells of creatures and beings born of blood that isn't pure. That aren't strictly fae, lunaria, or vamryre. *Hybrids,* the author calls them. Rare things. Powerful beings, capable of things beyond any sole race.

Creatures of power.

Creatures of dangerous, evil power.

CHAPTER 41
Caspian

Her voice is a fucking melody. I hate it. Despise it.

Crave it. Like a thread or a lifeline, I can grip it tight. Drag myself along this desolate landscape and find some semblance of clarity again.

Or not.

If I resist her, I could stay here forever in the quiet, far from Cassius or any other probing mind. Here, no one can ever own me again.

No one but her.

"...inception after the vamryre were all but wiped out," she says. "Only three of their 'pure' lineage remained. Cassius, Nataniel and Pol. By that time the fae had also been decimated with just twelve houses remaining..."

She speaks on and on, painting words into the air. Creating magic with that gentle voice. I could spend an eternity listening to her.

Never again would I have to go back and crawl into that ruined shell of a mind.

Never again.

"...hybrids."

Something is wrong. Pain laces that voice, dulling the beautiful song. Some part of me prefers it—her pain. It's so damn sweet to these evil, rotten ears.

Then, she continues to speak. The pain gets sharper. The hungry creature in my skull dies down. Although her pain is beautiful, it does not belong. Not here. Not now.

"Hybrids are rare creatures known for the unique properties of their blood, for it transcends the power imbued in any other race. A single drop of hybrid blood can transform the mind of even vamryre. The affected creature is then bound to the will of the monster who tempted it..."

She trails off and another part of me rails. Rages.

I want that voice. I need it.

To find my way out of this empty, useless skull, I need to hear it.

Hear her.

CHAPTER 42
Niamh

I wake up slumped against Caspian's shoulder, the infernal book still open on my lap. After Poppy cheerfully knocks on my door, I wash up, put on that pink, flowy dress, and head down to the shop.

The day proceeds normally, with the usual amount of customers. When Poppy returns at the end of lunchtime, she happily dances past. "I am going to a concert. A boy asked me to one. A pretty boy. But I am taking Daisy! Oh, you can come too if you want?" She beams at me, dreamily sighing at the thought of her concert.

"I can't," I say.

Because something is happening tonight. Something big is happening tonight. Something wrong.

The air in this place is all wrong. Stilted. Stifling.

Caspian. I don't like this air. I should take Caspian away. But where?

"Okay!" Poppy skips by into the main house. I hear a door open and slam with mindless, innocent noise. A chorus of shushes rises up.

"Poppy! Damn it, Poppy! Hush, Poppy."

I wish the noise would wake Caspian. Bring him back.

But it doesn't.

I am left in the storefront alone. I have to tend to the next customer alone.

A woman with sad gray eyes shuffles to the counter and whispers to me, "Order for A. Geem." A. Geem. I find a parcel with her name written on it under the counter. I hand it to her. Extend my palm.

"Payment please," I request politely.

She nods and drops a hairpin onto my hand. "Payment given. Good day."

Good day.

Bad day.

Long, boring day.

More customers arrive, but none wake up Caspian. None of them alone seem to have an answer to who or what I am. They barely look at me, fixated on their mysterious orders.

Payment.

Order.

Payment.

It goes like that until darkness descends, and the customers, one by one, trickle away. An hour passes without a new one coming. Another hour.

I should leave the shop and return to Caspian, but I can't. Only Altaris can give the order, and he isn't around. Only he can free me from this monotony, but he isn't around.

So, I sweep. I tidy the already neat piles of knick-knacks and books. I sweep the spotless floor. I wipe the windows with a dry rag, and I wait and wait.

No one comes. It's too late for any shopping now. So very late. I should find Altaris and ask for this shift to end. I start to. I've barely reached the small hall when the bells above the door chime.

Ding. Dong.

Someone comes in. A customer.

Not a customer. There are three of them, and they do not seem to desire whatever could be in one of Altaris' paper bags. Their eyes fixate on me. Greedy, dangerous eyes.

"Hello, beautiful," one of them says. "You're a ways from your home, ain't you?"

Ain't I? No. Because I have no home. Nowhere without Caspian. Except without Caspian. Unless he wakes up and changes. Unless he decides he no longer wants me.

I swallow hard. Try to remain polite. "Can I help you?"

"We came to buy something," a second man grumbles, his voice devious and rasping. It crawls over my skin like dry, scraping fingertips.

"Yeah," the third man laughs, looming tall above the other two. "Buy something."

Run! The voice comes from nowhere, whispered at the back of my mind. As if I were part of a vamryre collective, it comes. Commands.

Niamh, run!

I reach for the door.

The three men laugh in unison. They stalk toward me. Reach toward me.

I tug on the doorknob, but it doesn't turn. The door won't open. I bang on it, but it refuses to open.

"Altaris?" My voice rings out. Silence answers. "Altaris!"

I bang on the door.

The men descend.

One of them snatches my wrist and drags me back, lays me flat on top of the counter beneath three sets of peering eyes.

"A beauty, ain't she?" One of them hisses. "Bet she'll fetch a nice right price."

"She better," the first man replies, rummaging through his black coat. "But the bastard wanted us to check her first. Catalog her and what not. Stupid vampire prick. Thinks he has us on a leash or something." He finds what he's looking for and raises it. A knife, gleaming and wicked.

He raises it. Another man extends my wrists and raises it.

The knife descends and bites and tears.

"Jesus, Ace! Don't cut er' fucking hand off. We need her intact. At least somewhat. We need her holes intact, at least."

The man with the knife lowers it. Hisses in annoyance. "Didn't work. The sample must not be large enough or sumthin."

"What do you mean, it didn't work?" The second man snatches the blade. Lowers it.

Straight down into my chest.

I breathe blood. Bleed it out in torrents and drops—but beneath my skin. The knife in my chest keeps it all in.

Until the man rips the blade out and lowers it again. A noise sounds. Above my screaming, a noise sounds. Ding. Ding.

The door opening?

No. Something else. A device the men hold between them and eye with confused, frowning expressions.

"What the fuck does that mean?" One of them wonders.

"Don't care," another snaps. "Whatever she is, she's pretty and young and will fetch a nice price. Help me grab her."

Grab me. To take me away. From Caspian. From the mortal realm, perhaps.

They aim to take me away.

"No!" I kick out with flailing legs. Lash out with one whole arm and one gaping and bleeding. I shout. Scream. Fight. Bite a hand that comes to cover my mouth.

I won't go. They can't take me.

"Stupid bitch!" One of them howls, painfully bitten. He steps back, holding his hand to his chest. He steps back in fear of me.

"She's a wild, little thing. Hold her still. A bit of happy medicine will send her right off."

Right off. Away.

I can't go away.

"No!" I kick. I scream. I bite. "No! No! Let go of me! LET GO OF ME!"

I scream. So loud that I drown them out. So loud that it doesn't matter if I am fae or not-fae or nothing at all. I scream so loud that those in the other realm could hear.

I scream and scream because I am not nothing. I exist. I can scream, and so I exist.

No one will take that from me.

No one will ever take me away.

Not from anyone. Not from Caspian. Especially not from Caspian.

Yes, I hear him whisper. In my head, I hear him whisper it. *No one will ever take you away.*

Because the men holding me down are gone. They've been ripped away by an unseen force and I am left panting and gaping at a garish, purple ceiling.

I am crying. My chest hurts. My arm hurts. But pain is not why I am crying.

Relief is.

Because I can hear him. His voice, in my skull and in my ear.

"I am here," he says. Angry. Bitter. Vengeful. "Stop crying. Stop crying! I am here."

Caspian. He is here, and he will never leave me again.

I will never let him leave me again.

CHAPTER 43
Caspian

I hold her. Stupid little fae. Spoiled, greedy, selfish fae. I hold her in my arms and make her go silent. I press my mouth to hers. I kiss her so deeply it hurts just to make her silent.

But she isn't. I will never be able to silence her again.

Because...

She is in my skull. In the place that Cassius used to rest, linger, and slither. She is there now, all mine, gentle and soothing. Frantic and panicked. She is in my skull now, Niamh, and she says...

Caspian. Caspian. Don't leave me. Caspian. Caspian.

"Shut up," I tell her out loud. Hiss it against her quivering throat. I ignore her bleeding blood, and I tell her over and over again. "Shut up. I am here. Shut up!"

I am here, with her in a room that is unfamiliar, around bodies that are unfamiliar. With other vamryre that are unfamiliar.

Not part of the collective. Part of me. They don't reek of Cassius.

They are different. Broken toys that wiggled free of the all-encompassing web. They escaped into the mortal realm. Hide here like vermin. Free but fearful and scurrying. Always scurrying.

I don't know this. Don't know their names. She does.

Altaris. Poppy. Scythe. Her thoughts unfurl to me like those books she loved to read. Loves to read, still. Her mind is unending to me, cleaner and neater and emptier than Cassius'.

Her mind is the most beautiful fucking thing I have ever felt in all of existence. Even her body didn't feel as welcoming and soft. As inviting. As tempting to break and tear.

But I won't. Her mind is a paradise, and I won't tear it. I won't break and destroy. Not yet. Maybe not ever.

I lurk in her mind, and it is a safe place. A beautiful, perfect place.

Cassius can never touch me here. In her mind, he can never find me again.

"I missed you," she tells me. Over and over, she says it, her voice rasping, tears still spilling from her eyes. "You left me. You left me. I missed you..."

She missed me. A greedy, stupid emotion. Selfish. Wrong. Disgusting. Missed.

I would never ever miss Cassius. He misses me. Misses owning me. Controlling me. Misses smothering me.

Her desire, however, differs from his. It feels cleaner than his. As gentle as her thoughts are, there is a desperation in her loneliness. Her longing for me is genuine, not boastful. Prideful. Jealous.

Her longing for me is so damn sweet, like honey. Wine. It makes my mouth water, and my blood starts to pump and surge beneath my skin. Or perhaps it is her blood? Her mind is connected to her body and therefore, I feel it the same way I can feel my own. Pulsing and alive and free.

Not dead.

Not decaying.

Not endless, wallowing Cassius chasing after dreams and things he doesn't truly want and can never have.

Her mind is so damn sweet.

Her body is so damn soft.

She is all mine. All mine.

Apart from Cassius, I will never know hunger again.

CHAPTER 44
Niamh

I am at peace. I know him, and I am at peace. Peace becomes a part of me, such a fragile little thing. It slips into my skull, unaware. It blots the bad things out.

Poof.

Misery and fear no longer exist. In my mind, there is Caspian, a brilliant, blazing thing. He makes the darkness vanish. He makes the fear insignificant.

He makes it no longer matter whether I am fae or not.

Whether I am a monster or not.

I hold onto him, and I can breathe again. I hold onto him, and I feel again. I hold onto him, and I forget...

All of the dark, ugly things that threaten to swallow me.

I hold onto him, and I can forget.

Not everything, of course. Altaris is still here, watching and waiting. I hate him, and he is still here. I hate him. Want to kill him. Want to rip.

He took me away from my Caspian, almost. He almost took me away.

"Why?" The voice isn't mine, but the question is. It's in my head, glaring and wailing. But I don't ask it. Caspian does. My face is pressed to his chest, his arms around me, mouth low near my ear so I can hear him speak.

Even though I can also hear him think.

I will protect you from him, he says. *Kill him for you. Protect you from him. But you want to know why.*

So I will ask him.

And he did.

"We had an agreement," Altaris explains, his voice muffled, coming from across the room. A room strewn with blood and groaning, writhing creatures in their death throes.

A room of death.

"I think you understand that, or you would be at my throat right now, boy. I had a theory to test and I have. How marvelous a test it was."

"A test?" I whisper.

Caspian grips me tighter. After days of lost staring, he stands rigid and tall. I'm the one who is shaking on my feet. I'm the one who can barely stand up. I press my face to his chest as if I mean to burrow inside of him and steal his strength.

I can't stand up on my own.

So he holds me tight and keeps me standing.

"A test," Altaris echoes. "One we agreed to enact. To bring him back. Remember? You offered me an exchange, and I accepted. You wanted him back sooner rather than later, and so he is. You are a very interesting, singular creature. Very interesting indeed."

He moves. I can hear him floating across the room with excited, graceful steps. He stoops for something, hissing under his breath. Then he sighs.

Din. Din. Din. It's that noise again. A constant ringing that has never ceased. Not since the men fed that device, whatever it is, my blood.

Din. Din. Din.

"Inconclusive," Altaris murmurs, his voice trembling with shock. "Oh my. What a surprise this is. A marvelous, wonderful surprise. You, my dear, are inconclusive."

"What does that mean?" Caspian is the one who demands it. No longer can I speak. I just hold onto him. Hold him. I close my eyes and hold onto him.

"It means that she is even stranger than I expected," Altaris explains. "Oh my, this is strange. You both are so strange. I'm sure you know why, little Caspian. I am sure now that you know why. This creature plucked you from your old collective and made you hers. Made your mind a part of its own. Oh, how devious. How marvelous. How very interesting."

No more. I don't want to hear him anymore.

I want him silent. I want him gone.

But we can't kill him. Because Caspian alone wants to hear more.

"Explain," he says.

Altaris chuckles. "You, my dear boy, are the explanation. She sobs over you for days, but when her life is in danger, when she truly needs you. You come. For her you will always come. You are one in her collective, that corrupted little mind. I hope you don't come to regret the choice you have made."

One of her collective. A corrupted mind.

Nonsense. I want him gone. I want him to shut up. I want to make him shut up!

"Hush," Caspian hisses to me. In my head, he promises, *I will protect you. I will always protect you. Trust me.*

I will always protect you.

"You two should go," Altaris says. "I will clean up this mess. But you need to leave and stay somewhere safe. I have another home on the other corner of the city. Go there. Stay there. I will come to you with answers."

No! He will come to us with lies! With devious villains and stabbing knives. They will hurt me. Kill me. Take me away from dear Caspian—

"Don't let her mind corrupt yours," Altaris says. Hateful, evil Altaris. "You can hear me clearly enough, boy. Your will is still intact. That is the marvelous thing. The most wondrous thing. Your will is still intact and you can hear the truth in what I say. As long as you are in its twisted little mind, I will help you. I will protect you. I owe it to you, after all."

"Why?"

"You don't remember," Altaris says sadly. "One day you will. One day you will know full well why you have every right to hate me, Caspian. But not now. Go. The address is Cage's Street. The number is 621. A whole building, just to yourself. Stay there and wait for me to come. Go now. Before the sun rises."

Before the sun rises, go now.

But the sun has already risen, and he is all mine.

Caspian is all mine, unchanged, unbroken.

He is all mine.

Even as I die, he is all mine.

"Wait," Altaris says before letting us fade away. "There is something you should know. Both of you."

"What?" Caspian demands. Impatient. Restless. He's sat idle for too long. Sat still for too long. He needs to pin me down and see if I've changed. Inspect my body inch by inch. See if I have changed in my time without him.

"There is a bounty on her head," Altaris says. "On you both. You think Mo Farley sent you here to square some debt? That was never the case."

We know.

"She sent us into a trap," I say. Not Caspian. My voice is so broken and frail. I laugh at the sound of it. Laugh and laugh.

"Hush." Caspian grips me tighter. Then he lifts me off my feet and cradles me to his chest like he did that first night in the mortal realm. He holds me now as he held me then.

Even tighter.

"What's wrong with her?" he asks.

"She is dying," Altaris explains. "Which is why you need to listen. Why you still need my help. I will save her, but for a price. That we can discuss later. After you go."

"Bounty," Caspian grates. "What bounty?"

"The fae wants her for the death of her litter mate, I suppose. The heir to house Aurelius. He is dead. It happened the night you left."

Dead.

Day.

Day is dead, but how? But why?

Caspian knows. He thinks of an answer to himself and squares it away in his corner of our huddled, fragile mind. Cassius...

Cassius did something.

For him. To punish him.

"They say that she killed him and then corrupted you. Dragged you off into the mortal realm. Made you her accomplice. Cassius has demanded you back, but it is out of his hands, of course. The council wants you both. Oh, how badly they want you both. They've even held off on their little ceremony of the ages, or whatever the hell it's called. They've called it off, until they've brought you both back."

To punish.

To kill.

To steal away and hurt.

"Never," Caspian tells me.

Never will they have us again.

"Now go," Altaris demands. "Go now. Before the sun rises—"

"Her," Caspian hisses. "Save her."

"I can't... But you can," Altaris says. "You give her your blood, or you let her die. It is your choice to make. Your sin to commit—just keep that in mind. You know the risks."

A sin. One even Cassius wouldn't let me commit.

"Now, I told you where to go," Altaris snaps. "Go!"

He does, my Caspian. He takes me in his arms and carries us out into the night.

He carries us away, where the council and no one can ever find us again.

CHAPTER 45
Caspian

Dirty fae. Stupid fae. My fae.

I have her.

I hold her tight, and I have her. She is mine. Mine.

But I am hers—a bargain I didn't ask for. Didn't want.

Need to have.

I am hers, and her possession is stranger than mortals and their so-called art. Stranger than any prize or reward Cassius could wave before me.

Her heart is stranger, still. Even bloodied and gaping and pumping noisily, I can see it. Hold it. But even if I reach into her chest and crush it in a fist, I won't have it. It won't be mine, not truly.

Only she can give it to me. In those frantic little whispers of my name. In the way she grabs me tight. Begs me. Pleads.

To save her again, I will have to break the rules.

Bend the rules.

Ignore the rules.

Because here, in this mortal realm with her, no other rules matter.

So I rip my wrist open with the tip of a nail, press it to her mouth, and make her drink.

I command her. Beg her. Insist she does it.

We'll sin together, her and me.

We will sin together, and no one will tell us right from wrong.

No one will rule over us again.

So, I press my blood between her lips, and I command her, "Drink!"

She does. Slowly and weakly, lapping at my wounded skin. She cringes in disgust. Then gasps. Takes another delicate sip. So fucking delicate she is. Making sure not to hurt. Making sure not to bite and tear.

She feeds from me, and I am the one who is hungry. She presses her lips to me, and I am the one who craves more. More.

I would let her feed from me for an eternity if she wanted to.

"Drink," I tell her, and she does.

And she heals.

Color returns to her cheeks. The wound on her chest ceases to bleed. The one on her wrist remains, but that's because she's taken only a few drops. She needs more. Don't know how I know that.

I can feel it, the resistance in her to clamp down over rent flesh and truly feed.

"Drink," I tell her, sinking my hand through her hair and seizing a handful of it in a fist. I press on her skull. Will her to take.

But she is stubborn as hell, my fae. She writhes until I let her go. Those black eyes fixate on mine, her lips smeared a vibrant, ruby red.

An oddity, this moment is. A momentous, strange moment, though I'm not sure why. It takes my brain seconds to process it. Then I realize: *this* is the first time in decades I have seen my own blood. Bright. Wet. Red.

So many years since I've seen it outside this hollow shell.

How many exactly? Too many to count. Too many years to stomach spent in Cassius' domain.

But I am free...

Alone in my skull, I can think and only hear myself thinking back. Me...

And her. She dwells in this space with me, unobtrusive. A quiet, pensive thing. Her thoughts are whisper-soft and thread together like brightly colored ribbons. Just out of my reach, but distinctive from my own.

She is not like Cassius. She shies away in her own corner of this shared, false collective. Even in her own mind, she's used to shirking and hiding.

Until now. Our eyes meet, and I can sense her intentions clearly. Guilt and regret. She fed from me. Took from me. It is only fair that she gives me something in return.

"Stupid," I tell her out loud, pressing my palm to her cheek. "Stupid. You owe me nothing."

Because all of her is already mine. I'll take every last piece. She will never wander alone again. Whether or not she wants to. I will keep her.

Or will I? Cassius was one to take and keep his captive toys on invisible chains. I am not him. Never will be.

But I *will* keep her.

I just can't make her stay. She is right; this must be an exchange. A melding of bodies and minds.

"We share everything," she murmurs against my fingertips. Without meaning, too, my thumb seeks out the corner of her mouth, feeling my blood drying there. The scarlet hue seems at home on this mouth. It belongs here. On her. In her. In me.

An exchange is what she craves. That way...

We don't own each other. I am not Cassius, and she is not the monster Altaris claimed she is. Fine.

I relent. I press my forehead to hers and let her have her wish. She wants to exchange. My blood for hers. I'll let her. I'll bite her. Drain her.

I won't stop. Won't stop.

"You will," she tells me, her eyes on my throat. She doesn't want to admit it: this festering itch that begins to take root in her, wherever my blood flows. Down her throat into her belly. A hunger begins to gnaw there. Take root there.

And it shouldn't. She is fae. Not a creature that craves blood. Not a vamryre...

Because this is a hunger I know well. But only a shadow of it. I knew hunger only under Cassius, and he kept us sated and plied on mental lies. If I feed from her now...

I don't know if I can stop myself.

"You will," she murmurs, reaching for me, already craving more. Her tongue flits across her lips, tracing the remnants of me. She still needs to heal. Her wrist is severed, bleeding away. She'll bleed out if we aren't careful. If I don't help her.

Give to her. Take from her.

"Here." She reaches up with her unblemished hand and swipes a lock of dark hair from her throat. This throat I've longed to sink into. Her blood I've craved for so damn long...

No. I pull back. Copy her by going for my own throat and using my own nail to rip it open. Her delicate fae teeth aren't strong enough to bite through flesh. But I have no trouble when I lean in and press my fangs to her tender neck.

Fuck, she smells so damn good. Hell, she feels so damn good, leaning into me, her hands reaching around my shoulders to hold me close. Her mouth finds my bleeding wound. Her tongue tentatively licks.

She hesitates. I can hear her thoughts, spoken in our shared mental space rather than out loud. *Please...*

So, I please her. I bite. I sink my fangs deep.

I taste her blood.

And the entire world unravels. The old rules and roles we played by cease to matter. A new world unfurls between us here and now. A new realm.

Our realm.

One where no one can take us from.

Separate us, ever.

A world of violence and sin and hate and all of those things we both learned to feel in the shadow of our masters.

I feed from her, and I live again.

In her, I become something different from a man or a mere vamryre. Something terrible and new.

A monster with two minds.

Two hearts.

Two souls.

Yet she won't be mine alone for long. I can sense them in the air in ways she cannot: smell them, hear them riding on the wind.

Vamryre.

And fae—just one. *That* one. Her cries of pain woke me up but drew him to her as well.

Right from his supposed grave.

The Story Continues...

The Story continues in **book 2, Lux**, coming sometime in fall of 2024.

About Lana Sky

Lana Sky is a reclusive writer in the United States who spends most of her time daydreaming about complex male characters and parenting her Cockapoo Joey. She writes dark, twisted romance across several genres. Her titles include everything from mafia romance to vampires.

facebook.com/AuthorLanaSky
x.com/lanasky101
amazon.com/author/lanasky
pinterest.com/lanasky101
goodreads.com/lanasky
instagram.com/lanasky101
bookbub.com/authors/lana-sky
tiktok.com/@author_lana_sky

Also by Lana Sky

For more titles by Lana Sky, please visit:

https://www.lanaskybooks.com

www.ingramcontent.com/pod-product-compliance
Lightning Source LLC
Chambersburg PA
CBHW070643310726

48982CB00001B/402
9798890150035